A CLONE DISCOVERS HIS IDENTITY

How Alfred Johnson Embraces His Roots

I0587666

Jayesh Shah

Also by Jayesh Shah
David Wallace Goes to India
(Available on Amazon.com)

A CLONE DISCOVERS HIS IDENTITY

How Alfred Johnson Embraces His Roots

Jayesh Shah

ISBN-13: 9781732937017
Library of Congress Control Number: 2018913710

This book is dedicated to my daughters,
Monica and Payal

Acknowledgments

While working on this book, I have been blessed with the help and well-wishes of many people. I would like to thank them.

Khushroo Suraliwala, my best friend for four decades, for his encouragement, suggestions, and best wishes for this project.

My wife, Vanita; and my daughters, Monica and Payal; for their patience and tolerance while I was working on this book.

Dr. Tarachandra Narumanchi, geneticist from West Virginia University School of Medicine, for helping me understand the genetics of the cloning process.

Drs. Chang and Ramakrishnan Iyer for their help in writing about Korean culture.

Heather McChesney for editing, critiquing, and offering valuable suggestions.

Arlene Hudson for reviewing the manuscript and offering valuable suggestions.

Amnet Systems for copy editing and formatting the book.

Preface

Alfred Johnson is a young boy who is trying to discover his identity after learning that what he knew about his birth parents was a lie. His clues are his mother's bizarre confession about her involvement in a surrogacy and his uncanny resemblance to Steven Kincaid, whom he had never met. To make matters worse, Steven Kincaid is the only son of an infamous tycoon, Michael Kincaid.

When Alfred is offered millions of dollars by Michael Kincaid in exchange for giving up his quest, the courage of his conviction is tested. To Mr. Kincaid's surprise, he refuses to compromise his character.

Alfred's mother Angela, once a devout Christian, runs away from law enforcement, has a fake marriage, and commits one sin after another.

Brittany Wilson, an infant adopted from South Korea by an American family, feels she is betraying "my own people" by living away from the country of her birth.

Dr. Betty Sue Lawson is tormented by her twin sister during her childhood and adolescence. In the end, Dr. Lawson manipulates her twin into taking her own life. She could have forgiven her sister and moved on, but she chooses not to.

Michael Kincaid, once an ethical businessman, is not able to handle the untimely death of his wife and degenerates into a ruthless manipulator. He starts destroying people around him. Till the end, he does not learn that money cannot buy everything or everybody. (Here, I must clarify that I had envisioned Michael Kincaid's character years before the US presidential election of 2016. People have asked me if President Trump was an inspiration for this character. He was not.)

Alfred's integrity also forces Steven Kincaid to choose between inheriting billions of dollars of his dad's money or walk out of his dad's house and live on his own.

Stephanie Anderson struggles to become a "real woman."

And, finally, there is Patricia Sharp, a competent business associate of Mr. Kincaid, who is unable to understand for decades what kind of person her boss really is, until her "mitochondrial" son, Alfred Johnson, opens her eyes.

In his quest to discover his identity, Alfred meets many people whose ethics and morals are tested by unusual circumstances. Not everyone survives the challenge.

The book also describes the science and ethics of cloning.

Contents

The World According to Michael

No one can transcend their own individuality.

— ARTHUR SCHOPENHAUER, GERMAN PHILOSOPHER

Michael Kincaid was the happiest man in the world. He felt like he was in the seventh heaven. In a few weeks, he and his wife, Lucy, were expecting their first child. They planned to have three children. Ultrasound examinations had revealed the child to be a boy. He would be named Steven Joseph Kincaid—Steven was in honor of his father and Joseph was in honor of Lucy's father.

Besides a father-to-be and husband, Michael was a successful business-man—much like his own father. His life was planned meticulously. His businesses were running according to his projections. He strongly believed that one must have vision, planning, and an ethical work attitude to suc-ceed in life.

Michael Kincaid's empire was diverse in nature. His company was involved in the mining of precious metals, agriculture, the steel industry, and the manufacture and distribution of weapons to name a few. Charitable activities by his companies made him popular in many parts of Africa. Almost every business in third-world countries had to bribe government officials, but Michael's businesses, proudly, did not. In Michael's opinion, a man's true identity rested in the integrity of his character.

His MBA thesis was titled, "Demographic Changes in the Developing Countries and Their Impact on Their Economic Growth." Michael completed his studies during a time when people were focused on the impending collapse of the Soviet Union and the effects of the end of the Cold War on the political landscape of the world. President Reagan's call to Mr. Gorbachev to "break down that wall" echoed in their minds. In those days, people did not talk about emerging economies or the consequence of the younger population in the developing world as opposed to the aging population in the developed world.

When Michael talked to his friends and colleagues about the potential rise of the third-world countries, they laughed at him. His friends ridiculed those views as "the world according to Michael," but Michael took that as a compliment. He could foresee that the importance given to education by parents in third-world countries and their manpower were destined to benefit them.

Michael was never into partying, and he was never a womanizer. He dated very little while he was in college or, for that matter, even after he finished college. He was not interested in activities that wasted his time. Three years ago, he met Lucy Dent at a New Year's Eve party given by Bill Martin, owner of The Galaxy Casinos in Las Vegas. Lucy was a successful fashion model. It was love at first sight. Michael knew, right there and then, that he had to marry her. They started dating immediately. While dating, they learned about each other. They discovered that their interests and ambitions were slightly different. Lucy wanted to travel the world, whereas Michael wanted to own it.

A few weeks after they met, he proposed, she accepted, and they got married. Michael was well known as a successful businessman, and Lucy as a model who had appeared on the cover of many fashion magazines. Together, the young newlyweds became the most famous couple in Columbus, Ohio. Their marriage was the envy of the town. Michael could not imagine his life without Lucy.

Lucy took great care of herself during her pregnancy. She watched her diet, abstained from alcohol and coffee, and followed every instruction from her obstetrician. Her pregnancy was uneventful until she was more than eight months pregnant.

Unfortunately, for Michael and Lucy, things went downhill from there. Despite Michael's meticulous planning and Lucy's disciplined behavior during her pregnancy, they hit a roadblock. Lucy's obstetrician, Dr. Patrick Slim, told them that her blood pressure was high, she was leaking protein in her urine, and she had edema over her legs. "Nothing to worry about," he assured them. "It happens frequently in the first pregnancy," they were told. A few days after seeking treatment for complications, her blood pressure did not normalize, so she was admitted to Beth Israel Hospital. Again, they were told not to worry. Obstetricians and perinatologists were treating her around the clock under the watchful eyes of Michael.

Once hospitalized, her condition worsened. "I am afraid we will have to deliver the baby now," Dr. Slim announced. He explained that the preeclampsia, which caused high blood pressure and swelling of her legs, had worsened and that she was developing HELLP syndrome. The couple had never heard of HELLP syndrome before. Dr. Slim explained that in HELLP syndrome, the pregnant woman experiences high blood pressure, liver damage, and problems with the coagulation of blood. It develops in less than one percent of pregnancies, and, just like Lucy, many pregnant women suffer from preeclampsia before developing HELLP syndrome.

Dr. Slim told them that immediate delivery of the baby was required to help the mom. Lucy and Michael did not hear much of what Dr. Slim told them and understood even less due to the shock of such an unexpected turn of events. They agreed with the medical advice, and Lucy signed consent papers for surgery. This meant that Steven would be born prematurely, something that was not in Michael's planning.

Within minutes, the OR was ready. Michael kissed Lucy while she was being rushed to surgery. She was placed under general anesthesia, and the baby was delivered by cesarean section. Steven Joseph Kincaid was born roughly five weeks early. He weighed five and half pounds. He was delivered prematurely because of his mother's illness, but ironically the stress of that illness also helped his lungs mature. He had no breathing difficulty at birth, and apart from being small, he was healthy. His mother's condition, however, continued to deteriorate.

Michael stayed in the hospital with Lucy. He ran his businesses from there with the help of his very competent administrative assistant, Patricia Sharp. Patricia was so vital to him and his family that Lucy once said, "It's easy not to notice Patricia's presence, but her absence is always felt." Michael had another opinion. He joked that Patricia knew how to keep her job by making herself too indispensable to be fired.

Patricia consulted experts in HELLP syndrome to ensure that Lucy got the best medical care. When she learned more about this condition, she knew the prognosis was poor. She started looking for nannies to care for baby Steven after he would come home. Being pragmatic, Patricia knew that whether Lucy survived or not, the Kincaid family would need people to take care of the baby.

Two days after Steven's birth, Lucy died. Mr. Kincaid's planning and his money could not save his wife. In his grief, he failed to learn a valuable lesson that money could not buy everything. Even the men with vision have blind spots.

Baby Steven came home one week after his mother's tragic death.

$$*\quad*\quad*$$

Meanwhile, a few miles away from Mr. Kincaid's mansion, Angela Johnson lived in a small one-bedroom apartment. Angela was recently divorced. Her marriage was in trouble from the outset, and after five long years, it finally ended. Her husband Mark's infidelity, alcoholism, and inability to hold a steady job eventually took its toll on their marriage. Mark was from Canada, and after his marriage with Angela, he had become a US citizen. Angela's sister Melanie had cautioned her that maybe Mark was interested in her because he could become an American citizen after his marriage with her. Angela had yelled at her for being so rude and narrow-minded. As much as she resented the divorce and believed it was against her religion, she finally came to terms with it. Before she filed the paperwork, she sought the advice of Senior Pastor George Watson. It was Pastor Watson who had presided over her marriage with Mark. After listening to her reasons for divorce, he absolved her.

Angela hired a young attorney, Robert Newman, to help her with the legality of the divorce. He was one of the few divorce attorneys that she could afford. On top of that, Mr. Newman assured her that she could pay his fees in installments.

Angela came from a conservative family. Her parents were Baptists. Her mother was a homemaker, and her father was a factory-worker. They were seven siblings. Angela's parents wanted to instill Christian values within their children, so they homeschooled them. Alcohol and cigarettes were forbidden in their home. Angela and her siblings married and settled in southern Ohio. Angela worked as a cashier in a supermarket after graduating from high school.

Angela had always imagined a long, blessed marriage. Unfortunately, she had trusted the wrong man, but she was not bitter. She accepted her divorce as God's will and decided to make the best out of it. She obtained custody of her young son and received a lot of support from her church family. She took comfort in these blessings.

Michael Kincaid and Angela Johnson had both experienced joy that erupted into heartache and pain. Happiness and sadness know no class or dollar amount. Two people were living mere miles apart in physical distance, but their worlds were light-years away from one another. Yet, unbeknown to them, their destinies would somehow manage to become entangled.

2

Michael Kincaid in Shock

A clone of Einstein wouldn't be stupid, but he won't necessarily be any genius, either.

— JAMES D. WATSON, CO-DISCOVERER OF
STRUCTURE OF DNA

Michael Kincaid buried Lucy with a heavy heart. He had no idea how he was going to raise Steven. Mentally, he was not prepared to comprehend what it meant to take care of a newborn baby. Luckily, he had help. His administrative assistant, Patricia, handled everything. She hired nannies to raise Steven. Meanwhile, Michael's personal physician, Dr. Larry Parker, placed him on antidepressants.

What bothered Michael the most was the fact that he and Lucy had planned to have three kids and to grow old together. That's how he had pictured his future. The reality that he was now a widower and had to be content with one child was not acceptable to him. *It was not supposed to happen this way*, he lamented repeatedly.

Patricia knew what was troubling her boss and mentor. She had a relationship with Mr. Kincaid that very few others enjoyed or understood. Five years ago, when she took this job, she was a naïve, wide-eyed twenty-three-year-old woman. She idolized her boss. She viewed him much like an older brother at times and at other times as a father figure. Mr. Kincaid was a few years older than her. Under his tutelage, Patricia had become an adept and efficient employee. She had also become a valuable source of support to Michael.

After Lucy's death, Michael was barely functioning. Most days, he stayed in his bedroom. He neglected to shave, bathe, or sometimes even eat. People around him advised him to seek psychiatric help, but he refused to leave his room. After consulting with Dr. Parker, Patricia managed to have Dr. Pierce, a psychiatrist, make house calls. Dr. Pierce took over treatment for his depression. He visited Michael frequently.

During his visits, Dr. Pierce also discussed with Michael the way the mind copes with loss. He explained that when faced with a major loss, we go through five stages of grief: denial, anger, bargaining, depression, and finally acceptance. Michael and Dr. Pierce didn't always see eye to eye on psychological theory.

"What do you guys know about grief?" Michael balked. "You're telling me that a person goes through five stages of grief! Let me tell you something, Doctor. I go through all these stages about hundred times a day, every day, since Lucy passed away! Anger, denial, acceptance, bargaining, depression—like a ping-pong ball bouncing back-and-forth! All day long! There's no relief," he shouted while walking back-and-forth agitatedly!

"Maybe, the people who wrote your textbooks never went through the grieving process themselves. You know what, Dr. Pierce? *It hurts.* You have no idea how much it hurts. You see the top of my head?" Michael pointed at it with his fingers while still stalking back and forth. "That's where it hurts. It feels like it's vibrating painfully. I get a feeling of emptiness there. I've had headaches before, but this is different. It doesn't ache! It hurts," he shouted even louder, even more agitated now.

"You know another thing, Doctor?" Michael went on, quieter now. "Most people in my place would visit the grave of their deceased spouse, but I don't have the strength to leave this room. You can see Lucy's picture on the wall there." Michael looked in the direction of the picture and continued in a small voice, "I can't look at it without feeling odd about it. Every time I see the picture, I think she is going to walk out of the picture and materialize in front of me."

The psychiatrist nodded in agreement and told him that depression in each patient is different and that every patient doesn't go through these stages in order. Michael thought it was gibberish. Dr. Pierce warned that depression caused by the loss of a loved one can take weeks or sometimes months before it comes under control, so patience was required. Michael agreed with that statement. He was sane enough to understand that he would probably need medical treatment for a long time. Therefore, despite his disagreement with the psychiatrist and his theories of the grieving process, he took the medications.

Dr. Pierce had explained to Michael that he feared he would harm himself if he did not comply with his medication. Michael believed him. He had thoughts of suicide frequently since Lucy's death. It felt as if it would be a relief from this never-ending pain. In his rational mind, he knew that if he were to die, his son Steven would not be raised the way he and Lucy had envisioned. He had to take care of their son. He owed her that much. In order to do that, he had to take care of himself. Dr. Pierce had mentioned something that gave him hope for better days. He told Michael that his depression was secondary to a negative event as opposed to a primary depression, which is not triggered by a specific event and is sometimes associated with genetic predisposition. Depression borne of grief is easier to treat than depression that occurs without any obvious precipitating factor.

In the depth of his melancholy, Michael gradually developed animosity toward the whole world. He blamed it for his misfortune. The idea of punishing the world began incubating in his mind. His desire to survive was nourished by this growing hatred. By now, Steve was few months old. Every time Michael looked at him, Steve smiled. In his smile, Michael could see Lucy's smile. He felt better during these moments.

Since Lucy's death, Michael spent a great deal of time, alone in his room, watching television. One day, while flipping through the channels, he stumbled across something that excited him.

He saw a program on the Discovery Channel. The first successful cloning of a mammal from adult cells was in the news. The program described the cloning of Dolly, the sheep. He jumped off his bed! *This is exactly what*

I need! If scientists can clone a sheep, they should be able to clone a human being! Money was no object. He would pay anything to clone his beloved Lucy.

Cloning is the ticket. Suddenly, the empty feeling, the vibrations, and the hurt on the top of his head were gone. He looked at Lucy's picture and smiled. For the first time in months, he felt better. More accurately, he felt *normal*.

Michael walked to his bathroom. He looked at himself in the mirror. He was appalled at what he saw. An unshaven man wearing wrinkled clothes was staring back at him. Michael was shocked. He could not believe that he had allowed himself to fall this low. He locked the bathroom door and started shaving. Only after showering, shaving, and putting on clean clothes, did Michael dare unlock the bathroom door.

First thing after he entered his room was to walk to Lucy's picture and kiss her. Then, he called Patricia Sharp. John, her husband, answered the phone, "Hello?"

"Hi, John, this is Michael, Michael Kincaid. How are you?" Michael asked.

John recognized the voice. He was surprised to hear Mr. Kincaid's voice on the other end. He paused for a second before answering, "Hi, I am fine. How are you?"

"I am better. Thanks for asking. Can I speak to Pat?" Michael asked in a hurried tone. In the past, he would usually chat with John, but this time, he was too excited to even make small talk.

"Sure, please hold on," John told him and called Patricia. "Pat, you wouldn't believe who is on the phone," he told Patricia while holding his hand over the mouthpiece of the phone.

"Who is it?" she asked.

"It's Michael, and he wants to talk to you," John answered, smilingly.

"Michael? You mean Michael Kincaid?" She was shocked. "You know he's too depressed to pick up a phone. That's not funny, John," she scolded John while lightly hitting him on the shoulder in exasperation.

"No, I am not joking. Here, talk to him," John said as he gave the phone to Patricia.

"Hi, this is Patricia Sharp. May I ask who is calling?" Pat said, still not believing that it was Mr. Kincaid on the other end. She still thought that John was just playing a cruel prank.

"Hi Pat, this is Mike. How are you?" Michel said.

"Oh, Mike! I'm fine. It's great to hear your voice on the phone," she told him as she rushed around the house trying to find a notepad. She still couldn't believe it was him.

"Pat, listen, I have something important to talk to you about. Can I see you in the office at eight o'clock tomorrow morning?" Michael asked.

"Sure, I will be there. Do you really want to come to the office? I can meet you at your home." She was not sure if Michael could leave his house in his mental condition. He hadn't been out in months, and she wondered if the strain of coming to the office would be too much for him.

"No, I will come to the office. It will be better there. I need you to look up some information there," Michael insisted.

"Okay, I will see you there," Patricia agreed excitedly! Maybe this was the light at the end of the tunnel for which she had hoped. Watching Michael's rapid decline after the loss of his wife had been excruciating to Pat. She had always thought so highly of Michael and Lucy.

Michael woke up early the next day, just like he used to before Lucy's death. He got ready and had his butler make a nice breakfast of eggs and toast for him. Then he drove to his office. On his way to the office, he was thinking about cloning and the possibilities open to him now. He could bring his wife Lucy back to life and have more kids with her, exactly as they had planned. He had learned over the years that money could buy anything, and he was prepared to put that lesson to the test.

Once at the office, news of his arrival spread like a wildfire. People were delighted that their boss had recovered from his melancholy and that he appeared eager and ready to get back at it. Patricia was already there waiting for him. She greeted him with a big smile and a hug. Michael seemed cheerful. He thanked Patricia profusely for taking care of him, his son, and his businesses. He knew that without her pragmatism and dependability, his life and his businesses would have fallen into ruin.

After he sat in his chair, he asked Patricia if she knew anything about cloning. Patricia replied that she did not, except for Dolly the sheep, which she had seen on the news. Patricia thought this was a strange subject to discuss under the circumstances.

"Michael, I don't understand why you are interested in cloning. Can you please explain?" Patricia asked, her forehead creased in a frown.

"Last night I saw a television documentary on cloning. The program discussed how Dolly, the sheep, was born. I think through cloning, I can get my Lucy back," Michael explained excitedly. Patricia could tell that he could barely remain seated in his chair.

"Oh, I see. Forgive me for asking this, but are you sure it's a good idea?" Patricia wondered. Obviously, she was not comfortable with the idea. She was unsure of the consequences. Soon after she said it, she realized that she should have worded the question differently. She didn't mean any disrespect to Michael or Lucy, and Michael, despite having returned to the office that day, was still obviously quite fragile.

"I see nothing wrong in it. I am sure it will cost me an arm and a leg, but I will pay them any amount they need to bring her back," Michael answered curtly.

"I am not talking about money," Patricia stated evenly. "I am talking about the ethics of the whole process and whether it's even possible or not. I don't think cloning in humans has ever been done," Patricia cautioned him. She was highly alarmed with this turn of events and shocking change in Michael's personality. In the past, before Lucy's death, he would have never even considered such an outrageous idea.

"Well, first of all, it's my money, and I don't care what people think," Michael retorted. "Even if no one has cloned a human being yet, I'm sure some scientist somewhere would be willing to attempt it for me. It's worth a shot," he said with optimism. In Michael's grief-stricken mind, he could not recognize how skewed his ethical views had become.

"Before I go any further, I would like to know more about it. Can you have someone from OSU explain cloning to me?" Michael asked. OSU or Ohio State University was his favorite college.

"Sure, I can do that. Do you want me to call the president of OSU to find someone to meet with you?" Patricia asked. She was still shell-shocked from this revelation, but she knew that Michael was holding onto this idea like a lifeline.

"That's fine. He would know the best person for this job. After all, if I don't use my clout at OSU for something important like this then when am I going to use it?" Michael had donated millions of dollars to OSU over the years for many of their programs. His name was on a health sciences facility there, and he had started a scholarship fund for students from developing countries to attend this prestigious university.

Patricia called the president of OSU. He referred her to Dr. Jihoo Lee, a senior professor of genetics. She arranged the meeting between Mr. Kincaid and Dr. Lee. Dr. Lee couldn't understand why a businessman would want to learn about genetics and cloning, but he knew how much respect the university had for Mr. Kincaid, so he agreed. They set up the appointment for the following Saturday. Patricia informed him that Mr. Kincaid would pay him for his time, which Dr. Lee declined. They were to meet in Mr. Kincaid's office. The next day, Dr. Lee received a check in the mail from Mr. Kincaid's office. He was surprised to see the payment for his time not only because he had refused the money, but also as they had yet to meet.

Once Patricia had set up the appointment with the geneticist, Michael met with his staff. His employees greeted him warmly. They brought flowers, candies, and cakes. They were genuinely happy for him. Michael was touched by the love and affection of the people around him.

Mr. Kincaid then evaluated the current financial situation of his businesses. His mood soured immediately at what he found. In his absence, many of his businesses had sustained substantial losses. He called Patricia into his office; she could sense immediately that he was unhappy. He told her of his discovery and demanded that they begin to fix everything immediately! Patricia tried to convince him that people in the office had done their best under the situation. She defended them strongly, but it was in vain.

The next morning, Mr. Kincaid fired 10 percent of his staff, including people working overseas. Until that day, he had hardly fired anyone. His employees were stunned. Suddenly, they realized that they were no longer working for the same man.

3

What Is Cloning?

The greatest history book ever written is the one hidden in our DNA.

— Spencer Wells, geneticist, anthropologist, and former head of Genographic Project with National Geographic Society

The following Saturday morning, Dr. Lee appeared promptly at the appointed time and was greeted by Mr. Kincaid and Patricia. Before he began, Professor Lee asked, "Mr. Kincaid, I don't know what you want to specifically know about cloning?"

"Everything. I want to understand this subject in detail," Mr. Kincaid answered with determination.

"Let me set up my slide projector and we shall begin," Dr. Lee said while bustling around the office with his slide projector.

"Sure, take your time," Mr. Kincaid said.

Patricia jumped to assist Dr. Lee with his equipment. After a few minutes and with the help of some other office staff, Professor Lee had the projector and the screen set up and ready to go.

He began his presentation by saying, "Now Mr. Kincaid, this presentation is designed for medical students who already have basic knowledge of genetics, so we will go slowly, and I will explain several concepts in between the slides." He went to the first slide which showed the title of his presentation, his name, and his degrees. He waited for a couple of seconds so that his audience could read the slide and become acquainted with his title and his credentials. Then he changed the slide.

"You see, the word clone comes from the Greek word, Klon, which means twig. It actually refers to the process of creating a new plant from a twig," Dr. Lee stated while pointing to a graphic of a twig on the slide. It showed the twig being cut from a branch and growing roots. Patricia started taking notes. Dr. Lee found this very unusual. He never had a student who had someone take notes for him. He had never had such a wealthy student, either. *Maybe, that's how millionaires live. How would I know!*

"So when a new plant is created from a twig of the original plant, it's actually cloning!" Mr. Kincaid was surprised.

"Exactly," Professor Lee exclaimed. "Most people don't know this when they talk about cloning. There is a common misconception that cloning only occurs in laboratories. Some people argue that cloning should be banned because it is against the laws of nature, but in reality, when we create a tree from a branch sapling, we are creating a clone. A clone is a genetically identical organism. Bacteria and some insects also reproduce by this method," explained Dr. Lee.

"Cloning is a form of asexual reproduction," he went on. "Just as identical twins share the same genetic makeup, clones also have the same genetic makeup. So, basically, you can describe cloning as delayed twinning," said Professor Lee as he advanced to a different slide depicting a full-grown tree and a sapling planted side by side. "In the case of cloning, the twinning process can be delayed by years or decades or theoretically by centuries," he explained as he advanced to another slide. "Another difference between twins and clones is that in the case of twins, their environment is usually similar, whereas in the case of clones, it may not be. I am referring to their environment in the mother's belly as well as outside," said Dr. Lee, once again pointing to another slide showing a woman with an obviously pregnant belly showing two fetuses growing in her womb.

"Before I describe the process by which clones can be created, let me describe how the so-called test-tube babies are created. That will explain how cloning in mammals was developed. You know in 1978, British doctors created the first test-tube baby," Dr. Lee said.

"Yes, I remember that. It was quite an event. Newspapers and television channels talked about it endlessly," Mr. Kincaid said. "By the way, Dr. Lee, your slides are beautiful."

"I think you have made them in Harvard Graphics. Am I right, Dr. Lee?" Patricia asked.

"That's correct. Do you know Harvard Graphics?" Dr. Lee was surprised.

"Patricia knows everything. She is very resourceful," Mr. Kincaid informed the professor.

"I am impressed," Dr. Lee confessed. "I find Harvard Graphics easier than other programs. I am awful with computers, so I don't try a new program unless I don't have a choice," he said while making a pained expression.

He turned back to his slides and resumed his presentation. "The first test-tube baby was named Louise Brown. Her mother could not conceive because her Fallopian tubes were blocked. In order for a woman to conceive, the ovum, or egg, has to pass through the Fallopian tube. Before modern advances, women who had blocked Fallopian tubes could not become pregnant, because the ovum could not pass through the tubes. Thousands of women were infertile because of this problem. As you see, this slide describes how it was done," Dr. Lee explained while pointing to the slide. The slide showed a woman's body with reproductive organs visible. An ovum was shown being removed from it.

"Her doctors, Edwards and Steptoe, removed her egg via laparoscopy and placed it in a petri dish. There, it was fertilized by her husband's sperm," continued Dr. Lee. The slide showed the ovum in a petri dish. Next slide showed sperm being injected into the ovum. Finally, there was a slide showing embryo being transferred into the uterus.

"How successful is fertilization of the egg in the laboratory as compared to natural process?" Mr. Kincaid asked.

"It's fairly successful. In fact, we say that the only time it's not successful is when the egg has a headache," Dr. Lee explained, laughing. Mr. Kincaid also laughed.

"Really, Dr. Lee? Don't you think it's a stereotype about women?" Patricia complained. But she was happy to see Michael laugh. She had not seen him laugh since Lucy's death.

"I'm sorry, Ms. Sharp. To keep the students from getting bored, I insert jokes every now and then," Dr. Lee explained sheepishly.

"I have to admit, it was funny. Coming from someone who has a doctorate in science, it was also unexpected," Patricia said. Then she continued, "I have a question, Dr. Lee. How is it different from the test-tube babies described in the book, *Brave New World*?"

"There are some similarities between the two," Dr. Lee conceded. "Unfortunately, science fiction books and movies have twisted people's perception of true science. That book describes test-tube babies as well as cloning. But there *is* a difference," he said while raising his eyebrows and raising up onto his toes. He resumed once he rocked back onto his heels, "Unlike in Huxley's *Brave New World*, the first test-tube baby in the real world grew in her mother's uterus. Mrs. Brown's doctors transferred the fertilized egg into her uterus where it could develop into a full-term fetus." At this point, Dr. Lee raised his hand with his index finger extended as if to make a point and said, "Also, unlike *Brave New World*, in the real world, the Bokanovsky Process was not used. You see, when these so-called test-tube babies are created, they are not creating multiple babies." In *Brave New World*, the method by which multiple fetuses were created was known as Bokanovsky process.

"So fertilization of the egg was done in the lab. Other than that, this was just like a normal pregnancy. Is that correct?" Mr. Kincaid asked.

"Yes, it was," answered Dr. Lee. "She was delivered by cesarean section a few days before the due date. The mother had developed high blood pressure, so the doctors had to deliver the baby sooner. Mrs. Brown had developed a condition known as preeclampsia," he further explained.

"I know what preeclampsia is," Mr. Kincaid stated quietly. "Actually, my wife suffered from preeclampsia and then she developed HELLP syndrome. Unfortunately, in her case, it was fatal," Mr. Kincaid informed the professor.

"I am sorry to hear that," Dr. Lee said. He could feel the tension increase in the room at this point.

For a second or two, Dr. Lee did not know what to do, so he reached for his glass and took a sip of water. Meanwhile, Patricia fluidly redirected the conversation by asking, "So, Dr. Lee, this baby was not actually a clone though, is that correct?" Of course, she knew the answer, but she wanted to quickly change the topic.

"That's right. This was IVF or in vitro fertilization," Dr. Lee answered. "I described the case of Louise Brown, the first test-tube baby, so I could more easily explain the cloning process," he continued. Dr. Lee then advanced to the next slide.

"Before we discuss how cloning is done, let me explain another mode of reproduction," he began. "I think it's very interesting. It shows how nature finds ways to propagate different species. This process is called parthenogenesis," Dr. Lee said while showing a slide of lizard crawling among the ruins of the Parthenon. "Just like cloning, it's also a form of asexual reproduction. This method is used by females of some species of crustaceans, insects, and even lizards. Only the female of the species can reproduce by this method, and the offspring produced are always female," he said as he advanced to another slide showing several lizards.

"Oh, when you said that Nature allows asexual reproduction in animals, I was thinking of some other possibilities. But you say that the babies they produce are females only, so it's kind of disappointing." Mr. Kincaid was laughing as he said this.

"I know where you are going with this, Mr. Kincaid. Let's stick to the science and not discuss mythology," laughed Dr. Lee. "Sorry, I take it back. I will make an exception. Let me say a little bit about the mythology behind the word parthenogenesis. It is derived from the Greek word 'Parthenos,' which means virgin. Greek mythology describes a goddess named Athena, as Athena Parthenos, because she was a virgin," Dr. Lee added.

"Yes, Athena, the Virgin! Her statue was in the Parthenon in Athens, Greece. I am fascinated by Greek mythology," Patricia was very excited.

"Yes, that's the one. The Parthenon, as we all know, is the most famous example of Greek architecture." Dr. Lee continued, "Although there are debates over ethics of cloning of higher animals including humans, the process of cloning has been extensively used in horticulture. No one has questioned the ethics of cloning in that field. As you probably know, genetic information is carried on the chromosomes, which are located in the nucleus of a cell. Humans have forty-six chromosomes or twenty-three pairs of chromosomes, which consist of two sex chromosomes. In females, there are two X chromosomes, and in males there is one X chromosome and one Y chromosome. Different species have different number of chromosomes. . ."

"I am sure that human beings have maximum number of chromosomes," Mr. Kincaid interrupted.

"That's a misconception," answered Dr. Lee. "Chimpanzees and gorillas have forty-eight chromosomes. Cows and goats have sixty chromosomes. The number of chromosomes does not have much to do with how far a species has evolved. As I mentioned, the chimpanzees, our closest relatives genetically speaking, have one extra pair of chromosomes. But the second chromosome in humans is a combination of two chromosomes found in primates like the chimpanzees. You see, evolution is very clever," he stated.

"Chromosomes have a number of genes. Hundreds or thousands of genes can be located on each chromosome. Genes are made of DNA. This DNA molecule stores the basic instructions. It essentially contains the code of life. It is believed that humans have approximately one hundred thousand genes located on these forty-six chromosomes," Dr. Lee continued (*This number is revised to 20,000 genes*).

"Before we talk more about genes and genetics, we need to learn our alphabet. The English alphabet has twenty-six letters, but our alphabet contains . . .," Dr. Lee was explaining. Michael interrupted him in mid-sentence.

"I am confused. As far as I know, the Mandarin language does not have a traditional alphabet," Michael stated.

"That's true. I am actually talking about the alphabet of geneticists. Most people have no idea about Chinese languages. I am surprised that you know it," Dr. Lee was amazed. In addition to being very wealthy, Mr. Kincaid also appeared to be quite knowledgeable.

"Well, Dr. Lee, I have learned a lot about developing countries during my college years. In fact, due to my interest in Asian countries, I wrote a thesis for my MBA on the demographic changes in developing countries and the impact it would have on their economic growth," Mr. Kincaid explained. The professor was impressed.

"Dr. Lee, what part of China do you come from? I am familiar with some of the major cities of China, thanks to my studies and my travels," he said.

"Actually, I am from Taiwan, Mr. Kincaid. Most people, in the United States, don't know the history of China and Taiwan, so they think I am Chinese," Dr. Lee answered.

"Oh, I am sorry. I am familiar with Taiwan's history. If someone calls you Chinese by mistake, then you should educate them," Michael said. Like everyone else, he had also assumed that Dr. Lee was from China.

"Due to the contentious relationship with the People's Republic of China, Taiwanese people hate to be called Chinese. It used to offend me when someone called me Chinese. Now I tell people that I am a *Chinese professor from Taiwan*," Dr. Lee laughed.

"That's funny. Has your family always lived in Taiwan, Dr. Lee?" Patricia asked.

"We are Han Chinese. My family moved to Taiwan more than a hundred years ago. Living in the United States has taught me that people don't intentionally insult someone by saying something like that. Once you correct them, they make an effort to understand and respect your identity. Although, I must confess that most Taiwanese people who live in America feel like they live with an identity crisis. For outsiders they are Chinese, a label they strongly despise," the Professor explained.

"That's interesting," Patricia replied. "As an immigrant myself, I must say Dr. Lee, that we can't expect American people to know about every part of the world," she mentioned.

"We Americans learn about those parts of the world where we are at war," Michael said jokingly. "And, we are always at war somewhere."

"Let me go back to our discussion on genetics. The alphabet of geneticists contains four letters. The four letters are A, C, G, and T," Dr. Lee explained. "These are the four bases that form nucleotides in the DNA molecule. They stand for adenine, cytosine, guanine, and thymine, respectively. There is actually a fifth letter, U, which stands for uracil. It replaces thymine in RNA molecule. Now, let me explain how this genetic material is transferred from the original organism to its clone." Dr. Lee had not changed the slide for a few minutes since his presentation did not contain information regarding chromosomes and genes. His students at OSU knew that already.

"Normally during reproduction, the information is transferred via the sperm of a male and ovum of a female. This way genetic information is obtained from each parent, so the new organism does not become a genetic copy of any one of the parents. This provides genetic diversity.

"Cloning of mature individuals is done by Somatic Cell Nuclear Transfer technology or SCNT. An ovum is taken from an adult female's ovary. The nucleus is removed from the ovum. Then a mature cell is taken from the donor, and its nucleus is transferred into the egg or ovum whose nucleus has previously been removed as I mentioned. If the cell continues to divide, then it is implanted in the uterus of a surrogate. So we have one donor individual and two other individuals, one from whom the ovum is removed and one who acts as a surrogate mother," said Dr. Lee. The slide showed the technology. There was a drawing of an ovum with a nucleus, followed by the drawing in which the nucleus was removed from it. Next to that there was another cell labeled, somatic cell, from which the nucleus was being removed, followed by this nucleus being injected into the ovum. Dr. Lee kept pointing at the proper parts of the slide as he explained the process. Then, he continued, "So that's . . .," he paused because he could tell that Patricia had a question.

"Can the same individual act as the egg donor and the surrogate mother, Dr. Lee?" Patricia asked.

"That's a good question. Yes, she can. Actually, if an adult female is cloned, then she can be a donor of tissue for cloning, as well as an egg donor and a surrogate mother," answered Dr. Lee.

"Wow, that's fascinating. I am trying to figure out what the relationship between that woman and her clone would be. Would she be the clone's mother? Would she be her twin? That's pretty weird," Mr. Kincaid mentioned.

Mr. Kincaid listened intently and asked interesting questions. The professor was excited because he hadn't had such an enthusiastic student in a long time.

After hours of discussion, Mr. Kincaid dropped the bombshell. He asked the professor, "As I mentioned earlier, my wife passed away a few months ago, and I want to bring her back by cloning. Can it be done? Can the scientists who created Dolly the sheep by cloning, clone my wife?"

The professor was stunned. Now he understood why a businessman would be interested in science and why both Mr. Kincaid and Patricia had grown so tense when Mr. Kincaid mentioned his wife's death. Professor Lee explained that there were no known cases of human cloning. There were always unsubstantiated rumors about cases of successful human cloning, but that's what they were, just rumors.

"When cloning is done, the cloned animal is not the same age as the original subject. Hollywood and science fictions writers have misguided the public on this issue," Dr. Lee explained. He was growing a bit agitated. "A new movie called, *Multiplicity*, was released recently. In that movie, the main character creates multiple clones of himself. As you would guess, all his clones begin as adults. I had a laugh when I saw that movie," he said.

"In reality, the cloned animal starts as an embryo. So even if they can clone Mrs. Kincaid, the clone will start as a fetus and not as an adult person. Besides, they will need her DNA sample. Whether the scientists involved in cloning of the sheep would attempt human cloning or not is a question that I cannot answer. As far as human cloning is concerned, there are many ethical issues involved with it, so most scientists may not be interested in it at present," Dr. Lee said while trying to remain as cool and detached as possible. This was a touchy subject for him as it was for many people, but obviously, for Mr. Kincaid, the idea held great hope.

Mr. Kincaid was visibly disappointed. Dr. Lee saw it. He further emphasized to soften the blow he had just delivered, "You see, Mr. Kincaid, Hollywood teaches junk science. People should also understand that when a person is cloned, his or her clone may not be exactly like the original person. For example, a clone of Einstein may not be a genius like him or even have a proclivity for science. Similarly, a clone of Hitler, if someone would dare attempt it, may not grow up to be an evil person like Hitler."

"No one should take a chance to see what Hitler's clone would be capable of," Mr. Kincaid reacted.

"No question there. We could try cloning Einstein and fail to create a genius, but with Hitler, no one should attempt cloning," Professor Lee agreed. Mr. Kincaid's curiosity was over. He thanked the professor profusely for his time.

I am back to square one, he thought. He was not going to get Lucy back into his life, so having more kids with her was out of question. Then, he suddenly had an idea. What if they could clone his son, Steven? Even if the clone starts as a fetus, he would be less than two years younger than Steven. If Lucy had survived, their second child would have been two or three years younger than Steven too. The professor had said that there were no known cases of human cloning. What if there were unknown cases of human cloning? What if someone could be persuaded to experiment secretly and produce the first human clone? He wouldn't mind if the scientist wanted to do it clandestinely, for money. He could spare a few million dollars to have more children, more of Lucy's children.

Michael told Patricia the next day to call Dr. Lee again. He wanted to know if Dr. Lee had heard rumors of any scientists who had experimented on human cloning or were currently working on it. He wanted to know if anyone had the technology to produce a human clone. He explained to Patricia that maybe he could try to have his son, Steven, cloned instead of Lucy. Patricia was shocked to hear that information but decided not to respond. He also asked her not to mention it to Dr. Lee.

Patricia called Dr. Lee. She asked him if there could be cases of human clones not known to mainstream scientists or to the general public.

Dr. Lee told her that he did not know of anybody who had produced an actual human clone. He gave her a few names of the scientists who were involved in animal cloning at the time. There were scientists from the United States, the United Kingdom, Germany, South Korea, and China. He again emphasized that Mr. Kincaid's idea of cloning his wife was farfetched. Over and above the ethical issues involved with cloning, Mr. Kincaid needed to know that cloning would not produce an adult; therefore, he could not expect to clone his wife and get an adult person. Patricia assured him that Mr. Kincaid understood that.

Dr. Lee also added, "I had an excellent time discussing cloning with you and Mr. Kincaid. Please tell Mr. Kincaid that he is a fascinating man."

Patricia replied, "He already knows that." Dr. Lee laughed at the other end.

*   *   *

After Lucy's death, the depressed and reclusive Michael languished in the cocoon of his bedroom for a few months. The man who emerged was a metamorphosed person nothing like the old Michael. When Michael was depressed, he learned that planning, ethics, and morals did not matter. If they did, he would not have suffered so much. The unexpected death of his wife destroyed his personality. He questioned his core convictions, his morals, and his way of life. He concluded that in the end nothing really matters: ethics, honesty, goodness. Nothing matters once you lose your reason to live.

The new Michael was a ruthless businessman. His employees were disposable, and he enjoyed terminating them. This was particularly shocking to everyone because until then, he had hardly ever fired anyone. Some of the top executives of his company advised him against his impulsive termination policies. They were afraid of losing their own jobs, so they were tactful in their suggestions. Patricia was an exception. She told him that it was unlike him to act like this and she didn't like the new Michael. In response to that, Mr. Kincaid laughed and told her, "What can I say? After such loss, there is bound to be some change in me."

4

Cloning for Cash

Human cloning is coming.

— MICHAEL PENCE, VICE PRESIDENT OF THE
UNITED STATES

Patricia was facing an arduous task. Mr. Kincaid wanted her to find someone who could accomplish human cloning. He was determined to clone his son. If that's what it takes to fulfill the promise he had made to his late wife, then so be it. Dr. Lee had told him that the scientists who were involved in the cloning of Dolly the sheep may not be interested in human cloning. Nevertheless, Patricia secretly contacted them at Roslin Institute in Scotland, United Kingdom. None of them were interested in human cloning just as Dr. Lee had predicted. They also stated that they were not aware of any institution involved in human cloning at the time.

Patricia came to know about an obscure religious movement called Raelism during her search on the Internet. Their aim was to create clones. She met some followers of this movement. She came to know that they believed that human beings were created by extraterrestrials. They were doing research on cloning but did not possess the technology to clone a human being yet. Another dead end.

Patricia searched for someone who would be willing to experiment on human cloning. With the cloning of a sheep, there were many news articles about cloning, including the possibility of human cloning in the near future. No one claimed that it had already been done. She concluded that if someone had successfully performed cloning on humans, it would be done clandestinely. People involved in that kind of work obviously wouldn't do it for fame, but would do it for money, lots of money. She knew that for her boss, money was not an issue. She looked at many tabloids which every now and then reported on cloning of human beings secretly done in some remote parts of the world. None of them gave any clue of an authentic case of cloning, human or animal. Patricia was becoming frustrated.

One evening, she was going through all the information she had obtained so far when she was interrupted by her husband. He asked her what she was doing. She explained that Michael wanted to clone his son, Steven. She described to him the discussions she and Michael had with a geneticist and her research up to the point to find someone who would clone a human being.

"First of all, let me ask you. Do you have any ethical qualms about cloning?" her husband queried.

"I sure have, but I am simply trying to help Michael. That's all," she answered.

"Cloning is, in my opinion, playing God. Did you ask Michael about ethical and moral concerns involved with cloning? Before you and Michael go any further, I think you need to discuss its ramifications," he said. John was very concerned about where this whole situation was going, and he feared for his wife's safety.

"I'm only helping Michael. That's my job. He's still grieving. He barely survived his wife's death. If having another child will make him functional, then I think it is all right. I am sure once this happens he will be back to his old self," Patricia said in a defeated tone.

"Pat, the old Michael is not coming back. He died with Lucy. The new Michael is quite different. Don't you see he's changed? This Michael has no morals, no ethics. He is everything that the old Michael was not," he cautioned her.

"I know he's changed," Patricia snapped. "I am sure after a while he will recover from all this and be his usual self. I am convinced of that," Patricia was firm. John left the room in frustration.

A few days after that conversation with her husband, Patricia received a typewritten letter advising her to visit someone in Geneva, Switzerland. The letter mentioned that if she was looking for a miracle of birth, then she could talk to them. The letter didn't mention any phone number or even the word cloning. Patricia booked a flight.

Patricia flew to Geneva. She visited the place mentioned in the letter. The office did not have a sign outside. A beautiful, young blond lady welcomed her. Her name was Dalia. She asked her for the name and other pertinent information of the person who wanted their services. Patricia tried to ask questions about cloning, but the woman interrupted her and told her to come back two days later to meet the geneticist, doctor Julien Lautens. Patricia asked Dalia how they had come to know that she was looking for someone to help her with "this process." Dalia told her that all she could say was that they had heard that she was looking for someone in this field. Patricia figured that maybe someone she had contacted while inquiring about cloning had given her name to Dr. Lautens. In her multinational search, Patricia had not heard of Dr. Lautens. She was suspicious. She did research looking for a geneticist named Lautens but didn't find one. She figured that he was working under a pseudonym.

Two days later, she returned to Dr. Lautens's office. Dalia was waiting for her. She drove Patricia to a remote location in Geneva. The area looked very sketchy and run-down. Dalia parked her car in front of an old, nondescript building. It looked like a warehouse. She then took Patricia to one of the rooms in that building. It was Dr. Lautens's office. Dalia introduced Patricia to Dr. Lautens. The room was not very well lit. It took her a few seconds to adjust to the semidarkness of the room.

"I am Dr. Lautens, Ms. Sharp," said Dr. Lautens as he extended his right hand to her.

"Please call me Pat," Patricia said as she shook hands with Dr. Lautens.

"Very well. Please be seated, Pat," Dr. Lautens said as he pointed to a chair in front of him. Patricia sat down. She looked around the room. Dr. Lautens was sitting behind a huge desk. There was a beautiful model of the double helix of a DNA molecule on his desk. There was someone's picture on the desk too. Patricia read the name of the person under the picture.

It was Gregor Mendel. *Of course! After all, Gregor Johann Mendel is considered to be the "father of genetics."* There were no certificates or awards or citations anywhere in the office. *That's a surprise!* On the wall behind Dr. Lautens, there was a huge picture of a majestic white tiger. *Why would a geneticist be interested in a tiger?* While Patricia was studying his office and getting accustomed to the semi-lit room, Dr. Lautens poured coffee for them.

"Dr. Lautens, I am surprised to see a picture of a tiger in your office. You must be an animal lover or a hunter," Patricia was curious.

"Please have some coffee, Pat. I am not a hunter. I do love animals, though. But that's not why this picture is here. I like white tigers because they represent an interesting genetic mutation, which was exploited to produce generations of these beautiful animals. You know, all white tigers in the world are descendants of Mohan, a white tiger from India?" Dr. Lautens probed.

"No, I didn't know that. That's interesting," Patricia said as she leaned forward in her seat and reached for her coffee.

"There are hundreds of white tigers all over the world now. I hate to see these beautiful animals used in performances or kept in zoos for our entertainment," Dr. Lautens said.

"Speaking of zoos, I remember seeing a white tiger in a zoo in Columbus, Ohio. I was mesmerized by his beauty. I must admit, at that time, it didn't occur to me that it was unethical to destroy the natural lives of such beautiful animals," Patricia mentioned.

"That's the problem. As long as people visit zoos and circuses, the exploitation of these animals will continue. There is another reason why I like the picture of a white tiger. These tigers appear white due to lack of pigmentation. By inbreeding over multiple generations, zoologists all over the world have produced hundreds of these animals. As expected, many of these tigers have genetic defects because of inbreeding. So just like anything else, there are two sides to the success of breeding these animals. It reminds me that what I am doing now to help people who want genetic copies of themselves or of their other children has a negative side, too," Dr. Lautens lamented.

Patricia did not follow, but before she asked him to explain, Dr. Lautens continued. "You know, Pat, the science of this method of reproduction is not perfect. The success rate of a normal birth is very low. Besides, many animals born by this method have multiple health problems and shorter life-spans. So there are two sides to everything," Dr. Lautens explained. *That's the chance Michael will have to take if he wants Steven cloned.*

Patricia noticed that Dr. Lautens appeared Caucasian and had a fake British accent. He was in his early fifties. She could not decide where he was from. She was curious to know more about him, but she was sure Dr. Lautens wouldn't reveal any information about himself unless he wanted to do so.

"That's true. This mutation you mentioned for their white color is a recessive condition, right?" Patricia asked.

"You are correct. If you are trying to show that you know a thing or two about genetics then I am convinced," Dr. Lautens laughed. Patricia chuckled.

"Now let me get to the business at hand," Dr. Lautens mentioned. "Dalia tells me that Mr. Kincaid wants to do this because his wife Lucy has passed away, and he wants to have another child with her genes. I understand that Mr. Kincaid is a wealthy man, a successful man," he bluntly stated.

"Yes, that's right. I think you've done your homework to know your potential client," Patricia answered. "Mr. Kincaid had planned to have more kids. However, since his wife had passed away . . . he would like to clone his son, Steven."

"Let me discuss some ground rules first. We do not mention the word clone unless it's absolutely necessary. I want governments and ethicists out of this office at any cost. We use the word IVF, which stands for in vitro fertilization as you must know. Another rule is that I do not leave Switzerland. My lab is here, and I can't move my equipment to another country. People from your side will need to travel here to see me," Dr. Lautens said unequivocally.

"I will convey all the information to Mr. Kincaid. After that, it's up to him to decide if he can agree with your conditions or not," Patricia cautioned.

"That's fair. I can guarantee you that these rules are nonnegotiable. If Mr. Kincaid can't accept them, then we will forget about the whole arrangement," Dr. Lautens was firm. "The most important rule I have is this. Under no circumstance is my name to be revealed to anyone. All payments and all correspondence will be done with that rule in mind. Dalia will explain how we will communicate. I strongly suggest that your attorney contact Dalia. Only then will I discuss the whole process and show my laboratory to you and Mr. Kincaid."

Three days later, Mr. Kincaid visited Dr. Lautens with Patricia and his attorney, Rudolph Drake. Mr. Drake told the doctor that his conditions were acceptable to his client. Dr. Lautens explained the procedure involved in cloning to Mr. Kincaid and his team. He would need to take eggs from one woman. The woman would be given medications so that she would produce multiple eggs. Then he would create embryos using Steven's cells. He would like to implant these eggs in five women. That way the chances of one successful pregnancy would increase. Again, he stressed the importance of secrecy and anonymity of all the parties involved. After some more meetings and discussions, the contract was signed, and payments were made.

Mr. Kincaid discussed the issue with his attorney in his hotel suite. Mr. Drake would conduct the whole operation through his law firm. Their first concern was to find a woman who would donate eggs. That woman had to be willing to travel. Mr. Drake told them that his firm would look for someone for that job although she would not be aware of the cloning process. Patricia thought of volunteering for that job. She decided that she should talk to John before talking to Mr. Kincaid or Mr. Drake.

*   *   *

After returning to the States, Patricia asked John, "Honey, I want to ask you something." She sat down on the couch next to her husband.

"Yes, what is it?" John asked. He put the newspaper down so he could focus on her.

Patricia took a deep breath and began, "For cloning, the geneticist wants a woman to donate her eggs, and then he will need five women to be surrogate mothers. He wants to implant embryos in more women because in pregnancies resulting from cloning, there is a higher incidence of fetal loss. There is also a higher chance of some babies not making it to the first year of life."

"What are you asking me?" John asked. He was afraid to assume where this conversation was going.

"I am thinking of donating my eggs and also of being one of the surrogates. Michael is desperate for another child and this way, I can help him get his wish. I want to know what you think." she said while reaching for John's hand. She could sense that he was becoming anxious and she wanted to comfort him, but at the same time she also needed his reassurance that they would be okay.

"I don't think it's a good idea. I don't understand why you should be in the picture at all. As you know, I am not even comfortable with the idea of cloning. I think it's against Nature," John stated emphatically.

"I know you don't like cloning. But we're not doing it. Michael is doing it. He needs someone to donate eggs. This whole process demands the utmost secrecy. Whoever donates the eggs is likely to suspect something because she will have to travel to Switzerland. The geneticist refuses to come to the States with his staff and his multi-million-dollar equipment. For the surrogates, it's a different story because the embryos will be implanted in them here in the United States. I think since both, Michael and Lucy, have done so much for us, I want to do this," Patricia said. She could see that John was growing stiffer and more uptight the more she talked about this subject. She braced herself for his next words.

"No, I don't agree with this. I agree that they have both been good to us, but that doesn't mean that you should carry a baby for them for nine months. I don't even know what you will have to do to donate eggs. Pat, tell me when we are going to have our baby?" John said as he stood up from the couch and began to pace the length of the room. He ran his hands through his hair.

"John, it's no big deal," Patricia said trying to placate him. "They will give me some medicine, so I will produce more than one egg in my monthly cycles; then they will remove the eggs by laparoscopy and fertilize them in a laboratory. I promise, after this thing is over, I will be ready to have a baby," she continued. "You know, when I was new in this country, it was Michael who hired me, and it was Lucy who mentored me. Thanks to their support, I got my MBA. I even got my green card, thanks to them," Patricia said, trying to make her case.

"True. But whatever they did for you or me doesn't mean you are expected to do this. I want you to think about it some more," John opined.

At this point, Patricia stood up so she could catch his eyes. "I know that. Neither Michael nor his attorney, have asked me or even indirectly suggested that I should consider this. I want to do it. I feel it is my duty," Pat insisted.

"I don't understand your 'hero worship' when it comes to Michael Kincaid. Why have you put him on a pedestal?" John wondered. John's hair was standing up all over his head from repeatedly running his hands through it. He looked slightly like a wild man.

"John, ever since I was a little girl, I was in awe of the United States. When I came to this country and met Michael Kincaid, he represented America to me. He is a mover and a shaker just like America is for the whole world. By immigrating to America, I have fulfilled my life's dream. Michael has helped me tremendously in this endeavor," Patricia said. She was emotional. She felt like it was the least she could do to help a man who had been so kind to her and had had such a huge impact on her life.

"I think your problem is deeper than I thought. Pat, don't take it the wrong way, but I think when it comes to the Kincaid family, you act like you don't have a will of your own," John explained.

Patricia was stunned to hear something so cruel from her husband. She became red-faced and started shaking from anger. She regained her composure after a few seconds and answered him. "John, I have never been so insulted in my life. That was totally uncalled for," she said while walking away from him into the bedroom. Maybe if she put some distance between them, they could both calm down.

"I am sorry, Pat. But this is how you always act when it comes to the Kincaids. I apologize for saying this," John said as he followed her into the bedroom. He couldn't believe she was walking away from him.

"An apology doesn't fix the insult you have inflicted upon me. It was very hurtful," Patricia yelled. She walked into the bathroom and slammed the door. *Divorcing him right now will show him how strong her will is.*

"Pat, my dear, you are in for a rude awakening. Michael manipulates people. Explain to me why his actions are frequently contradictory? Have you thought of that?" John yelled through the door, so she could hear him. He couldn't understand how she could be so naïve.

"John, it's a simple business practice. I have asked him about it in the past few weeks. He explained that if you don't manipulate people, they will manipulate you. According to him, the best way to remain in control is to keep disturbing others. Although I will never do it, I understand his logic," Pat explained.

"His policy is to do unto others and keep doing it. Or, do unto others, before they do unto you. And that's wrong," John replied. Then he continued.

"You claim that Michael Kincaid symbolizes America to you. Let me tell you something, my dear. As great as the United States is, you need to admit that this country was built on the genocide of one race and enslavement of another. You know that Michael frequently goes out of his way to help people around him, but he also manipulates their lives for no apparent reason. What Michael does to people is what the United States does to other countries. Look at our foreign policy. We give billions of dollars in aid to other countries. But we also interfere in their elections, their internal affairs, and we make them go to war with one another. When there is any major disaster in the world, we donate millions of dollars. At the same time, we have hundreds of military bases spread out across the world. We are always at war with one country or another. We have used hundreds of thousands of land mines, and we have used tons of poisonous gases on innocent civilians in other countries. What our CIA does in other countries is a whole other matter. Do you think that's the way to treat people?"

John was angry. Patricia did not reply. This had obviously been building for quite some time, and she had no idea how to respond.

"Perhaps, Michael Kincaid is like that Mr. Jekyll or something you told me about some time ago," John mentioned.

"You are referring to the story of Dr. Jekyll and Mr. Hyde. I don't think Michael is anything like Mr. Hyde. Edward Hyde was pure evil. It's absolutely unfair to compare Michael to him," Patricia corrected him.

"Pat, one day you will realize that Michael is not what you think he is. I don't know what is with you smart women. If I had a nickel for every time, a beautiful, smart, competent woman was mesmerized by a ruthless, arrogant, evil man I would be a millionaire. I think you should think about your priorities, not others'. Don't try to live for other people. I would rather you punch someone in the face than compromise your life to keep everyone happy," he stated.

"Anyway, you do what you want to do. I am not going to stop you. For the record, I am not happy with this idea, but it's your body and your health. You need to decide soon where you will draw the line when it comes to doing things for Mr. Kincaid," John conceded. He knew that Patricia was strong-willed and young. She had to learn from her own mistakes. Although, she could understand John's point of view she did not change her mind.

The next day, Patricia went to work and told Michael that she was willing to participate in this experiment. She told him that she would love to donate her eggs if it was all right with him and Dr. Lautens. Michael thanked her for that but declined the offer. He assured her that in his opinion there was no one better than her and he was honored that she wanted to help, but he didn't want her to feel any obligation to help him. He even informed her that neither Mr. Drake nor he had even thought of her providing these services. Patricia insisted. Finally, he agreed.

The office of Mr. Drake contacted some people to hire as surrogates. They had to find four women since Patricia was going to be one of the five they were looking for. After they were done with their search, contracts were signed by the women with the help of their respective attorneys. Then the women were examined by different obstetricians.

Patricia was placed on ovulation inducing medications. Then she flew to Switzerland to meet with Dr. Lautens. This time Dr. Lautens's office was in a different location. Patricia was not surprised. When she was ovulating, Dr. Lautens removed seven eggs by laparoscopy.

Steven was flown there at the same time. Cells from his tissues were removed. When the cells were fertilized and started dividing, they were brought to Columbus, Ohio, where they were to be implanted into the surrogates.

5

Angela Becomes a Surrogate Mother

From the beginning, each human embryo has its own unique genetic identity.

— Robert Casey, US Senator

Angela Johnson was struggling to survive. She was raising Jeff, working part-time, and attending church activities. Her husband's child support payments were never on time. Bills were piling up. Then one day her divorce attorney, Robert Newman, called her. She still owed him some money. *He must be getting impatient*, she thought.

"Ms. Johnson, this is Robert Newman. I have some news for you. I am not sure how you will take it, but I think I should at least ask you," Mr. Newman said.

"What is it, Mr. Newman? If this is about money then let me assure you that I am doing my best to pay you in full," she said to him.

"No, this is about something else. I called to discuss with you an interesting proposal. It is something totally unexpected, so please hear me out. You can give your answer after you think about it. An attorney from another law firm contacted me. He has a client who needs help. The client's wife, I believe, is not able to have children. They are looking for someone to carry the pregnancy for them. The person, known as a surrogate mother, must be young, healthy, and cooperative. My lawyer colleague, Mr. Drake, has assured me that there is good money for whoever is willing to do it. I am wondering if you would be interested," Mr. Newman said.

"This is something strange. I've never thought about anything like this. I mean, I've heard about test-tube babies and so on, but this is kind of weird. Can you explain to me how it works?" Angela asked.

"Sure. As I understand it, they fertilize the ovum or egg in a test tube. Then, they implant it in the surrogate woman. The surrogate's role is to carry the baby for nine months. The husband and wife are the biological parents of the child if that's what you are concerned about. Surrogacy is required when the woman has some problem with her uterus, or she has other health issues that make pregnancy too risky for her. After the baby is born, the surrogate's job is done. If you are interested, then first you will have to go through a physical examination. The doctor will inquire about your medical history, assess your mental status, and determine whether you are a proper candidate or not. The law firm has informed me that the client is very rich and is willing to pay a lot more than what is currently being paid for this job," Mr. Newman explained.

"Is this moral? Is this against Christianity? I will have to think about it. For the sake of money, I don't want to do anything sinful. 'Is it legal or not?' is another question that comes to my mind," asked Angela.

"Many people have been surrogates. It's completely legal. I am not an authority on Christianity or any religion for that matter. I am a lawyer not a religious leader, so I can't tell you what is moral and what is not. But to go through nine months of pregnancy for somebody else is definitely a great service to them in my opinion. Why don't you think about? If you agree to do it, call me, and we will go through the contract. They need an answer in few days," he said.

"Oh, that is kind of sudden. But I understand. I will get back to you soon," she said to him and hung up.

Angela could not sleep that night. Sure, she could use some extra income. But she had to look at the morality of this situation. She was helping a needy family who was desperate to have a child. If her sister or cousin were in this situation, she would definitely do it. Well, in that case, she would do it for free. In fact, it would be her moral obligation to offer her service. People donate their kidneys to family members and sometimes even to strangers. If she would accept this offer, she could make some badly needed money. After tossing and turning all night, she knew what she had to do. She had to seek the advice of her pastor.

The next morning, she went to her church to see Pastor Watson. When she was going through her messy divorce, he had helped her a lot. She explained the situation to him. The pastor asked her a few questions to determine whether she was comfortable with it. Finally, he advised her that if she was comfortable, then this was the Christian thing to do. That's what she wanted to hear. If it was all right with the Church, then it was all right with her. She called Mr. Newman and told him that she was willing to participate. Mr. Newman asked her to come to his office immediately.

In Mr. Newman's law office, she found Mr. Rudolph Drake. Mr. Drake represented the couple who wanted to hire a surrogate mother. He was in his fifties. He was a fierce-looking man with a penetrating gaze and a sharp tongue. Mr. Drake informed her that the couple wanted privacy, so their identity would not be revealed. Mr. Newman informed her that even he was not privy to that information. Mr. Drake told Angela that additionally her identity would be kept secret from his clients. He added that the only reason he wanted to meet her was that during her pregnancy, it was important that he was able to contact her.

They had a long contract for her to sign. Mr. Newman had already reviewed it. Angela glanced at it and signed it. Mr. Drake's clients were to pay her medical bills. She was paid half the amount up front, and the remaining was to be paid after the infant was born. From the money she received, she settled her account with Mr. Newman. Angela was assured by both attorneys that she was not the first surrogate mother in the United State. Thousands of women before her had done it either for a fee or had volunteered their services.

Two days later, Mr. Drake's assistant took her to meet her obstetrician, Dr. Beverly Adkins. Dr. Adkins was a very pleasant woman in her late thirties. She told Angela that she would eventually implant the fertilized egg in her uterus. First, she was going to perform an ultrasound study to make sure that her uterus was normal in shape. Then, Angela was placed on hormonal treatment to prime her uterus for implantation.

Angela returned to Dr. Adkins's office for check-ups and when she was ready, the fertilized egg was implanted in her uterus. A few days later, it was confirmed that everything was progressing fine. Angela was pregnant.

What Angela Johnson, Mr. Newman, and Dr. Adkins didn't know was that they were participating in human cloning. That information was kept secret by Mr. Drake, Dr. Lautens, Patricia Sharp, and Mr. Kincaid.

* * *

While the efforts to clone his son were going on, Mr. Kincaid became embroiled in a scandal. He gave a huge Christmas party. Senators and congressmen of the state of Ohio, prominent businessmen of Columbus, and many Hollywood celebrities were invited. At the party, he flirted with many women. People laughed it away thinking he was drunk or he was recovering from his wife's death.

Among the women, he flirted with was Veronica McHenry, First Lady of the State of Ohio. When he was dancing with her, the Governor joked that Michael was trying to steal her away from him. Everyone within earshot of the Governor laughed politely. When you are a governor, people will laugh at your jokes even when they are not funny.

Three days later, Mr. Kincaid was in bed with Veronica in his hotel suite. The affair continued for a couple of months until one day a tabloid published the story of their affair. Photographs accompanied the article.

The affair caused a huge public scandal. Veronica McHenry accused Michael Kincaid of leaking the information about the affair to the press by colluding with a hotel employee. She mentioned that some of the details of their affair could have come only from one of them. Since it was not her, it had to be him. When the story was published, Patricia asked Michael about it. In response, all he did was laugh. Patricia was surprised. She understood that her widower boss wanted a female companionship, but she couldn't understand why he would go after the governor's wife. When she saw Michael laugh at the news item, she concluded that he wasn't bothered by the gossip. The scandal resulted in a very ugly divorce of Ohio's First Couple. In an interview, Mr. Kincaid even claimed, "She fell head over heels in love with me. What was I going to do?"

Michael Kincaid's roving eyes didn't spare Patricia either. One day, Patricia noticed that her boss was ogling her legs. She was too smart for him. As soon as she saw him looking at her with lust in his eyes, she coughed violently, retched, and then spit on the carpet. Then she looked at Michael, who was repulsed by this action, and told him, "Something blocked my windpipe. I almost died." A message was conveyed as disgustingly as possible and was unquestionably received because after this incident, Michael never looked at her that way again.

6

Angela's Pregnancy

The greatest deception men suffer is from their own opinions.

— Leonardo da Vinci, inventor and artist

Angela was pregnant. There were four other women in this project, but Angela was not aware of it. Different obstetricians were assigned to each of them. Mr. Drake's office was managing payments and contacts with the physicians involved in the care of these women.

Angela's pregnancy proceeded smoothly for the first few weeks. By the second month of her pregnancy, she developed morning sickness, bloating, and craving for spicy foods. *All the good things that happen in pregnancy*, she thought.

She remembered her first pregnancy. She had enjoyed it, but that joyfulness was tarnished by the problems in her marriage. It's hard to enjoy pregnancy when you are not sure if you have married the right guy, your husband is unfaithful, and your siblings are advising you to divorce him.

This time, things were different. Mark was now her ex-husband, and he was out of the picture. She loved every minute of her pregnancy. As weeks went by, she gained weight and started to "show." People in her church started noticing it. There were awkward stares at her bulging belly followed by some whisperings. Angela was becoming uncomfortable. She talked to Pastor Watson for his advice on how to deal with this situation.

The pastor told her that if it was acceptable to her then he would inform the congregation the reason behind her pregnancy. She was fine with that.

The following Sunday Pastor Watson announced in the church that Angela Johnson was doing a great service for an infertile couple. She was doing a "Christian" thing by carrying a baby for them, so they could have a family of their own. Everyone applauded her for this noble deed. From that day onward, people came to her and offered their support. Everything was going very smoothly, again. She took good care of herself, and she was thoroughly enjoying her pregnancy. She was glowing, literally. Some women look more beautiful when they are pregnant. Angela was one of those women.

Fifteen weeks into her pregnancy, the baby "moved!" Angela now felt a life inside her. *What a feeling!* Angela was in heaven. It had been almost three years since she had that feeling. She could tell when the baby was awake and when it was sleeping. As time passed, the baby moved more frequently. She enjoyed her pregnancy more and more too. Her son Jeff was with her. She could imagine that the baby kicking inside her belly would grow up to be like Jeff in three years.

Whether it was her hormonal status, her religious upbringing, or the maternal feelings in her heart, she could not tell, but she decided that she could not part with this child. She had to keep it. She had gone through a few ultrasounds, but Dr. Adkins did not divulge the baby's gender to her. She told her that even though she could tell by the ultrasound; her contract with Mr. Drake forbade her from revealing the baby's gender.

Boy or girl, Angela did not want to part with the baby. What if she keeps the baby? That will mean breaking the contract. It will also be immoral. She should not deprive the couple who wanted this baby desperately. Could she keep the baby? She had to seek advice of someone soon. She met with Pastor Watson. She told him that she had to talk to him, or she would go crazy. She explained her dilemma. She told him how much she was attached to this unborn child and how much she wanted to keep it. She asked him if she can go back on her contract and keep the child.

Pastor Watson asked her why she wanted to keep this baby, she already had Jeff. Angela told him that she could take care of both the kids. Having Jeff did not change what she felt now when the baby moved inside her.

The pastor contemplated for a few moments. He was stumped. Finally, he told her, "I think you should not keep the baby. It's morally and legally wrong. I understand that you have become attached to the unborn child, but you did not plan to have a child for you. In the eyes of God, this is sin. God may still forgive you, because you are acting like a mother. But you should consider your obligations to that family." Angela was disappointed, but she realized that Pastor Watson was right even though he was not telling her what she wanted to hear. She thanked him for his advice.

She kept on struggling with the idea of keeping the child while the clock was ticking. Now she was almost eight months pregnant. The baby was more and more active. She decided that no matter what, she would keep it. If she had to fight for the baby in the court, she would do it. Then it dawned on her that she did not have any money, and the couple who was expecting this child must be loaded or they would not have gone through this whole process to create a child this way. How was she going to fight with them in the court of law?

Angela went to Mr. Newman's office. She talked to him about her desire to keep the baby. He was furious! He told her that it was totally unacceptable. She can't do this! Not only would she have to return all the money she had received, but she stood to lose everything she had if the couple were to sue her. He also told her that once he talked to Mr. Drake, things will become unpleasant. They will drag her to court. He told Angela that before he would even make a phone call to Mr. Drake's office, he would like her to reconsider her decision. Clearly, Mr. Newman was very annoyed.

Angela tried to reason with him. "I am emotionally attached to this unborn child. The pastor of my church and you are the only two people I have talked to about it. Neither one understands my situation. I know it's crazy to think of keeping the baby! I can't even tell anybody else about this. Do you have any idea how hard it is to have such feelings bottled up inside you and not be able to share with anyone? I am afraid I will implode."

Robert Newman laughed.

Angela got angry. "How could you laugh at a time like this?!"

"Ms. Johnson, I understand your situation. Many of us go through times when we have to bottle up our feelings or our secrets inside us. You have no idea how long I had to keep my feelings inside me and then how long I waited for my own parents to understand and accept me."

"I don't follow," Angela replied.

Mr. Newman continued, "Ms. Johnson, I am not sure whether you know this or not, but I am gay. After years of struggle, I finally accepted my sexual orientation. When I came out and told my parents, it was a long time before they accepted me for who I was. I can tell you this now because most people around me already know it. Believe me, I know how hard it is when you feel strongly about something but people around you don't understand it. Anyway, as your attorney, I must ask you to reconsider your decision."

"I didn't know that. To tell you the truth, I don't know how to handle this new information."

Angela's religious mind couldn't figure out what to do now. She was not sure if it was all right to continue the attorney–client relationship with a lawyer who was, well . . ., a homosexual. She was visibly disturbed. Mr. Newman could read her mind.

"Ms. Johnson, it does not change anything between us. I came out a long time ago and most of my clients either know it or suspect it, and they are fine with it. I thought you knew it too, but obviously I was wrong. I don't understand why my being gay makes you so uncomfortable. And please don't deny it. For the last few minutes, you have been rubbing your belly, but as soon as I mentioned that I am gay, your hand froze. It still remains motionless on your belly."

Mr. Newman paused for a moment. He wanted to help put her more at ease. "I find it fascinating that almost every pregnant woman loves to rub her belly. I distinctly remember my girlfriend did it all the time when she was pregnant..."

Angela interrupted, "Mr. Newman, you just told me about your being a . . . you know?" Angela could not use the word gay or homosexual. "Then how come you had a girlfriend?"

"True. In my early twenties, I was confused and was not sure of my sexual orientation. Long story short, I had a girlfriend, she got pregnant, and we had a son. Shortly after his birth, we broke up. He is a senior in high school now and lives with his mother, but I have a good relationship with him," Mr. Newman explained. He opened the drawer of his desk, took out a picture, and showed it to Angela. "That's me with my son," he said to her. Then, he put the picture back in the drawer.

"I appreciate your candor, Mr. Newman. It may be sometime before I can get used to who you are. Maybe, it's my conservative upbringing. I am sure that people who are not strongly religious also may consider it unnatural."

"Ms. Johnson, that's a common misconception. People always claim that homosexuality is against the laws of Nature. It's not. Hundreds of species of animals exhibit homosexuality. From insects and birds to mammals, there are many such examples. So it's not unnatural at all. Anyway, I was just trying to explain to you that I understand what you are going through," Mr. Newman explained.

"I don't see how these two situations can be even related. All I can say is this. As an attorney you should always keep your client's interests in mind. When someone comes to you after robbing a bank, you don't tell him that he should not have done it. You help him as his attorney and defend him in court."

"I guess you are right. You know, Ms. Johnson, you are not the only person to have the idea of breaking the contract as a surrogate mother. Occasionally, surrogate mothers change their minds and decide to keep the babies. There have been battles fought in the court of law in such cases. They have gone to court or have run away to Canada or Mexico or anywhere else they could go. As your attorney, I must advise you that it's illegal." He paused and took a deep breath before continuing. He wanted to make sure that she fully understood the magnitude of her decisions. "People change their names, assume a new identity, and sever ties with their friends and family and so on. It's not legal, it's not the right thing to do, and it's risky. Let me give you an example to illustrate how far people go when they are determined. You may have heard of doctor Elizabeth Morgan. She was in news few years ago."

"No, I have not. What has Dr. Morgan to do with my situation?" Angela was perplexed.

"I am coming to that," Mr. Newman continued. "Elizabeth Morgan's story has some similarities to yours. She is a medical doctor. She found out that her ex-husband was sexually abusing their little daughter. She refused to let their daughter visit her dad. Her ex-husband went to the court to force Dr. Morgan to allow the visitations. The court ruled in his favor. The judge asked Dr. Morgan to allow her daughter to visit her dad. She refused. The girl then disappeared with Dr. Morgan's parents. The court ordered Dr. Morgan to reveal her daughter's whereabouts, but she refused to comply. She went to prison for not obeying the court order. Sometime later, it was discovered that Dr. Morgan's parents had taken the child out of the country and moved to New Zealand."

Mr. Newman continued, "My point is, when Dr. Morgan realized that the court was forcing her to allow her daughter to visit her dad, she thought outside of the box, so to speak. She had to risk imprisonment or allow her daughter to continue being abused by her dad. She chose imprisonment. The girl was taken out of the country, so that the long arm of the law would not subject her to any more abuse. Eventually, Dr. Morgan was released from prison and reunited with her daughter. When people are determined to do something, they go to any lengths. But the consequences for those actions are severe. Therefore, I urge you, one more time, don't do anything rash."

Finally, the lawyer advised her that she should go home and sleep over what he had told her. She did. She knew that she should not keep the child. Then the baby kicked and all her rational thinking went down the drain. *The child would remain with her.*

Then she understood what her lawyer had told her. Maybe, instead of advising her to respect her contract, he was suggesting a way out. She remembered that his tone changed when she told him to keep his client's interests in his mind. Sure, Mr. Newman knew that if she would refuse to give up the baby, it will be a disaster. But if she would leave the country, then the legal system of the country she runs away to may protect her.

Even better, she may remain hidden forever. Of course, she couldn't prove that Mr. Newman was advising her to run away. He was too subtle for that. *What a sneaky, young man!*

Running out of the country was not easy. She needed someone's help. But who would help her? She thought Mexico was a not a good option. She did not know anyone there and also did not know the language. She knew her siblings would not be able to help. For the last few years, she had not listened to them, so why would they want to help her now?!

There was one person who might help her. She may have to pay a price for his help, but right now she was at a dead end, not at a crossroads. Whatever price she had to pay, she will do it. There was no other option. After much hesitation and soul-searching, she picked up the phone to call Mark Baron, her ex-husband.

7

Angela's Ex

When you break up, your whole identity is shattered. It's like death.

— DENNIS QUAID, ACTOR

Angela's ex-husband, Mark Baron, was from a small town near Toronto, Canada. He came from a broken family. His father, Mark Baron Sr., was an alcoholic. He worked as a truck driver, and because of his work and his alcoholism, he was never home. His mother, Martha, was disabled. She had multiple sclerosis. She spent the last ten years of her life in a wheelchair. Her husband barely took care of her. Mark's younger brother had run away from home at the age of fifteen, never to be heard from again. Mark lost his mother two months after his brother ran away. Last time, Mark saw his dad was at his mother's funeral. After his mother's death, he lived alone and managed to survive by doing odd jobs.

When Mark was in his early twenties, he went to Florida on a spring break. He was hitch-hiking his way back home when he spent a few days in Columbus, Ohio. He ran out of money and was surviving by doing whatever work he could find. While waiting tables in a restaurant, he met Angela. She and her friend, Gloria, had come there for lunch. While serving them, he accidentally spilled water on Angela. He apologized profusely. The restaurant manager saw this and yelled at Mark. Angela and her friend felt that the manager was going to fire the poor guy. Gloria looked at Angela and signaled her to say something so that the waiter wouldn't be in trouble. Angela was not sure if she should lie or let him get fired. As much bad as lying was, if it saved someone's job, "*God may forgive her*," she thought. She told the manager that while the waiter was serving food, she tried to pick up her glass and it slipped, resulting in the spill. She assured him that she was fine and there was nothing to worry about.

A few minutes later while the manager was not looking, Mark came back to the table and thanked her for saving his job. He told her that he was not doing too well there, and they were looking for an excuse to fire him. He then asked her if he could take her out for a cup of coffee to show his gratitude. Angela politely declined the invitation and told him that anyone in her place would have done the same thing. Her friend signaled her to accept the invitation and when Angela ignored her, she kicked her in the shin. Angela got the message. She wrote down her phone number on a napkin and gave it to Mark. When they left the restaurant, Gloria asked Angela what was wrong with her. Angela told her that she didn't like to go out with strangers. Gloria advised her to go out with him on a date. Later, she can decide whether to continue dating him or not. She agreed.

The next day, Mark called her. They went on a date. When Angela learned about Mark's family, she felt sad for him. She saw that this man was hurting and needed a shoulder to lean on. She was naïve and in love. Mark proposed, and she said yes. Interestingly enough, when Mark and Angela met Pastor Watson for premarital counseling, the pastor was not impressed with Mark. He talked to Angela privately after the meeting and told her that she should think hard before rushing into marriage. Angela didn't get the hint. Her friend Gloria met Mark a few times before he proposed to Angela. Mark hit on her. Gloria thought it was her duty to warn Angela before she married him. She told her that she should try to know more about her boyfriend before taking the plunge. Angela replied that for the first time in her life she had found happiness. Gloria dropped the matter.

Angela's siblings also met Mark before they were married and they didn't like him either. They advised her that they should know each other better before getting married. Angela assured them that they both were deeply in love, and they didn't want to waste any more time.

They married in a small church ceremony. Everything was great for a while. Gradually the trouble started. Initially, Angela dismissed the troubles as lovers' quarrels. Soon after their marriage began, she wanted to visit Canada to see where Mark came from, but he did not want to go there. After few months of bugging and nagging, he relented. They visited Mark's hometown. Angela was excited to see the place where her husband grew up. She liked Canada. She told Mark that she would not mind living there if he would want to move. Mark told her in no uncertain terms that he wanted to leave Canada more than he wanted to settle in the United States. He had lot of bad memories there; an alcoholic father who was mostly absent, a disabled mother who was no more, and a sibling who left him never to be heard from again. Angela did not push the issue further. If Mark wanted to live in the United States, that would be fine with her. She can always visit Canada in future.

Angela wanted to have kids soon after marrying, but Mark wanted to wait for a few years. Although they could not come to an agreement on this important issue, nature made the decision for them. Two years after their marriage, she got pregnant. She was ecstatic; he was upset.

Their fights escalated during her pregnancy. Angela continued her job as a sales-person in a department store. Mark did not provide any emotional support to her during her pregnancy. He seemed more and more aloof. After Jeff was born, Angela found it difficult to take care of him and continue to work full time. She started working part-time so that she could take care of Jeff.

Few months later, Angela realized that even though she made a baby with Mark, they had nothing in common. They hardly talked to each other. When they did, it was only about the baby. His infidelity was becoming more and more noticeable. Finally, she saw the writing on the wall. She filed for divorce. She told him that she wanted full custody of Jeff. Mark agreed for divorce. He was a US citizen now; he didn't have to live in a pretend marriage.

Angela hired Robert Newman as her attorney. She was happy when the court gave her full custody of Jeff. Mark could see him every other weekend. She was to get alimony and child support. She began a new chapter in her life. She worked part-time, raised Jeff, and spent time in her church.

Her role as a surrogate mother changed everything. She wanted to raise this child after its birth. She reasoned with herself all the time that this was not her baby and it was the Christian thing to give the baby up after delivery. One little movement in her belly, and she was immune to any reasoning or any potential legal complication. How was this pregnancy different from a normal pregnancy? Except for the way in which she became pregnant, everything else was same. She felt the same morning sickness, cravings for food, bloating, weight gain, and fatigue.

Why could she not keep this baby when she could keep the baby from her previous pregnancy? Anyone who looked at her could not tell whether she was the biological mother or a surrogate mother. *I have every right to keep this baby*, Angela concluded. The easiest person to fool in the whole world is our own self.

How will she do it? *I must think outside of the box just as Dr. Elizabeth Morgan did. Hell no, I mean, heck no, I must think outside of the Book.* What she wanted to do was contrary to the teachings of her holy book. Angela also knew that if she ran away to another part of the United States or to another country, it will be difficult for her to raise two little kids with no money. Maybe, she can ask Mark to take care of Jeff for the time being. Once she settles down, she could have him back.

Finally, she called Mark. He already knew about Angela being a surrogate mother and that she was almost eight months pregnant. Angela told him that she wanted to keep the child even though she was supposed to be a surrogate only. Mark couldn't believe this. He questioned her sanity and her ability to raise two kids. She explained to him that if he would take care of Jeff for some time, maybe a few months or a year, then she may be able to manage everything. Mark was stunned.

"Do you understand what you are doing? Are you prepared to give up your own son to raise someone else's baby?!" He was yelling.

"Calm down, Mark. Only a mother can know what I am going through. Pregnancy is the same whether you are carrying your own baby or someone else's. I am emotionally so attached to this baby that I can't give it up. I want your help only for a short time. I need to run away from here, so they cannot catch me. After everything is settled down, I will take Jeff back," Angela pleaded.

"Well, the way my life is set right now, I can't see taking care of a toddler 24/7. I don't have the time or money for that. Besides, who is going to babysit him when I am at work?"

"How do you think I manage it? While you are at work, put him in day-care like I have been doing or get a babysitter."

"I can hire a babysitter, but then I can't afford to pay you alimony," Mark told her.

Without any source of income, it will be difficult to survive. Angela had intended to return the advance money she had received from Mr. Drake's law firm because it was the right thing to do. But if she could not receive any financial support from Mark then what was she going to do? How was she going to survive? If she would run away with the money she had received so far, she would be fine for some time. She was already breaking the contract by running away with the unborn child. Taking their money is just one more thing she had to do.

"Okay, how about this? You take care of Jeff. You don't pay any alimony as long as he is with you. After about a year when I take him back, we will work out the arrangement. It's possible that I can take him back sooner than that."

Mark tried to explain to her the consequences of breaking the law. Angela told him that she was prepared to take that risk. Finally, they agreed that Mark will take care of Jeff and would not pay alimony. He agreed to take her to Canada. Mark's cousin, Mary, lived near Mississauga. Angela would live with her for a while.

8

Age of Reason . . . or the Lack Thereof

God has no religion.

— MAHATMA GANDHI, LEADER OF INDIA'S
INDEPENDENCE MOVEMENT

A few months after the Veronica McHenry episode, Mr. Kincaid had a surprise for Patricia. "You know, Pat, I read this book, *The Age of Reason*, by Thomas Paine. I think it's a wonderful book," Mike announced.

"Yes, I know. I have read it. There are some interesting arguments against the Holy Bible in that book," Patricia replied.

"I think every priest should read it. People who preach from the Bible should know how their holy book is interpreted by a philosopher," Michael dropped a bomb.

"Mike, that book trashes the Bible. Why do you think the priests should read it?" a confused Patricia asked.

"I want the priests to know how their scriptures appear from a different point of view. They need to read the criticism of their holy book. I plan to donate a copy of this book to thousands of churches across the country."

"I didn't know you are an atheist. No, I know for sure that you are a religious person."

"I am not an atheist. I believe in God. Although, I can't say with certainty that God does exist. I think the existence of God or a Superior Power is a great concept. My idea of God is that He or She is a Supreme Entity, pervading the whole universe. This entity is ultimately the reason for everything in the universe. God is a wonderful concept," Mike tried to explain.

"Then why do you want to gift *The Age of Reason* to all these churches? It's contrary to your own beliefs," Patricia asked.

"No, it's not. I believe in God, I don't believe in religions," Mr. Kincaid said to Patricia. "There are two very important concepts people need to understand. One is that there is a God, a Creator, who is responsible for everything in the universe. This God created the laws of physics and mathematics. He or She also created all the stars, galaxies, and so on."

"What is the second concept," Patricia could not wait to hear.

"The second concept is that there is no God," Mr. Kincaid answered with a smirk. "In my opinion, they are both amazing concepts. Only one of them can be true, but either one of them makes the universe exciting."

"It sounds interesting," Patricia admitted.

"For the record, I believe in the first concept. I believe that there is a God. But my problem is with the religions. They have spoiled the image of God. Why this beautiful concept of a Supreme Deity had to be ruined by religions? I believe that if God exists, then He or She will not be anything like the biblical God or, for that matter, the God of Hinduism. Why do we need a church or a priest or a holy man to be an intermediary between us and our idea of God?" Mike explained.

"I think it does kind of make sense; however, I don't see why you want to declare a crusade against organized religions," Patricia gave her opinion.

"It's because I hate when people don't use their own minds. It's the habit of blindly following the scriptures that I abhor. You are forbidden to question them. What kind of nonsense is that?" Mike asked.

"Don't you believe that millions of people live decent lives because of the inspiration they get from their scriptures?" Patricia was stunned by Mike's logic.

"Pat, you are a well-read person. Don't you think that if more than a billion people have one concept of God and religion, and another billion people have totally different concept on the same issues, then one or both of those concepts are wrong?" Mike asked. "Even within the same religion, there are problems. You know that the most segregated hour in the United States is nine a.m. on Sunday."

"Yes, I do. But people should be allowed to believe in the religion or the scriptures that they want to believe in. There is nothing wrong in that. Freedom of religion is one of the most basic civil rights," Patricia argued.

"I think when people say freedom of religion, they actually mean freedom to worship. There is nothing wrong in the freedom to worship. It does not hurt anybody. A person may worship his God in the privacy of his home or, for that matter, in a church or a temple, as long as it does not violate anybody else's rights. Freedom of religion is a totally different thing."

"I think there's not much difference between the two," Patricia opined.

"Actually, there's a huge difference. It's because we have freedom of religion that people try to convert others into their religion. It would be all right if people were allowed to believe in their religions, but they are not. Religions themselves do not believe in the freedom of religion. If they did, they would let other people follow the religion they want to follow or believe in atheism if that's what they prefer. The average person has no idea what goes on when the religious people proselytize others. Next time you see Jehovah's Witnesses or Christian Evangelists, tell them to leave other people alone in the name of freedom of religion. Let me know if you can convince them. You know something? People need to do with religion what they have done with government," Michael mentioned.

"I don't have any idea what you mean by that statement." Patricia was confused. *Maybe they need to increase the dose of his medication.*

"Man has experimented with many different types of governments, like totalitarian, monarchy, autocracy, dictatorship, communism, and finally democracy. Over the millennia, people have realized that in spite of all its shortcomings, democracy is the best form of government. They need to do the same for religion. Currently, organized religions are practiced the way totalitarian governments function. I am not against the belief in God or, for that matter, religion as long as it does not oppress its followers. We need to democratize the religions so that people are not persecuted by the church. Many people believe that we should have minimum government so that people can live their lives without interference from the government. Similarly, we need minimum religion so that a person is free from the tyranny of religion, his own or others."

"You know, Mike, we have a political party that believes in minimum government. Unfortunately, it believes in more religion instead of less."

"True. The Republican Party wants minimum government, but they want to control many other things, all the way to the reproductive rights of people. There are millions of people who do not believe in the Darwinian evolution because it does not agree with Creation as described in the book of Genesis. That's how strongly the religion controls us. If the reality is different than the scripture, then the religious people will question reality and not the scripture."

Mike continued after a pause. "Mankind needs to modify religion in such a way that people can practice it without being blackmailed by the Church. People should not have to fear the priests. A book like, *The Age of Reason*, can make them think about their beliefs," Michael explained.

"I understand your argument. But I don't believe for a second that anything in the world may make some people think with an open mind. So it's not going to work," Patricia opined. *His arguments made sense; maybe they do not need to change his medication.*

"It does not matter if people will read Thomas Paine's book or not. At least, let the book be available to them. Let's buy one hundred thousand copies of this book and mail them to different churches. I think it won't look good for my image if my name is involved with this project. So you should create an organization with a name you like and mail copies of the book on its behalf."

"Mike, if you want me to do it, I will do it. But you need to understand that even when we are at the end of the second millennium, organized religion has a very secure place in this world. Millions of science graduates also are religious people. Can you explain that?'

"Pat, I think people should accept that science has helped them more than religion can ever hope to do. I want people to think scientifically," Mike countered.

"Okay, let's think scientifically. Can you explain on the basis of science why religions play so much part in our day-to-day life? Why is the influence of religions increasing instead of decreasing?"

"Simple. It can be explained by the second law of thermodynamics," Mike answered laughing.

"What? You mean the entropy principle! You mean the influence of religions is evidence of increased disorder in our society?!" Pat was shocked. The second law of thermodynamics states that the entropy (or a disorder) of a system always increases. By invoking the second law of thermodynamics, Mike was obviously indicating that there is a gradual disorder in the world and that the increasing influence of religion was the evidence of that increasing disorder.

"*Bingo!*" Mike answered.

* * *

Patricia created an organization called *Thomas Paine Society for Critical Thinking*. She bought the books and mailed them to thousands of churches under the name of that organization. Within days, there was a lot of media attention. Apparently, for some inexplicable reason, someone had spent almost a million dollars to insult the churches! Due to the publicity, thousands of people bought and read the book and talked about it. Large numbers of them agreed with Paine's arguments.

Churches across the country condemned this deplorable act by some heathen from Ohio's capital. People of Columbus were divided on this issue. Many of them believed that under the First Amendment, a person has a right to spend his own money, however, he desires. They argued that this book was available for centuries and was not the only such book that criticized the Bible. Others argued that since this book and many such books were already available, sending a book like this to churches was insulting and provocative.

Few weeks later, Michael Kincaid called a press conference. There, in front of the media, he declared that somebody from this great city of Columbus had mailed such trash to the churches and damaged the reputation of the city of Columbus and that of the great State of Ohio. He emphasized that Columbus is located in the heart of America and is named in honor of the great explorer Christopher Columbus whose voyages eventually resulted in European colonization of the New World and created the greatest country on earth. He announced that as a small gesture to restore the city's image, his company will donate one million dollars to major religious organizations across the country. Patricia's jaw dropped.

Media hailed Mr. Kincaid as a hero. People of the city of Columbus thanked him for this beautiful gesture. They forgot that just a few months ago, this same person had destroyed the marriage of their Governor.

Patricia was shocked with these two contradictory actions by her boss. This was beyond comprehension. She discussed it with her husband. John told her that Michael Kincaid had lost it. He added that Mr. Kincaid's personality had split in two ever since his wife died. He has had contradictory views on everything.

"Pat, Michael does not need any medication. It's his other personality that needs it, and lots of it! You love mythology, so let me explain by giving an example from mythology. Michael Kincaid is like the Greek god Janus. He has two faces," John explained.

"John, please don't use mythology when you talk to me. Janus was a Roman god, not a Greek god. Mythology is your Achilles' heel. If you understand what I mean by that, then we both know I am right. If you don't understand it, then so be it," Patricia answered. She did not like the criticism of her boss.

9

The Missing Surrogate

Canada is the only country in the world that knows how to live without an identity.

— MARSHALL McLUHAN, CANADIAN PHILOSOPHER OF
COMMUNICATION THEORY

It was Monday morning. Dr. Adkins' secretary called Angela Johnson to remind her of her appointment. Her phone was disconnected. She informed Dr. Adkins about it who in turn called Mr. Drake's office to inquire about her.

Mr. Drake was surprised. He thought it must be a mistake. He tried to call Angela, but he too found that her phone was disconnected. He called Mr. Newman, Angela's attorney. He was not aware of his client's whereabouts either. He suspected that Angela must have run away, but he was not going to tell Mr. Drake about his suspicions. If she really ran away, then he certainly did not know where she had gone. Also, Angela's discussions with him about her desire to keep the baby was protected under attorney–client privilege, and therefore, confidential.

Mr. Drake and a couple of his security officers went to Angela's apartment and asked the building manager about her whereabouts. He informed them that she called early that morning and told him that she had vacated the apartment. He added that when he opened the apartment there was nothing there. It was completely empty. He did not know anything more than that. Mr. Drake was seething with anger.

Where could have she gone, he wondered. He called Mark, her ex-husband. Angela had given Mark's number as an emergency contact. Mark told him that Angela dropped Jeff off to him on Friday evening and since then he has not heard from her either. She was supposed to pick him up this morning, but he could not find her. He told them that he was worried about her, although, Mr. Drake did not believe he was. *Something was rotten in the State of Denmark*, he thought. *Maybe, something was rotten in Canada or Mexico.*

That weekend, Mark and Angela had gone to Canada. Mark returned Sunday morning. He left Angela with his cousin Mary. To corroborate his story, he had even placed calls to Angela's apartment before she disconnected her phone. If the police were to find out that he had gone to Canada, then it was no big deal. He could say he was visiting his friends there.

When the news made it back to Michael Kincaid, he was furious! He wanted the cloned child back, and he also wanted to teach Angela a lesson. Mr. Drake had his people follow Mark Baron for months to see if they could find some information about Angela.

In the meantime, Patricia delivered a baby boy. Michael named him Chuck. News began to spread in the world of genetics. When Chuck was born, many of the geneticists that Patricia had earlier approached heard that Michael Kincaid, the tycoon, had a newborn baby boy. The mother of the baby was not identified. During the last months of her pregnancy, Patricia was supposedly handling overseas operations, so the local staff didn't notice she was pregnant. She mostly remained home in Columbus.

In the geneticists' labs and conferences, there were murmurs that maybe the newborn boy could be a product of cloning. Slowly, the news started spreading and gained momentum. More and more people were talking about it. Rumors were going around and gossip papers and late-night talk shows mentioned it frequently.

Some geneticists came forward with claims that they were approached on behalf of a wealthy man who wanted to clone his child. They suspected that the person could be Michael Kincaid. Some of them even remembered that it was Patricia Sharp who had contacted them. When reporters asked Mr. Kincaid about the rumors of cloning, he told them that with his money, why would he use his wife's frozen eggs and go for IVF or use artificial insemination which would cost pennies compared to cloning which would cost millions. He claimed that something simple like IVF would diminish his status. On the one hand, there were geneticists claiming that Chuck could be a clone; on the other hand, Mr. Kincaid was joking that Chuck is certainly a clone and not a product of IVF or artificial insemination. Eventually, the rumors of cloning were laughed at by media. No one took them seriously.

When Professor Jihoo Lee heard that Mr. Kincaid was a father of another newborn baby, he was curious too. He remembered his meeting with Mr. Kincaid. He called Mr. Kincaid's office to congratulate him. Patricia talked to Professor Lee. He reminded her about their meeting in which Mr. Kincaid had inquired about cloning. Patricia understood that Dr. Lee was curious as to whether cloning had anything to do with Chuck's birth. She told Dr. Lee that Mr. Kincaid decided to have a child by artificial insemination and that he had hired a surrogate woman to bear the child. Dr. Lee didn't ask anything else.

Even though, these rumors were not taken seriously, they didn't stop. People who lived on conspiracy theories kept them alive. News about Mr. Kincaid and Patricia's visits to Europe, Patricia's rumored pregnancy, her absence for few months around the time of Chuck's birth kept on leaking into the media. Most people considered these leaks as pointless attempts on the part of gossip columnists to malign the character of Mr. Kincaid because he was wealthy and powerful. Professor Lee's name also came up. No one knew how his name was dragged into the mess. When asked by a tabloid, the professor revealed that sometime ago, he had talked to Mr. Kincaid about cloning. He emphasized that Mr. Kincaid was curious about the subject and, if possible, he wanted to clone his late wife Lucy. The professor also noted that so far there were no known cases of human cloning. Media made up stories about Dr. Lee's interest in human cloning.

Dr. Lee was hounded by the media for months. OSU asked Dr. Lee about his association with Mr. Kincaid and the issue of cloning.

Finally, the "Chinese professor from Taiwan" resigned from the university and left the country. Patricia was sad to see the innocent scientist pay the price for his involvement with Mr. Kincaid. She wished the media had left him alone. When she asked Mr. Kincaid about Professor Lee, he denied any involvement in Dr. Lee's resignation. Since she didn't know otherwise, she believed him.

Unfortunately, Chuck Kincaid was sick from the very beginning. He had respiratory problems. Dr. Lautens had told Mr. Kincaid that cloned animals are frequently unhealthy. Science of cloning was still in its infancy. Several weeks later, when Chuck eventually died, Mr. Kincaid tried to contact Dr. Lautens, but he was nowhere to be found.

After they realized that Chuck was not healthy and may not survive, Mr. Kincaid and his attorney increased their efforts to locate Angela. When they could not find any trace of her in the States, they suspected that she could be in Canada. Their plan was to take the child and replace him as Chuck. That way they didn't have to invent any stories to explain his existence. There were three other women hired as surrogates, but none of them ever became pregnant. Success rate with cloning was small anyway as Dr. Lautens had warned Mr. Kincaid. After Angela and Patricia got pregnant, those three women were released from their contracts.

While Chuck was alive, Patricia cared for him as her own child. After all, she had carried him for nine months. She thought of him as her own son. When he died, she understood how painful it was to lose a child. Her pregnancy and Chuck's sickness resulting in his death made Patricia realize why Angela might have run away to keep the child. She sympathized with Angela. The strain of taking care of a sick infant ultimately resulted in conflicts with her husband. John had it with Patricia's devotion to her boss. He frequently tried to pull his wife away from Michael Kincaid, but he got nowhere. Finally, he divorced her and left the company.

10

Birth of a Clone

You lose your individuality a huge amount when you have no money, and I certainly had that experience.

—J. K. ROWLING, AUTHOR OF HARRY POTTER SERIES

Angela went to live with Mary, Mark's cousin, in Canada. Five days later, she moved to a motel in another town. Within days, she went into labor and rushed to the emergency room. She delivered a baby boy. She named the child Alfred Johnson.

She spent three days in the hospital with mixed emotions. She was delighted to have a child, but at the same time, she was afraid that someone would come from the United States and lay claim on the child. She told the hospital authorities that she was a victim of domestic violence and that she didn't want her boyfriend or his family members visiting the child.

The hospital authorities respected her wishes. After all, it was not an unusual request. Frequently, women who were victims of domestic violence didn't want their boyfriends or husbands to visit them. Hospital security was alerted to prevent anyone from visiting Angela or her baby. Social workers of the hospital helped her get an apartment and a monthly allowance. Once she was out of the hospital, she told everyone her name was Helen Porter. Porter was her mother's maiden name.

She even didn't allow Mary, Mark's cousin, to visit her in the hospital and didn't let her know where she went after she left the hospital. Angela practiced the first rule of selfishness – sever ties with the person who is no longer useful. For selfish people, gratitude is a waste of time. Angela was learning fast.

Alfred was now just a few weeks old. Unknown to her, the other child born by cloning, Chuck, had died recently. One day early in the morning, Angela had just finished bathing Alfred and was feeding him when the phone rang. She answered, "Hello?" The person on the other end replied, "Hello, Ms. Helen Porter. Or should I say, Angela Johnson? How are you? I am sure you recognize my voice, but I will still introduce myself. I am attorney Rudolph Drake."

Angela was frightened. How did he find her? Did she leave any trace that led him here? Did Mark betray her for money? *Damn it, I mean, darn it, Mark.*

"You have the wrong number," she said in a feeble voice.

"Angela, don't hang up and don't play games. We know it's you. Look outside of your window."

Slowly she walked toward the window and peeked through a gap in the curtains. Sure enough, Mr. Drake was standing outside, flanked by two big men. *They must be his bodyguards.*

"I will come down in few minutes. I need to get dressed," she told Mr. Drake and hung up. She didn't know what to do. If she did not do anything soon, they will come upstairs, break her door open, and take the child away from her. Or they could do something worse. If she asked the law enforcement to help her, then at least she could buy some time. But in doing so, she will expose herself. After that it will be difficult for her to hide. The laws of Canada may or may not protect her, but eventually she may lose in the court. Either way she will always be at risk from Mr. Drake and his people. She must think fast. Once again, it was time to think outside of the box or the Book or whatever.

Angela called a cab. The dispatcher told her that the cab will arrive in ten minutes. Quickly, she gathered all her important stuff; money, her

American passport, Alfred's birth certificate, his clothes, baby food, her clothes, and whatever else she could think of. She started packing everything in a bag. The bag was getting full. She put some diapers in the bag. She closed the bag. Then she looked around the apartment to see if she forgot to pack anything important. She saw her family Bible. It was on the end-table near her bed. She picked it up and put it in the bag. Then she tried to zip the bag. She couldn't. She looked at the contents of the bag to see if she could remove something to make room for the Bible. She didn't find anything that she could take out. She took the Bible out of the bag and zipped it.

While packing, she called police and told them there was a car outside of her building that belonged to drug-dealers and that they came there frequently to sell drugs. She also gave the description of the car and its occupants. Then she waited. Somewhere between two minutes and eternity the police came. Three police cars surrounded Mr. Drake's car.

While police were interrogating Mr. Drake and his party, Angela saw her cab pull up. She ran downstairs holding Alfred in her right arm and her bag in her left. She jumped in the cab and told the cab driver to speed away. She told the cab driver that there had been shooting and police were talking to the suspects. That was enough incentive for the cab driver to get the heck out of the area and not ask any questions. A minute later, she told him to take her to the hospital. At the hospital, she paid the cab driver and then took another cab to the bus station.

At the bus station, she found the first bus that was leaving. It was going to Etobicoke. She bought the ticket, walked toward the waiting bus, but at the last moment she changed her mind. She took another cab and went to Toronto. When she reached Toronto, she had the cab drop her off at a busy shopping center. She did not know what to do now. *Time to think outside of the box, again.*

Angela decided to go to a shelter for abused women. She asked a police officer about it. She found out that they were called transition homes and that they allowed women to stay there with their kids. She told them that she was a victim of domestic violence. One lie leads to another and over time, it gets easier to lie. At the center, she made up names for her and her son. She was Peggy Baldwin, and her son was Elijah.

The transition home was very helpful. The people there were used to taking care of women who were not forthcoming with personal information. Many women hid important details to keep their privacy. They did not question Angela's story. They did not care to inquire about her legal status either. All they were interested in was to assure that she and her child were safe and well fed. Angela learned a lot during her stay. She heard the stories of many women who were staying there. There were women who were sexually assaulted by their family members, women who were beaten up by husbands or boyfriends or their pimps, women who feared for their lives, women who were homeless, and so on. She saw it all. She also learned a lot about Canada's social programs—how much it pays if you are homeless, how much it pays if you have two children vs. one, etcetera. Angela came to know that if she wanted to live in Canada, she would need to have legal status there. After spending some time there, she moved out and rented an apartment.

The next several years were tough for Angela. She lived in the perennial fear of being caught. She had figured that Mr. Drake was not an average attorney. He was more like a gangster than an attorney. She changed her name and the baby's name. She knew that Mr. Drake already knew the baby's name. When the baby was three months old, she started calling him Jaden. For a three-month-old infant, it would not matter. He would answer to anything. She moved around a lot. Anytime she saw a car with an Ohio license plate in her neighborhood, she panicked. She associated those cars with Mr. Drake or his people. She would move as soon as she could. She survived on the money she had received from her surrogacy contract and social programs of Canada. In the middle of all this chaos, Alfred was growing up.

*   *   *

Mark Baron had never been responsible in his life. He was an alcoholic, and he could not hold a job. Even though he liked having Jeff around, it was impossible for him to take care of a young child. Jeff was often neglected. He was not getting proper nutrition. Sometimes Jeff was not bathed for days. When Mark was at work, he had babysitters take care of him. Due to Mark's unstable lifestyle and inability to make prompt payments, babysitters would leave after a few weeks.

One babysitter, Debra, saw the appalling conditions in the apartment. She often warned Mark about his dirty apartment and neglect of his son's hygiene. Mark didn't listen. Then one day, she saw lice crawling on Jeff's head. She had had enough. With her cell phone, she took pictures of lice, the dirty kitchen, the disgusting bathroom, and the mess in the living room. Then she contacted Child Protective Services (CPS). The CPS worker visited the apartment. She was shocked when she looked at the kitchen and the bathroom.

When Debra called Mark and informed him that CPS was in his home, he rushed home. He tried to explain to the CPS worker that he was trying his best to work full time and take care of his son. The CPS worker understood Mark's situation, but she could not ignore how bad things looked in the apartment. Jeff was taken away immediately. Mark could not handle the kicking and screaming of his son as he was taken away by strangers. Jeff was scared. He did not know the people who were taking him away. Mark tried to explain to the little kid that he is going for few days and that Dad will get him back, but he continued to scream. He was terrified. Mark stood there helpless.

CPS told him that they would find a family to take care of him until they could figure out whether Mark could get him back or not. They told Mark that if things did not change with him then he would lose his son forever.

Mark realized that the apartment was filthy. He did not have proper food in the refrigerator. His clothes were dirty. Then it dawned on him that the root cause of all his problems was alcohol. His alcoholism prevented him from having a steady job. His alcoholism resulted in the neglect of his son. He tried to stop drinking. He lasted six whole hours. On his own, he was not going to remain sober. He remembered his dad was an alcoholic too. He had never seen a stable family life. His mom was sick and disabled for years before she passed away. He may have inherited alcoholism from his dad. He remembered his dad always blamed his father for his alcoholism.

Then Mark had an epiphany. Twenty years from now, his son Jeff could be alcoholic and live the kind of life he lived now. On top of that, Jeff could blame his dad for his failures just as Mark was blaming his. Mark didn't want that on his conscience. Possibly his own dad deserved a lot of blame for the problems he was facing, but he needed to stop the cycle. He did not want his son to blame him. It was his responsibility to assure that his son was cared for the way his dad should have cared for him.

Mark knew he needed help. But who would help him? Desperately, he looked at the list of his contacts. He did not want to involve his former or current employers. The past employers did not like him and had fired him. The current employer may fire him if he finds out about him neglecting his own child. There was his friend Keith, but he lived in Canada and presently he was serving time. There were names of his past baby-sitters who had stopped answering his phone calls. There was one name on the list that gave him some hope. It was Debra, Jeff's last babysitter. She was the very person who had called CPS, which began his downward spiral. Mark was at a dead end. He decided to call her.

He dialed the phone with some trepidation. Debra answered. "Hello?" she asked.

"Hi, Debra, this is Mark. I need to talk to you," he said.

"Mark, hi. How are you? Did you get Jeff back?" she sounded surprised.

"No, I did not. I called for some other reason," he said.

"You know it's 10:00 p.m.? It's past my bedtime. And, I do not understand why you would call me if Jeff's not with you."

"Debra, I am in trouble. I need your advice," Mark admitted.

"You got some nerve calling *me* for advice. Last time I was there, I called CPS because I was fed up with your behavior. Do you remember that? You are an alcoholic, you cannot hold a job, you don't know the difference between a clean apartment and a filthy apartment, and you can't take care of a child if your life depended on it. I thought it was in Jeff's best interest that he was taken away from you. That's the reason I called CPS. And you want my advice!" Debra was shocked.

"Yes, I do. I want you to tell me how to straighten my life out," Mark pleaded.

"Mark, if you need advice, you should talk to your friends, your priest, your counselor, or your psychiatrist. Don't call me for advice. Good bye." She hung up.

Mark redialed the phone and said, "Please, don't hang up. Listen to me," Mark begged.

"Okay, tell me one reason why I should listen to you?"

"I have only one other person I can call. It's my friend, Keith, but he is in Canada and . . ."

"So? Call him in Canada."

"No, you don't understand. I can't reach him. He is incarcerated."

"Why am I not surprised?" Debra taunted him.

"I deserve that. I do not have a priest, because I don't go to church. I don't have a counselor or a psychiatrist. You are the only person who can tell me what to do with my life."

"Oh my God! You can't be serious. You really need help. You should have a support system. You got to have two or three people that you should be able to call anytime in case of an emergency or a crisis. It's common-sense. And, no, a babysitter should not be one of them. Tell me, what do you want from me?" Debra asked.

"I want you to tell me what I should do with my life, so that I can get my son back. I am willing to do anything in my power to get him back," Mark answered her.

"Mark, listen to me. It's late in the evening, and I need my sleep. I can meet you tomorrow morning. Is that okay?" Her tone was sympathetic now.

"Sure, that would be great. Can you come to my apartment tomorrow morning?"

"Yes, I can come on one condition. Clean your apartment. If it's clean, I will come inside and talk to you. Is that a deal?"

"Yes, it's a deal," Mark agreed.

"I will be there at eight."

Mark went to Walmart. He bought everything needed to clean the apartment. Then he went back to his apartment and started cleaning. He worked for hours. Finally, he saw some order in his apartment. It appeared clean. It did not smell. He looked at the time. It was four in the morning. He went to bed. He had three hours before he had to wake up.

Mark heard Jeff screaming. He was yelling, "Please don't take me. Dad, I don't want to go. Please, Dad, please stop them." Mark was crying and pleading with CPS workers to give him one more chance. They did not listen and took Jeff away. But the screams continued. It was more than a minute before he realized that it was his alarm clock. *Man, these nightmares must stop.*

He showered, put clean clothes on, and got ready for his big test. Two minutes after eight o'clock, the doorbell rang. Mark walked to the door and opened it. "Please come in," he said.

Debra couldn't believe her eyes. A well-dressed man was standing there asking her to come in. She looked at Mark in total disbelief.

"You . . . you . . . must be Mark's good twin," she stammered.

"Thanks for the compliment," Mark answered.

"You look good. Well, the kitchen looks great too. You must have worked the whole night."

"I want to make a good impression for my parole officer," Mark joked. Debra laughed.

They sat down on the dining table. Mark served coffee, toast, and scrambled eggs. After breakfast was over, Mark explained his predicament to Debra.

"Listen, I want to turn my life around. I want to live a normal life, whatever that means. I want my son back. I will appreciate if you could guide me."

"Mark, this is not something you can accomplish overnight. It takes time. There are a number of things you need to change about you," Debra tried to explain.

"I know that. I want you to tell me how I should do it."

"First of all, alcohol is the root of most of your problems. You need to stop drinking."

"I know. The longest I have been without drinking while awake is six hours. I can't help it."

"You need to join Alcoholics Anonymous. AA is a wonderful organization. They can help you quit drinking. Once you are sober for a few weeks, you will see the change in your life. Look what you did to your apartment in one night. Obviously, you have determination. Put your mind to it, and you will be able to survive without alcohol. I am sorry, I called CPS, but a child's welfare is of the utmost priority and I had to do it," Debra explained.

"You think I am mad at you for that? On the contrary, I am glad that you opened my eyes. Night after night, I wake up with a nightmare. I see my child being snatched away from me, because I am not a fit father. Those nightmares motivate me. I am determined to get him back. I wish Jeff was still with me, but you are not at fault that CPS took him away. It is entirely my fault."

Mark continued, "Let me tell you a secret. When I was going through the divorce, I did not want to keep Jeff. I knew my ex-wife Angela wanted full custody of Jeff. I used it to my advantage during our divorce. I didn't want him, because I did not want the responsibility of taking care of a child. But now that I got him, I don't want to lose him," Mark confessed.

"You have been horrible and selfish. Man, you have a long way to go."

"I know. But I guarantee you that the way Jeff was screaming when CPS workers took him away from me has opened my eyes. I will never let that happen again."

Debra left the apartment feeling better about Mark and Jeff.

*   *   *

"Hi, I am Mark, and I am an alcoholic," Mark announced to a group of strangers in his first AA meeting. What a silly thing to say in an AA meeting where everyone knows that you are an alcoholic. Yet, it was not easy for him to say that. When he stood up, looked around the room and cleared his throat, he found his voice betray him. He had trouble saying those words aloud. When he finally said them, he felt like he was confessing his sins.

After weeks in AA, he became sober. He learned a very important lesson in AA that he will always be a recovering alcoholic. There is no such thing as an ex-alcoholic. For the rest of his life, he had to fight the temptation to drink. Until he joined AA, Mark had hardly thought about God. His parents were not religious. He had rarely set foot in a church. The twelve-steps program of AA made him think about God. AA emphasized the importance of believing in a power greater than us. He started reading about his religion. He acknowledged his failure to control his addiction to alcohol and depended on help from above. He accepted his weakness and trusted that God will help him.

Mark felt that when a person leaves all his problems to God, he feels unburdened. He started going to church. While he was married to Angela, he had been to the Baptist church where Pastor Watson was preaching, so he decided to attend the services there.

While working on his addiction, Mark had to apologize to the people he had wronged. He called his friends, his ex-girlfriends, and his ex-wife Angela. Apologizing to Angela was the hardest thing he had to do. He told her that he was sorry for neglecting her during their marriage and for having affairs while they were married. It didn't do any good to Angela but did a lot of good to Mark.

Angela and Mark had established a system to communicate with each other. Every few weeks at a predetermined time, they would talk to each other via pay phones. With Mark's history of being irresponsible, communication was not very reliable. Often, he would forget to call Angela or simply neglect it. After he joined AA, he became reliable.

When Jeff was taken away by CPS, Angela was furious. She wanted to come back to Columbus to get him back. But she was afraid of losing Alfred, and she didn't want to face Mr. Drake. She also thought that if she was in legal trouble for running away from her surrogacy contract, she would lose Alfred and Jeff both. Mark promised her that he would do everything possible to get Jeff back and take care of him. Angela didn't believe him, but she had no choice but to wait and see what happens.

Mark wanted to learn how a "normal" family lives. When he was growing up his family was dysfunctional at best. He did not have any relatives or friends who could be role models. After some thinking, he decided that if he cannot find any normal family in real life then he would look for it in fiction. He started watching television shows depicting stable families. He watched episodes of *Family Matters*, *Family Ties*, and *The Brady Bunch*. From these shows, he learned how to talk to kids, how to celebrate their birthdays, how to help them in their homework, etcetera. He knew the difference between reality and fiction, but he figured at least he could learn from these shows and apply some of the lessons in real life. He was also able to keep a job as an auto mechanic and began to save money.

Angela was losing her faith while she was trying to keep Alfred though she had no right to do so. Mark, on the other hand, was gaining his faith while he was trying to get his son back who was rightfully his. God has a sense of humor.

11

Mark's Recovery

*Recovery is something you have to work on every single day, and
it is something that doesn't get a day off.*

— DEMI LOVATO, SINGER AND ACTRESS

With the help of AA, Mark became sober. Night after night, he was
tormented by nightmares of his son screaming and being taken
away by CPS. In a way, these nightmares helped his resolve to stay away
from drinking. Mark also learned how to keep his apartment clean. Off and
on, he called Debra for advice. She helped him make his apartment look
presentable. Per Debra's advice, he hired an attorney to get his son back.

His attorney was George Clemens. Mr. Clemens presented to the
court that his client had been sober for few months, attended AA meetings
regularly, and held a steady job. Mr. Clemens also called Mark's supervisor
and coworkers to testify in his favor. They were familiar with Mark's struggles with alcoholism and were impressed with his recovery. Mark regained
custody of his son with the stipulations that CPS would supervise him
periodically. For Mark, that was not a problem, since he knew he was not
going to fall off the wagon.

Finally, Jeff was back. Mark asked Debra if she would come back to
work as Jeff's babysitter. Debra declined because she was now working full
time elsewhere. However, she arranged for her niece, Kelly, to help Mark.

Months later, one evening, Mark asked Debra out for dinner. He told her he wanted to thank her for helping him put his life on track. Debra accepted. Mark had Kelly babysit Jeff. Mark picked her up from her apartment and took her to a fancy Italian restaurant. Debra was pleased with the way Mark had changed his way of living. When Mark dropped Debra off at her apartment, she invited him for a cup of coffee. Hesitantly, Mark went in.

He told Debra that maybe he should call Kelly and tell her that he would be late picking Jeff up. Debra informed him that it was already taken care of. Next morning, Mark woke up in Debra's apartment. Weeks later when they were steady in their relationship, Mark told Debra that as soon as CPS cleared him, he wanted to move away. He didn't want CPS or the attorney of people who hired his ex-wife as a surrogate to haunt him. Just as he didn't want to live in Canada, he didn't want to live in Columbus or anywhere in Ohio. Debra agreed.

CPS didn't find any problems with Mark over next one year. They cleared him and stopped supervising him. They cautioned him that his case would be in the file. Mark didn't care. Finally, two years after Angela left Columbus and went to Canada, Mark was free. Now he was sober, Jeff was with him, and he had a girlfriend. His life had changed for better. He moved to Buffalo, New York, with Debra and Jeff. Buffalo was close enough to Canada that if Angela needed to see Jeff, he could cross the border and meet her. Angela had told him that she was not comfortable crossing the border and entering the United States, just in case there was an outstanding warrant for her. Mark, on the other hand, was fine visiting Canada occasionally so Jeff can see his mom. After they settled in Buffalo, Mark and Debra got married.

*   *   *

Mr. Kincaid had businesses in many African countries. He sold weapons to some of those countries. He also had established NGOs to perform charitable work in those countries.

One day while in one of his moods, Mr. Kincaid talked to the head of his company in Africa. He told him to buy every morsel of grain he could buy from countries in central Africa. He was interested in buying wheat, rice, and millet. Farmers were happy as they were making more money. The company, which was buying all these crops, had no traceable connections to Kincaid's businesses. His company had bribed the government officials, so they allowed this to happen. Once they bought everything, they stored the grains in warehouses and did not sell.

Within months, people couldn't buy any of these life-sustaining crops. For one, it was not available in most areas, and two, if it was available, it was too expensive. World Health Organization and United Nations had to donate millions of dollars and tons of food to the starving people to prevent a humanitarian crisis. Mr. Kincaid bought some crop from his own secret company and gave it away to starving people.

Then Mr. Kincaid fired a manager of his warehouse. The manager told everyone that Mr. Kincaid's company was responsible for the famine. No one took him seriously. Everyone thought he was making things up, because he was a disgruntled ex-employee. Mike also had his people plant rumors that it was his company that had created the famine. News spread like wildfire. The best way to hide something is to put the outlandish truth in front of them. Then they will never believe it. Patricia was distressed to see so many people starve to death, but sadly decided to do nothing about it. She realized her husband was right about Mike.

12

Alfred Grows Up

I am Chevy Chase and you are not.

— CHEVY CHASE, ACTOR

"Peter, I want to call you Alfred from now on. Is that all right?" Angela asked.

"Why? My name is Peter," Alfred answered.

"Yes, but I want to change your name. Okay?" Angela asked.

"Mom, I like the name Peter," Alfred answered.

"Yes, but I think Alfred is a better name."

"No, I am Peter," Alfred insisted.

"Listen, Peter, I mean Alfred, I want you to go to school in a few months. Peter is your nickname. Your real name is Alfred. You are five years old. I should call you by your real name," Angela explained.

"Mom, what is wrong with Peter?" Alfred was confused.

"Alfred, the teachers in the school know you as Alfred. They want to admit you in the school as Alfred."

"But I like Peter. Zach also calls me Peter." Zach was Angela's ex-husband. She married him when Alfred was about two years old. Alfred loved him. Zach also loved Alfred. They had a good father–son bond between them. Just before Alfred turned five, Angela divorced Zach. When Angela met Zach, she was telling everyone that her son's name was Peter. For a little infant, it didn't matter. She wanted him to go to school with the name he had on his birth certificate.

Alfred missed Zach a lot. Angela explained to him that Zach had to move to another town because of his job. The truth was that Angela was now a legal resident of Canada and didn't have to stay married. She created fake affairs to make Zach mad enough to divorce her. Alfred was very sad for weeks after Zach moved out.

"But, Mom, whaaaa-y he had to move away?" he protested. Angela explained why. Alfred would listen to the explanation and then repeat his question, "but, Mom, whaaaa-y he had to move away?"

Angela compromised with Alfred, "I will call you Peter at home if that's what you want." Alfred was happy to hear that.

"But, Mom, whaaaa-y he had to move away?" Alfred asked.

"When Zach calls, I will let you talk to him. Are you happy now?" Angela answered.

"Yes," Alfred was happy to hear that. He never got a chance to see him or talk to him on the phone again.

Angela took him to kindergarten. She told him that her son has some imaginary friends and also he likes his friends to call him "Peter." His teachers didn't see anything alarming for a child that age.

Gradually, Alfred adjusted to his *new* name. His teachers, his classmates, and now Angela were also calling him Alfred. He all but forgot that for a few years, he lived as Peter.

Thanks to Angela's unstable life, Alfred was moving from town to town. As a result, he also moved from school to school. Frequently, for months at a time, he was home-schooled by Angela. Alfred did not have a steady friend.

By age ten, Angela thought that it was time to settle down. She figured that if Mr. Drake would want to take Alfred away, she could take him to court. If the crime she committed had a statute of limitations, then it would perhaps be over by now. Besides, for last few years, there was no credible threat to her or to Alfred. She decided to finally stop running.

Alfred was enrolled in a public school. He began to have a steady life. He also began to make friends. His best friend was Jagdish Chandra

Mathur. They met in sixth grade. They had something common between them. Jagdish had emigrated from England and felt out of place in the new country. Alfred had always felt out of place thanks to his moving around, occasional home-schooling, and unstable life. They did not fit with other kids who had normal childhood.

*   *   *

Ross Drew, news anchor of Columbus' Channel 3, broadcast an investigate report on Mr. Kincaid. He discussed his business practices, scandals in his personal life, and bribes he had allegedly given to the leaders of the third-world countries. It was very damaging to Michael Kincaid's reputation.

Michael Kincaid was outraged. Many of the allegations made by Mr. Drew were true. Michael knew that he couldn't sue the news anchor or the TV channel for libel. He found a way to embarrass him. Drew was a conservative reporter and a staunch Republican. On top of that, there were some incidences in his past, which showed his hatred for minorities, including African-Americans.

Michael donated one hundred thousand dollars to the United Negro College Fund in the name of Ross Drew's late mother, Miranda. The money for the donation came from a company called Miranda for Minorities. The company was located in the Bahamas. It also donated money to some charitable projects in the Bahamas in memory of Miranda Drew. Michael's people spread the rumor that Ross Drew donated money in his late mother's name for many projects involving African-Americans.

Ross Drew was livid. He called Michael and started yelling. Michael congratulated him for his generous donation. He also advised Ross that the NAACP was also a great organization. Maybe, Ross should donate some money to them too. Ross accused Michael of insulting him by donating money in Miranda Drew's name. Michael denied it saying he didn't have a hundred thousand dollars to spare. The public laughed at Ross for being humiliated like this. Others thought that the bigot got what he deserved. Ross was frustrated for months. That was the last time Ross talked about him.

13

Mom, Where Do Babies Come From?

What's in a name? That which we call a rose by any other name would smell as sweet.

— WILLIAM SHAKESPEARE, ENGLISH POET AND PLAYWRIGHT

Alfred was in the last month of his senior year in high school. A few short weeks and he would be a high school graduate. Then, unexpectedly, life took an ugly turn for him and for Angela.

One day Alfred came from school looking very angry. Angela asked him if something was wrong. Alfred told her that something happened at school and he wanted to talk about it. "But before I talk about it, I want to ask you something," he added.

"Sure, but why don't you eat something first?" Angela suggested.

"Maybe later," Alfred answered.

Angela said, "Okay, you said you want to ask me something. Go ahead." She figured that Alfred must have had a fight with some students or a teacher might have given him a bad grade or something.

"Mom, where do babies come from?" he asked.

"What! What are you talking about? You are a senior in high school, and you don't know that? What kind of a joke is this?" She was flustered. Alfred's demeanor shocked her more than the stupidity of his question. She had a feeling that there was something more to his question.

"That's not the answer I was looking for. Who is Michael Kincaid and when was the last time you saw him?"

"I have heard of Michael Kincaid. I think he is a big shot businessman, probably a billionaire or something, but I have never met him. What has that to do with where babies come from? You are not making any sense today." She was confused.

"Sure, Mom, I knew you would say that. Let me show you what I found today. Look at this picture. Does that ring a bell?" Alfred asked as he pulled out a newspaper clipping from his bag. It was a picture of Michael Kincaid's son, Steven. It mentioned that he was critically injured in a skiing accident. But it seemed like they had printed Alfred's picture instead of Steven's.

Angela looked at the picture in sheer horror. She felt dizzy. Her hand reached for the chair for support. She never knew the identity of the couple who had hired her as a surrogate. It was obvious to her that it must be Kincaids. Why did it have to be the baby of a famous person? All her lies, all her manipulations, and all her deceits will be out in the open. The parallel universe she had created when she left the United States for Canada was merging with the real universe.

After a second or two, she sat down. Steven and Alfred looked like identical twins. But when she delivered Alfred in Canada, there was only one baby born. She was speechless. While she was trying to collect her thoughts, Alfred started talking.

"Come on, Mom, tell me. All these years you told me that my dad's name was Noah Clark and you had dated him briefly after your divorce. Why didn't you tell me that Michael Kincaid was my dad? Did he give you millions of dollars to keep your mouth shut? Where have you hidden the money? For your own selfishness, you have deprived me of my real family. How could you do that? Maybe the answer to my question is, 'Babies come from moms who are paid to carry them by rich philanderers.' Right?" Alfred asked her.

"Listen, Alfie. You are crossing the line. I never had affair with Mr. Kincaid. I have never met him in my life. Honest to God, I didn't know I was carrying Mr. Kincaid's baby. I realized I deprived you of being raised by a billionaire."

"First of all, do not bring God in the middle of this unholy mess. Second of all, this has nothing to do with Mr. Kincaid's money. It's about truth. I know it's hard for you to believe that but let me tell you something. I have envied everyone. No, I have been jealous of every kid who lived with his or her dad. A child does not care about money. He or she wants a father when they grow up. Jeff has visited us only a few times, and I have loved his company, but I hate when he talks to me about his dad. Whenever my friends complained about their fathers, I have told them they didn't know how lucky they were to have fathers. All these years, I have been trying to figure out who I am. I have felt that I was a man without identity. You have been telling me that you do not have any contact with my biological father and that I was conceived as a result of a brief relationship. Why?"

"Alfred, I am as much in the dark about this as you are. I think I will need to tell you what happened or at least as much as I know about this whole thing. You have to trust me. I am not proud of some decisions I have made, but I made them out of love for you. As far as money is concerned, you cannot be any more wrong than you are right now. Let me start from the beginning."

Angel continued, "After I went through a messy divorce, which you know a lot about, I could barely survive. Mark did not pay child support and alimony regularly. Only thing that got me going was that I had Jeff and I had emotional support from my church. My divorce attorney, Robert Newman, knew about my financial situation. One day he approached me with a proposal. He told me that a fellow lawyer was looking for someone to be a surrogate mother. He explained to me that when a woman is not able to carry a child because of medical problems, the couple could have a baby via IVF, or in vitro fertilization. A surrogate mother is required to carry the baby. He told me that they were going to pay good money. He also assured me that the whole process was absolutely legal. After some hesitation, I agreed. Before I signed the contract, I even talked with my pastor. By the way, Mr. Newman, my lawyer, was gay."

"What difference does it make if your lawyer was gay or not? We live in the twenty-first century," Alfred could not understand why it was important for her to mention the lawyer's sexual orientation at this time. Sometimes his mother baffled him. He worked to get her back on track. "Don't you have to give the baby back to them after delivery?" he asked.

"Yes, I will get to that. Have some patience. There was no intimate relationship involved. I would not have agreed to it, anyway." That instant Angela realized how moral her life was back then and how much she had fallen since then. She knew that Angela of that time would not have imagined things she has done in last few years.

What has she done in last eighteen years? Rather, what has she not done in that time? She has lied, cheated, taken advantage of the social programs of Canada, had a fake marriage to stay in the country, and broken number of laws in the United States and Canada. How low she has fallen to keep a baby that was not hers. She had not been faithful to God, to her family, and of course to herself. She has been incredibly unfair to her first son. How did this happen? During all this time why she didn't stop and think about what she was doing? She remembered all the lessons she learned in the transition home. *Why did she marry Zachary Roy?* Poor man had no idea that he was just a pawn in her scheme. Three years after marriage, she divorced him when it was inconvenient to her to stay married. The only reason for her marriage was to make her stay in Canada legal. Divorce made her eligible for alimony. The color on her face changed. She was pale and sweaty.

"Mom, are you all right?" Alfred asked fearfully.

It was too late to cry over that anyway. She gathered herself. "I am fine. I was just trying to think how this mess happened and what I would have done if I had known more about the people involved with this surrogacy." She was lying, of course. She didn't want Alfred to know that she was thinking about the sins she had committed in the last eighteen years.

She continued, "The lawyers did not tell me who the couple was. In return, they told me that the couple did not know my identity. I imagined it must be a rich couple with some reproductive issues and I was doing them a favor. Anyway, long story short, I got pregnant.

"At about fifteen weeks of pregnancy, I felt the baby move. It's called quickening. I suddenly realized how happy I was when I was pregnant with

Jeff. Even though I was not happy with my marriage at that time, I had
enjoyed being pregnant. Feeling the movements of a baby inside me was
the only happiness I had during my first pregnancy. When I was pregnant
with you, I was recently divorced, I had no money, and I was lonely. Sure,
I was being paid well to be a surrogate, but it was nothing compared to
the happiness I was experiencing being pregnant. I got half the amount up
front. I was to get the rest after the baby was born. I decided that I could
not give you up. I realized that it was not fair to that couple who hired me
and I was breaking my contract, which was against my own religious convictions. I knew all that, but I could not give up the child who gave me so
much joy. I told my lawyer about it. He went berserk. He told me that if I
didn't honor my contract, I would be sued. He also told me that the courts
might rule in favor of the couple. He warned me against breaking the contract. I believe while he advised me not to break the contract, he indirectly
suggested that if I leave the country, I might be able to keep the baby. Of
course, there is no way to prove that."

She continued, "Interestingly, my ex-husband, Mark, came to my rescue. Since he was from Canada, he helped me hide in here. That was not
without a sacrifice. I had to give up Jeff so I could take care of you. Mark
knew he couldn't take care of a child, but he agreed to do it for a short time.
As luck would have it, after he got Jeff, he kind of got used to having him
around and did not want to part with him, so I couldn't get him back.

"Except for the few times, he could visit me; I have not been able to be
a part of Jeff's life. I lived near Toronto under an assumed name. You were
born in a small hospital in a village near Toronto. Your birth certificate
does not mention your father's name because I did not know the name
anyway."

Angela's heart began to race, and she unfolded the rest of the story.
"When you were little, one time Mr. Drake came with some thugs to take
you back. Mr. Drake was the attorney of the couple who were trying to
have a child through surrogacy. I ran away from him. I was still afraid that
Mr. Drake could find us and harm us. Therefore, for a few years, we kept
moving. We changed our names also. The weirdest thing was that a few

times, I got letters or phone calls from someone advising me to move away immediately. The woman who called me knew the names we lived under, even though we changed our names frequently. She knew where we lived. It was obvious that she was trying to protect us. I never knew who she was. If I received a letter from her or someone else, it was typed, and it included cash. Phone calls were always very difficult to hear due to background noise. Maybe, she was trying to protect her identity that way. Whenever I asked her who she was or what Mr. Drake or his client wanted, she would not answer and would keep telling me to get out of there ASAP."

"Last time she called me, she told me that every time I withdraw money from my account in the United States bank, somebody informs them, and they are able to locate me. After that conversation, I withdrew all the money from the American bank. After that I did not hear from that lady or from Mr. Drake. You were little more than two years old at that time. I was still afraid of being exposed and get into legal trouble until finally; I learned to live with it.

"When nothing happened for almost eight years, I was feeling somewhat at ease. Of course, during that time, I married and divorced Zach. I remember you bonded with him soon after you met him. He loved you too. Unfortunately, the marriage did not work."

Angela began to pace with second guessing. "I still do not know if I did the right thing. From the religious point of view, I am sure I should have abided by the contract, but the truth is I did not. The thought of giving you up was gut wrenching." She paused and took a deep breath. "If I left out anything, you can ask me," Angela explained her story. She was crying.

"My God, what a story! So you are not my biological mother. It explains why I don't look like you. I really miss my stepfather. He was a nice person. I also understand some of my childhood. I understand why you called me by different names, why we lived at different places, and so on. But you know that a person's name is the most important thing for him. It is his identity. Shakespeare has claimed that *a rose would smell as sweet even if it was known by a different name.* That statement is stupid. Shakespeare should have said that *a rose is a rose is a rose is a rose.*"

Alfred sat in deep thought for a moment before continuing. "I believe that from my point of view, what you did was wrong. In addition, you could have told me all this years ago. It was humiliating to find out something like this in school. My friend Jagdish showed me the picture and told me that Steven Kincaid got hurt in a skiing accident. He asked me why he and I look alike. Can you imagine how embarrassing it is?" Alfred asked.

"I am sorry to hear that you were in an awkward situation. The choices I had in front of me were all bad. Whatever I chose, somebody was going to get hurt. Can you tell me more about Steven Kincaid?" Angela asked.

"Steven is the twenty-year-old son of Michael Kincaid. He had an accident while skiing in the Colorado Rockies. He fractured his skull, and he is in a coma. He is in critical condition. I found a lot about the Kincaids on the Internet. The media talked to his girlfriend, Stephanie Anderson; his dad, Michael Kincaid; and many other people. Pupils in my class had many jokes to explain how they placed my picture instead of his in the news. Then, I looked up some old news stories about Steven and found out that in all of his pictures, we look alike. That's when I figured that I must be Mr. Kincaid's son."

"Can you show me Steven's other pictures on the Internet?" Angela asked.

"Yes."

Alfred and Angela then explored the Internet. They saw many pictures and articles about Steven Kincaid. The resemblance was uncanny.

Late that night, Alfred also uncovered something even more disturbing. An Internet search revealed that Michael Kincaid's wife, Lucy, had died almost nine months before Alfred could have been conceived. How did that happen? He also found out that Mr. Kincaid never remarried. He had many affairs that resulted in scandals, but there was no information suggesting that he married again. Why he would want a surrogate woman if his wife was not even in the picture? This requires some detective work, he concluded.

Clearly, Mr. Kincaid wanted another child, and he had hired Angela Johnson to carry it. But if Angela was his biological mother, then he should look like her, but he did not. If she was only a surrogate, then where did the ovum come from? His wife, Lucy, had died a long time before he could have been conceived. The only way this was possible was if for some reason they had frozen Lucy's eggs before she passed away. There was no reason to do it, either. Why would someone freeze the eggs of a young woman who was healthy and was able to bear children herself?

Alfred kept on looking into it. For him and Steven to look so much alike, they must have not only the same parents but also almost similar genes. They were something like identical twins, except in this case they were born about eighteen months apart.

He searched on the Internet for identical twins and people with similar genetic makeup. Over and over again, he found the word, "clone." That is absurd, he thought. Cloning can explain this situation, but how could you explain cloning? *Human cloning is still science fiction*, he thought. On his search about cloning, he found frequent references that there are no known cases of human cloning. There were news items about successful cloning of mammals like sheep, dogs, cats, and so on, but humans? After surfing the Internet for few hours, Alfred considered the possibility that he could be a clone of Steven Kincaid. It sounded absurd but not impossible.

* * *

Michael Kincaid was invited as a keynote speaker for the graduation ceremony of the MBA program at Albert University in Los Angeles, California. Students were excited to hear from one of the most legendary entrepreneurs in the country.

Mr. Kincaid was expected to advise the students on how to become successful businessmen. He had prepared a beautiful speech for the event. Dr. Keaton, the president of the university, gave his speech congratulating the students on their graduation. Unfortunately, he mentioned in his speech that the new graduates should use their training and expertise toward helping the common man. He told them, money was not the only thing in life. The students, while making money to have a comfortable life, should also attempt to uplift the lives of average citizens across the country. Something in Michael Kincaid's mind snapped when he heard it. He glanced at his speech and decided to ignore it completely. It was his turn to address the students now.

Mr. Kincaid began his speech by thanking the university and the president for inviting him to address the students. He stated that he considered it his honor to be invited to speak on such an occasion. The president was visibly happy to hear it. So far, so good.

Things then took an ugly turn. Mr. Kincaid said that with all due respect to the president, it was his moral obligation to give his honest opinion even when it conflicted with his host's. He mentioned that everything we do in our lives is to get as far away from the common man as possible. The reality is that all of us, while talking about the common man, actually despise him. We educate our children so that their lives will be better than that of a common man. We try to have better friends, better jobs, and live in better neighborhoods than the common man does, because we look down upon him. Maybe what motivates us is our desire to be better than our neighbors, our cousins or our own siblings. Maybe we do all these due to envy, jealousy, or some other inherent vices within us. Perhaps, it is these very vices that help us improve our lives. Don't forget that the common man himself is too ashamed to acknowledge that he is a common man.

He further added that most of the students came from families which were better off than average American families. Those who came from average families were in this program so that they could live better than the common man did. When, collectively, we all try to increase our distance from the common man of this country, we raise the bar, and thereby uplift the country. But we don't do this out of altruism or sacred ideals; we do it because we loathe the common man and the life he lives. We dread the idea of becoming like him. Therefore, we strive to become better than him.

The president and the faculty were stunned to hear such words from their guest. They could not believe their ears. The students felt awkward because their president was being disrespected in front of them by their guest speaker. When Mr. Kincaid finished his speech, there was complete silence for a few seconds. Finally, the president started clapping out of courtesy. Students followed suit and applauded the speech half-heartedly.

The video of Mr. Kincaid's speech went viral within hours. Patricia watched it on YouTube. No one could be so thick as to insult his host in this manner. He did not have to endorse the president's views, but common sense dictated that he should not say anything that would insult his host either. Many people agreed with Mr. Kincaid's views, but stressed that after the president's speech those views should not have been expressed. Mr. Kincaid failed to keep social courtesy.

14

Alfred in Columbus

When I discover who I am, I'll be free.

— Ralph Ellison, novelist and critic

Alfred's first priority was to sort out the genesis of his existence. To accomplish that objective, he had to visit Columbus, Ohio. The Kincaid family was there, and the attorneys for Angela Johnson and Michael Kincaid were also there. He had graduated from high school and was waiting to start college once the vacation was over. Maybe, he will take off a year or two before starting college. As much as he wanted to obtain a college degree, this issue was more pressing. First thing he did was to obtain a passport.

One day, he told Angela, "I think I want to spend some time in the States. In Columbus, Ohio, that is."

"Dear, why do you want to go there? What good can come out of it?" Angela was perplexed.

"This is something I need to do for my own sanity. I need to find out the truth about my birth."

"What makes you think you will find what you are looking for in Columbus?" Angela asked.

"I don't know, but if I sit here, I am not going to know anything about my birth. In Columbus, I will try to meet Steven Kincaid, Michael Kincaid, and others involved in this matter."

"I can't blame you for trying, but I think there is more risk than reward in this situation."

"Whatever risk is there, I have to take it. I must know who I am. Until then, nothing matters," Alfred was firm.

"I have another idea. Nobody needs to go to Columbus. How about we contact Mr. Newman? I am sure he will help us. We can hire another attorney if Mr. Newman is not interested. Without an attorney, we can't negotiate any deal," Angela said.

"Let me make it clear. I am not interested in any kind of a deal. I am not in this for money. Also, I don't want you to benefit from this whole affair either. So please stay away from Mr. Kincaid and his money. I want to look Michael Kincaid in the eye and ask him why he messed up our lives. I want to learn about my roots and embrace them no matter how bad they may be. I don't think you can understand it. It's better that I go by myself."

"Well, I don't know what else to say. If you must go, you must go. If there is any problem, give me a call or just come back. I will not interfere at all. I promise you," Angela agreed. "Alfred, dear, sorry for everything. Please believe me, whatever I did was to make sure that I will not lose you. I could not imagine giving you up."

Alfred went to meet his best friend, Jagdish Chandra Mathur. He had to see him before leaving for Columbus. After he rang the doorbell, he heard Jagdish's parents arguing loudly. For a moment, Alfred thought it may not be the best time to visit. He thought of leaving, but before he could turn, Mrs. Mathur opened the door.

"Hi, Alfred, come on in. Jagdish is waiting for you," Mrs. Mathur welcomed him. Then she called out to Jagdish, saying, "Jaggu? Alfred's here." Then she turned to her husband and told him in a harsh tone, "All you need to do is to pick up the phone when it rings."

"Why do you want me to pick it up? Nobody calls me. It's always for you," he replied. Then turning to Alfred, he said, "Alfred, good to see you. Jagdish told us you are going to the States?"

"Yes, I am," he replied. By this time, Jagdish came to the living room and hastily escorted Alfred away from his arguing parents. He was visibly embarrassed that his parents were quarreling in front of his friend. A second after they entered Jagdish's room, his brother Satyendra suddenly materialized.

"Hey, Alfred, you look good with a moustache and beard," Satyendra said.

"Thank you. I am just trying a new look, that's all," Alfred explained.

Jagdish told his brother, "Satyu, would you mind leaving us alone? We need to talk about some grown-up stuff." Satyendra left the room with a nasty look on his face. Alfred found all these amusing. He was grinning. Jagdish saw that and got mad at him.

"Alfred, what are you smiling about?" he asked.

"Nothing. I find it funny that you are uncomfortable with your family whenever I visit you. It's weird," Alfred explained.

"Of course, I am uncomfortable. You see, my parents are always arguing. They won't stop even when someone is visiting us. And my brother, Satyu? He is always poking his nose in my business. He's very annoying," Jagdish tried to explain.

Alfred was now laughing loudly, "Jagdish, it's normal. Parents argue and brothers interfere in our matters. If you are not comfortable with it, I will trade places with you anytime."

Then, Alfred told Jagdish something else that Jagdish had not imagined in a million years. "You know, Jagdish, whenever I visit your house, I envy you."

"What? What are you talking about? How can anybody envy me?" Jagdish replied.

"Every time I come here, I see a normal family. I see your parents chatting. Your brother Satyendra and you always interact. I wish I had a brother or sister too. What would I not give for one day of a normal life like that?" Alfred lamented.

"Thank you for being so kind. But my parents don't chat, they bicker. I have not seen them have a normal conversation in years. And Satyu is an idiot. He and I fight all the time. We don't get along. So I don't understand what you are seeing in my family to envy me."

"That's exactly what I am talking about. I would love to have parents who would live under one roof even if they argue. I will like to have a brother or a sister to fight with. You have no idea what you have, Jagdish. You will know it when you don't have it any longer. Anyway, that's not why I am here. Let me talk to you about something very personal. I need your advice."

"Sure, tell me what's going on. Any idea why you and that Kincaid guy look alike?" Jagdish asked.

"That's what I want to talk to you about. You know, Steven Kincaid and I look alike in all the pictures my mother and I saw on the Internet. I want to figure out what happened. My mother or whatever relation I can describe for her in this mess told me as much as she knew."

"She is your mother, Alfred. She raised you. She has done a lot for you," Jagdish opined.

"I guess you are right. Anyway, after she told me what she knew, I found some huge gaps. I am going to the States tomorrow to find out more about the circumstances around my birth. I will go to Columbus, a city in Ohio State, to investigate this matter. I don't think I can sleep well until I get some information," Alfred explained.

"I understand. Obviously, millions of dollars are at stake here. As a friend, let me caution you. Michael Kincaid is a very powerful man. You need to be extremely careful."

"My goodness. You think I am doing this for money? Do you really think that if Mr. Kincaid were an average person, I will not be interested in knowing why his son and I look alike? As my best friend, I thought you would know me better than that," Alfred was mad.

"No, I don't mean that. Michael Kincaid is not just a rich man. He is a multi-billionaire. That's why money is the first thing that would come to anybody's mind. If you tell me you are not doing this for his money, I will believe you. You should think about what you want and how far you want to go. Certain avenues are better left unexplored," Jagdish warned.

"Thanks. I am really not doing this for money. As a matter of fact, the way my mother and the Kincaid family have messed up my life, I would love to spit on Mr. Kincaid's money. My mother confessed to me that she was a surrogate for some family. After she got pregnant, she decided to keep the baby and that's why she ran away to Canada. She tells me that she didn't know she was carrying Mr. Kincaid's baby. The whole thing stinks to high heaven. I want to talk to Steven Kincaid, Michael Kincaid, and who-ever else was involved in this. I want to explore my roots. By the way, I am growing a beard and moustache so that people won't suspect that I could be related to Steven Kincaid," Alfred was angry.

"Yes, I figured that much," Jagdish answered, "Kunta Kincaid!" Alfred and Jagdish laughed. Jagdish was referring to the character from Alex Haley's book, *Roots*, in which the author traces the roots of his ancestor, Kunta Kinte, all the way to his native village in Africa.

"That's really funny," Alfred agreed. "Anyway, looking at my situation, I hope you understand that I would switch my life with yours in a heartbeat if all I have to do is to put up with an annoying brother," Alfred told him.

"Come on, man, don't go philosophical on me. As far as my brother is concerned, I can't imagine getting along with him. You think you have problems? Let me tell you what my family went through a few years ago. It's so personal and shocking that even though you are my best friend, I have not told you about it. About three years ago, my brother Satyendra wanted to change his religion," Jagdish revealed a big family secret.

"Why? Why would someone want to change his religion?" Alfred was surprised.

"My parents wanted us to receive better education, so they had enrolled us in a private school. As you know, it was a Catholic school. In that school, many teachers and students could not see anything outside of the context of their religion. I was fine with that, but Satyu had issues. Atmosphere in school, where Christianity was always given huge importance coupled with criticism of other religions, messed up his mind. He was very frustrated and told our parents that he wanted to convert into Christianity."

"What did your parents tell him?" Alfred was intrigued.

"They told him that Hinduism is the oldest religion in the world. They also talked to him about many other religions, including Buddhism, Islam, and Judaism. They explained to him that people follow the religion they were born into and almost every religion claims that it is the only true religion. As

A CLONE DISCOVERS HIS IDENTITY

a matter of fact, Hinduism declares that people who follow other religions can also enter heaven. Hinduism says that there are many paths to the One Truth. My parents even talked to the school principal for his advice."

"What did the principal say?" Alfred was curious.

"He listened to my parents and then told them that they should let their son decide what religion he wanted to follow. My parents told him that he is a child and that they did not want him to be influenced by people around him. The principal mentioned that monotheistic religions are the true religions and that there cannot be more than one God, as western religions clearly state. He explained that western culture was based on Judeo-Christian beliefs, and other religions like Islam, Hinduism, and Buddhism have beliefs, which are contrary to western religions."

"But Islam is a monotheistic religion, and Muslims believe in the same God that Jews and Christians believe!" Alfred was surprised.

"Obviously, the principal did not know it," Jagdish explained. "He believed that except Judaism and Christianity, all other religions originated in the East. Then the principal asked something that I still cannot believe. He asked my parents how the scriptures of Hinduism handle the life of Jesus Christ."

"What? That doesn't make sense," Alfred was shocked.

"Exactly, but it gets worse. My dad told him that our scriptures were written more than two thousand years before Jesus was born. The principal, who has a PhD, told my dad that if he knew the first three words of the Bible, he would know why his question was relevant. My dad was speechless. He and my mom just walked out of his office. Then they took Satyu and me out of the private school and enrolled us in a public school," Jagdish explained.

"So because the first three words in the Bible are *In The Beginning*, the principal was expecting that your scriptures would mention the name of Jesus Christ? Is this what you think happened here?" Alfred was flabbergasted.

"Yes, that's exactly what happened. It was beyond stupid. Anyone should understand why Eastern religions would not mention the name of Jesus or for that matter any Biblical character. First of all, they were written long before the Bible was written, or revealed, depending on what you believe. Second, in the theology or mythology of the religions of the East, there are different gods and patriarchs. My dad told us that this is what happens when a person believes too strongly in his religious books. While telling us stories from our scriptures, he always tells us that this is what is written in our books, but we should not take everything literally.

"Now going back to Satyu, it took months of anguish for the family before he changed his mind. It's kind of funny that of all people, my semi-literate grandmother was able to convince him. She lives in England with my uncle. She came and stayed with us for few months and spent a lot of time with Satyu. She told him, we are who we are. We are Hindus because we are born in a Hindu family. If we believe that God is all-powerful, then if He wanted you to be a Christian, He would have made sure that you were born in a Christian family. We can't believe in God and also question His decisions. Grandmother also talked to him and me about hundreds of stories of our mythology. From that time on, we always have dinner together as a family and also do evening prayers. What we went through was nothing short of a nightmare," Jagdish explained.

"That's terrible. I didn't know that," Alfred confessed.

"We don't talk to anybody about it. Not to change the subject, but do you know what I am going through?" Jagdish asked.

"No, but I am sure it must be something serious," Alfred answered.

"You know, I was born in England, and both my parents are of Indian origin. But my dad was born in Uganda, and my mom was born in Kenya. They left their birthplaces when they were very young. They grew up in England. Years later, they met in London and got married. We have been living in Canada for many years. More than a billion people live in India and yet we are one of the few people who are called Indians, but have never been to India," Jagdish explained.

"I know that. I have heard it many times from you and from your parents. What is so problematic about that?" Alfred asked.

"The problem is, everyone assumes I am from India and expects typical Indian things from me. Even your mom acts that way with me. She talks about India whenever I come to your place. If she has heard anything about India on TV, she makes it a point to tell me about it. When I told her I am vegetarian, she asked me if only thing I eat is salad. She could not comprehend that vegetarian people can have anything other than salad on the menu. I had to explain to her that besides Indian food, Mexican food, and Italian food can also be made without meat. Vegetarian people enjoy those cuisines too. As if this were not enough, every time a child of Indian origin achieves something, my parents tell us about it and ask why Satyu and I could not do the same thing; whether it is spelling bee or inventing something in computer software, they wonder why we couldn't do it."

Jagdish continued after a pause, "Ethnically, we are Indians and we follow Hinduism. But I do not know anything about India. When I meet somebody for the first time, they ask me how many times I have seen the Taj Mahal. Every time there is some TV program showing something bizarre about India, I have to face lots of questions about it."

"It doesn't matter whether you have been to India or not, you have Indian genes. Why should all these things bother you?" Alfred asked.

"*Because I am not Indian*," Jagdish explained. "By birth I am British, by citizenship I am Canadian. My parents are Ugandan and Kenyan by birth. I have met many Britons and Canadians who know more about India than I do, and they are Caucasians. My family has practically no roots in India. If I visit India, I will have to stay in a hotel, just as you would if you were to visit there. I guess, what I am trying to explain to you is that I too have conflicts about who I am. I don't know what my true identity is. You know something? I follow the culture and religion of a place, which is thousands of miles away from where I live. It's weird looking at a country half a world away for the source of my beliefs."

"I know who you are," Alfred said. "You are someone who is trying to find issues where there is none. There are millions of people who ethnically belong to one part of the world but live in another part of the world. There are many Chinese people living in the Philippines. There are Italians who live in Argentina. Western civilization owes its roots to Greece, which is a very tiny and insignificant country these days. Christianity is the religion followed by most people living in the western countries, but its origins are in the Middle East. So my point is that more than a billion people are used to looking at two different parts of the world for the roots of their civilization and the origin of their religion. Most Indians, I guess, are not used to that. For them their civilization and their religion come from the same land. Your conflicts can be resolved by visiting India just once."

"Anyway, Alfred, I guess you are right. I am not implying that my problem is as serious as yours. What I am trying to explain to you is that we all have to face the question of our identity one way or the other."

After a few more minutes of chitchatting, Alfred left. When he was leaving the apartment, he heard Jagdish's parents arguing about something. He looked behind and saw Jagdish smiling at him. He was not embarrassed this time.

*　*　*

The next day, Alfred packed his bags and drove to Columbus, Ohio. At the border between Canada and the United States, he stopped at Niagara Falls. The beauty of the Horseshoe Falls always amazed him no matter how often he had been there. For a while, he felt that his problems were trivial in front of the beauty and the immensity of this world. After spending some time there, he crossed the border. For the first time in his life, he entered the United States.

I am entering the country where I was conceived, Alfred thought. Then it dawned on him that even though they lived only hours away from the border between Canada and the United States, his mom never took him across the border. Jeff lived in Buffalo, which is very close to the Niagara Falls. Mark occasionally brought him to Canada, so he can spend time with his mom, but Angela never went to Buffalo to visit him. Possibly, she didn't want to enter the United States, because she was afraid of Mr. Drake or other people hired by his client. Mark never came there with his wife Debra! Maybe, he did not want Debra to be implicated in this mess. How come it never occurred to him that he had never been taken across the border by his mother or by Mark? Why Mark had not asked him to visit him and Jeff in Buffalo? Maybe Angela didn't want him to leave Canada. What kind of web people weave around you while you are busy trusting them! What else might Angela have done with his life to hide her own crimes?

Several hours later he reached Columbus. The first order of business was to find a cheap motel. Thanks to penny-saver magazines he picked up at the rest areas, he found a hotel within his price range although it was in a far from ideal neighborhood. For a single guy like him, he could stay there for a while, as long as he was careful.

Alfred decided that he had to find a job to survive. He was a teen-ager and did not have any work experience. What kind of work could he do? He went to a few restaurants to apply for a job. Soon he realized that his Canadian citizenship was an obstacle in finding a job in a franchise res-taurant, so McDonald's and Burger King were out of question. He found some part-time work as a pizza delivery guy. He saw an ad for a cleaning company. They contracted with offices and hospitals. He went there to look for a few hours of work. They hired him and told him he will be paid in cash. The company hired undocumented people for cheap labor. They asked him to work in Beth Israel Hospital in downtown Columbus.

In between his jobs, he had to figure out how he was going to find the truth about his birth. Talking to Mr. Kincaid and his son was one way to do it, but before he would meet with them, he had to learn about cloning, genetics, and in vitro fertilization. If possible, he should figure out how he was born, by cloning or by IVF from Mrs. Kincaid's frozen eggs, before approaching them. He decided that a public library would be the best place to get the information he needed.

Alfred went to the main public library in downtown Columbus. He stopped at the desk and asked the librarian about books on science. The clerk was an elderly lady. From her name tag, Alfred knew her name was Marilyn and that she worked as a volunteer. Her face was expression-less. She looked at him indifferently and pointed him to the direction of science-related books. She further explained that the Dewey Decimal

System's code for genetics is 576. She also told him that he could check in the computers located everywhere in the building.

While the lady was giving the instructions in a monotonous voice, Alfred's eyes fell on a young girl pushing a cart-full of books in a room behind the desk. He could not see her face, but he noticed her clothes. She was wearing bright pink shirt and blue jeans. She had long black hair. There was a silver bracelet on her right wrist. He could not see her face. Alfred was not sure if one could say a person is attractive without looking at her face, but if one could then she was definitely attractive.

Alfred didn't listen to what this older woman was telling him because his mind was distracted. When she was done, he thanked her and walked away. He didn't remember what the lady had told him. He looked around. There were rows after rows of long, tall racks full of books. He checked some books randomly; they were history books. He saw some people walking around. He requested one of them to show him books on science. The man showed him the huge poster on the wall, which showed the location of books by subjects. He also showed him the computer terminals where he could search for the books. Alfred thanked him and went to the science section. While he was browsing, he saw that same girl with a cart-full of books. She was putting the books from her cart back on the shelves. He still couldn't see her face, but this time, he saw her beautiful black shoes.

Alfred found the section that had books on genetics. While he was selecting the books, he saw the girl a few rows away. He kept looking at her from the space between the shelved books. He could see her lips and part of her nose, but still not the whole face. He had to see her face. He picked three books on basic genetics he had selected already and walked toward that girl. He moved toward her, but she had started working on the opposite row so her back was toward him. He still couldn't see her face. *How this can be possible*, he wondered. He saw this girl almost ten times already and still could not see her face. He was standing about four feet from her. Maybe, if he would ask her a question, then she will turn around to talk to him.

"Miss, I have a question. Can you help me?" Alfred asked.

"Yes, of course," she answered with a smile as she turned around.

Finally, she was standing opposite him. He could see her face. She looked Asian, probably Korean. She had a beautiful smile. Her teeth were perfect. She was wearing a shiny necklace with a turquoise pendant.

"I am looking for books on genetics. Can you tell me where I can find them?" He asked.

"You mean, other than the ones you already found?" She asked pointing at the books he was carrying.

"Oh, yes, I mean, I am looking for a specific area of genetics. I am looking for books on in vitro fertilization. I could not find any book on that subject," Alfred said pointing at the books in his hand.

"Okay, let me see. I think the easiest way will be to look in the computer database." She noticed that Alfred was staring at her. "Are you all right?" She asked.

"Yes, yes, I am fine. I am just wondering where you are from."

"I am from around here." She then walked toward the computer with Alfred following her.

"In genetics, what topics you are looking for?" She asked.

"Actually, I want to learn about basics of genetics and in vitro fertilization," Alfred answered. She punched a few keys on the computer and printed list of books. Alfred was not paying attention to the monitor. He was looking at her fingers dancing on the keyboard. She had long fingers with beautiful nails.

"May I know your name?" Alfred asked.

"I am Brittany Wilson," she said pointing at her name tag. "Here's what you are looking for." She picked up the paper from the printer and pointed at the list of books. "In this column, you can find the location of each of these books."

"Thank you, Brittany, thank you very much," Alfred answered.

"You are welcome," Brittany replied with a smile.

"Can I ask you one more thing?" Alfred asked.

"Is it about books?"

"No. I want to know where you are from."

"I am originally from South Korea. I knew you would ask about something, you have no business asking."

"I am sorry. I was just curious."

"Don't be. I don't understand why boys try to impress me by asking me about books they cannot understand," She said smiling. *That was cruel.*

"Well, Brittany, I can tell you, you are wrong. I am trying to learn about genetics. Most people would want to talk to you because otherwise they would have to talk to Cruella DeVille sitting down there," Alfred said pointing at the front desk on the lower floor. Alfred began to laugh but stopped when he saw that Brittany was not laughing.

"You didn't tell me your name."

"Oh, I am Alfred. Alfred . . . Johnson." He wondered if he would take the name Kincaid if he discovered that he was indeed related to Mr. Kincaid. Maybe he should, because he told his mother that he wanted to embrace his roots. Funny that this thought had not crossed his mind. He extended his hand and she shook it.

"It's nice meeting you, Brittany."

"Likewise," Brittany answered and walked away.

Alfred selected some books and walked to the desk. That old woman from earlier was sitting there. Alfred asked her how he could borrow these books. She asked for his library card. He told her that he will like to obtain a card. She told him that he could apply for a card online using one of the computers there. Alfred started applying for the card, but soon realized that the applicant had to be a resident of Ohio. He went back to the desk and explained his situation. The lady told him that since he was just visiting there, he could not be considered a resident of Ohio and, therefore, was not eligible to obtain a library card.

Alfred took the books and dejectedly walked away from the desk. There were few chairs and tables where some people were reading books. He sat on a chair. He opened one of the books. In few minutes, he saw Brittany pass by that area.

She asked if he needed any help. Alfred explained his predicament to her.

"I am sorry, but the library policy is to issue cards to residents of Ohio only," she answered.

"I am planning to live in this city for few weeks only."

"You need an address in Ohio."

"Here, I am staying in a motel. I guess that is not going to help my case," Alfred wondered.

"I am afraid not. If you are renting an apartment you might be able to get a card," Brittany gave him an idea.

"Where am I going to find an inexpensive apartment?" Alfred asked.

"Your best bet is to visit OSU. In the main lobby of OSU, there may be lots of flyers from people looking for roommates," Brittany answered.

"What's OSU?"

"Ohio State University. OSU Buckeyes is my favorite football team," Brittany explained.

"Thank you very much. You are an angel. By the way, is Brittany a common Korean name?" Alfred asked laughing. He was relieved to get some help from a stranger in this new city.

"Ha-ha-ha! My first name is Sun, which means goodness in Korean language. But because it is spelled the same way as the sun in the sky, it is confusing, so I go by my middle name Brittany." Alfred smiled. He liked the sound of her name, *Sun Brittany*. He also felt better meeting someone with a friendly face in a new town. It made him feel a little less lonely.

"Thanks again," Alfred told her.

"Alfred, I will hold onto these books for you if you want me to. That way you don't have to search for them again."

"Sure, that would be wonderful. Thank you so much," Alfred said and left.

Alfred went to the campus of Ohio State University. In the main building, he found bulletin boards. On and around the bulletin boards, there were flyers from students looking for roommates. He called some of those students and found an apartment to share with two students. It was cheaper than motel and gave him more space and a common kitchen, too.

The following day, he went to the library again. He applied for the card and received it immediately. Then he picked up a book on genetics and started making notes. In few minutes, he saw Brittany go by with her cart. Her eyes fell on him and she smiled. He smiled back. She left her cart there and walked toward him and asked, "Did you find an apartment?"

"Yes, actually I did. I went to the university as you advised and found a place."

"Great. Now you can get a library card," Brittany said.

"Yes, I already did. I looked for you, but I didn't see you there. Thanks for your help." Alfred was happy. It became a routine for him to visit the library when he had time from his part-time jobs. He would chat with Brittany if she was there. Brittany could not understand why someone who just graduated from high school would be interested in genetics.

*   *   *

One day, Alfred was chatting with Brittany in the library. After a few minutes, she told him that she would love to talk to him, but she was on her break and wanted to go out for fresh air. Alfred understood and went back to his desk. Brittany started walking away, slowly. Then Alfred suddenly thought maybe he should ask her if he can join her. She said she was going out for fresh air, so if he asks her, she can't say she was busy. *Brilliant!* He thought.

He walked toward her and asked, "You know, I am somewhat bored. I need to go out too. Can we go out for a coffee?" *Boys are dumb. Even those who can read books on genetics*, Brittany thought. "Sure, that would be fine," she replied.

They went to a nearby restaurant for coffee. Brittany ordered hazelnut-flavored coffee with two packs of sugar and two containers of half-and-half.

"So it's a double-double for you?" Alfred asked.

"What do you mean?" Brittany didn't follow.

"Oh, in Canada a coffee with two creams and two sugars is called a double-double," Alfred explained.

"I didn't know that," Brittany replied.

Alfred ordered black coffee with sugar.

"Wow, you drink your coffee black? I can't do it," Brittany was surprised.

"I can't drink milk. I am lactose intolerant," Alfred answered.

"So you are Canadian and you are lactose intolerant. Is there anything else I should know about you?" Brittany teased him with a laugh.

"What's wrong with being lactose intolerant?" Alfred asked. He did not want to answer her question. What was really different about him was something he wanted to keep secret.

"Most people can tolerate milk. So I think people who are lactose intolerant are different," Brittany joked. "Anyway, why are you sporting a moustache and a beard?"

"Oh, I just want to know how it feels," Alfred answered.

"I think you will look better clean-shaved." *Well, lady, you have no idea how I look clean-shaved*, Alfred thought.

"I am not sure. Maybe, after few weeks, I will shave them. Let's talk about you. What can you tell me about yourself?" Alfred asked.

"Well, I am originally from South Korea as I told you before. I have a brother and a sister. I am a middle child. My sister is younger than me. I am working in the library this summer. In September, I will attend OSU. What about you?"

"I finished high school. Either this year or next, I will start college. I don't know whether it will be in Canada or here," Alfred gave some information about himself.

"How many brothers and sisters do you have?" Brittany asked.

"I have a half brother, Jeff. No sisters," Alfred answered. *He is not actually my half brother, but it's complicated*, Alfred thought.

"Your half brother lives in Canada, too?" She asked. Immediately, Brittany saw Alfred's facial expression change. She figured, this is the area where for some reason, he was not comfortable. She said to him, "I am sorry for being too nosy. Let's talk about something else."

"No, it's okay. Jeff lives in Buffalo, New York, but it is complicated. I am here due to some personal issues. It's complicated," Alfred replied.

"I understand. Want to see a picture of my brother and sister? Here it is," Brittany mentioned as she showed their picture on her cell phone.

Alfred looked at the picture. It showed Brittany flanked by her brother and sister. Her siblings were Caucasian. He looked back at Brittany, as if to confirm that she was still Asian.

"That's what I mean. We all have issues. I was adopted from an orphanage in South Korea when I was an infant. My parents are from here," Brittany explained.

"Oh, I am sorry. I didn't mean to ask you anything personal. When I said if you could tell me something about yourself, I was just making casual conversation," Alfred apologized.

"I know that. I want you to know that I have some issues, too. You have issues regarding your family, your half brother, or whatever else. But you are not alone. We all have some issues in our lives," Brittany comforted him.

"Alfred, you are not comfortable talking about your half brother, you are visiting all alone from Canada, and you are reading about genetics! Is there a common thread connecting all these things?" Brittany wondered.

"All I can say is that I want to get answers to some questions. That's all." Alfred replied without actually answering her question.

"What's going on, Alfred?" Brittany demanded. "Something mysterious is going on here. I have not seen any boy your age reading books on science. Some are still into *Harry Potter* books."

"True. I might have something to do with a family that lives here. It has nothing to do with Jeff or his dad. We are half brothers, because we have a common mother. Please, try to understand me," Alfred pleaded.

"So that's why you are trying to understand genetics! Do you think you are a product of in vitro fertilization? Is Johnson your real last name?" Brittany asked.

"I grew up with the last name Johnson. It's my mother's maiden name. I have never known my father. My mom told me that after her divorce, she had an affair with someone, but they broke up before she found out she was pregnant with me."

"How do I know you are telling the truth?" Brittany asked.

"That's easy to answer. It's not true. What I said is the story I grew up with. Only recently I found out that my mother was not truthful with me.

She confessed to me that she lied about having an affair to cover up certain things. She lived in Columbus prior to moving to Canada. That's why I am here. I am trying to find out who I am," Alfred explained.

"Looking in the mirror didn't help?" Brittany was sarcastic.

"I am serious. You have no idea how much heartache I have gone through," Alfred was angry.

"I am sorry to hear that. Listen. Everybody has a story. Try to live in a house where ethnically you are different than the rest and then tell me about heartache. I believe you were subjected to some deceptions by your mother, but I am trying to explain to you that some people have gone through worse. Luckily, I had a happy childhood. I understood that I looked different than the rest of my family, because I was adopted. My parents were and still are exceptionally supportive of me. My brother and sister love me. You know something? I have all that, but still at times it gets difficult for me," Brittany explained to him. "Now, what is it that you are trying to discover?"

"There are things that I can't share with anyone at this time. All I can say is this. I am trying to understand genetics, so I can sort out the mystery regarding my birth. Believe me, I told you lot more than I was prepared to share." Alfred continued, "Wow, my first cup of coffee with you and I am getting the third degree."

"I am sorry, Alfred. First of all, I had no right to get mad at you. It's just, I hate it when guys lie and cheat to go out with a girl. True, this is the first time we went out for a coffee, but we have talked a lot in the last few days and I thought at least you would be upfront with me," Brittany calmed down. "Maybe, next time I will order decaf." She laughed.

"Now, that's more like you. In time, I will tell you everything," Alfred promised.

"Okay," Brittany said.

"By the way, Brittany, I wanted to hear about your life in Korea. Now I know you left Korea when you were a baby. Having been raised by a Caucasian couple, I don't think you would know much about the country of your birth."

"Actually, that's not true. My parents learned a lot about Korean culture and taught my siblings and me about it. Three years ago, they took all of us to South Korea. They wanted to make sure that I knew my roots," Brittany said.

"Time flies! My break is almost over," Brittany said as she was getting up.

"Yes, we better go back. If you are late, Cruella will yell at you," Alfred joked. "She is always expressionless. Man, what's wrong with her?"

"You know, Marilyn is actually a nice person. I must admit, I, too, have made fun of her behind her back, but she is a sweet lady. She has been volunteering in this library for many years. Her face is expressionless, because she has Parkinson's disease. At least that's what my coworkers tell me. In a few years, she may develop tremors if her condition worsens," Brittany defended her superior.

"I didn't know that. I am sorry. I thought that's how she was," Alfred confessed. "I guess there is more to people than we know." He felt bad for making fun of Marilyn.

"Yes, it sure is. It's certainly true for you, me, and Marilyn," Brittany concurred.

15

How to Confirm Cloning

A four-letter alphabet called DNA.

— MATT RIDLEY, BRITISH JOURNALIST AND AUTHOR

After the initial blow-up, Brittany had calmed down. She liked Alfred. He was not pretentious like other boys. He was normal except for his obsession with genetics. He was easy to talk to. He never expressed desire to get intimate.

Maybe, if she would know what Alfred was looking for, she could help him. One day, Alfred and Brittany were walking in downtown Columbus trying to find a place to have lunch.

"How is your reading going, Alfred?" Brittany asked him.

"Not too well, I must admit," Alfred confessed.

Brittany asked him, "Can you tell me what specific genetic information you are looking for?"

"What do you mean?" Alfred asked.

"If you tell me exactly what you want to know about, I could find appropriate books and save you lot of time. Biology has been my most favorite subject throughout school, and I plan to major in biology. I want to go into medicine."

"I am looking into different methods of reproduction in human beings. I don't feel comfortable revealing anything more than that," Alfred answered.

"I guessed that much. The books you are borrowing are pertaining to in vitro fertilization and cloning. I know that because I have checked out some of those books to you. I have not pried into your account to see what kind of books you are reading. Oh my God! Do you think that you are a clone or *you* were cloned to create someone else? Man, that's heavy," Brittany was shocked at this thought.

"Brittany, please don't try to analyze what I am doing. I have told you time and again that I can't reveal what I am trying to find out," Alfred pleaded.

"My goodness! I am trying to wrap my mind around this. If you are a clone or you were cloned, then that's something major. My gut reaction is if cloning has anything to do with you, then it would be impossible to keep secret. I think you are wasting your time," Brittany explained.

Alfred had read about Chuck, another child of Mr. Kincaid, who was born around the time he was born. He had also read about rumors that Chuck was a product of cloning. While digging up the information on Mr. Kincaid, he had come across those reports in the crypts of the Internet. *You are right, Brittany. It was not a secret. Only thing is, no one remembers it now*, Alfred thought.

"In due time, I will explain what's going on. Please, don't speculate," Alfred said to her.

"Listen. You are working two jobs. You are living in a shabby apartment with two students, and you are spending most of your time going through books that you can't understand. I enjoy talking to you and look forward to your visits in the library, but as far as your goal is concerned, you are wasting your time. I think you may have reached a dead-end in your research in genetics. Have you thought about discussing with a geneticist? Maybe, he or she can explain to you what you need to do. If you have suspicions that cloning has anything to do with you, then a geneticist can help you."

"I will look for a geneticist in due time. At present, I want to understand the basics of genetics," Alfred replied.

They were walking on Broad Street. Suddenly, Brittany said to Alfred, "You know something? Right here, at the junction of Fifth and Broad, was the first Wendy's restaurant. I went there often when I was little. We used to visit the COSI museum, which is on the other side of the Scioto River. Then we would walk here to eat a burger. Unfortunately, they closed the restaurant a few years ago."

Alfred looked at her in astonishment. "Why are you staring at me like this?" Brittany asked.

"I can never understand women. If a man would say something like that, the woman would complain that he does not know what he should say when he is going out with a girl. But, apparently it's all right for a woman to mention something like this."

"Well, all you need to know about women is this. We make rules, and we change them as and when we please. Anyway, I told you about Wendy's because I thought you would find it interesting. From here, Wendy's expanded to thousands of restaurants across the country," Brittany added.

"Actually, I admit. It's interesting," Alfred confessed.

"Let me share one more thing with you then. Did you know that Dave Thomas, the founder of Wendy's, was adopted? I think it's interesting," Brittany mentioned.

Okay, Dave Thomas, Wendy's founder, was adopted just like Brittany was! That explains her interest in the first Wendy's restaurant, Alfred concluded.

They found a fast food restaurant and went there for lunch. While eating lunch, Brittany decided to ask Alfred again about his search in genetics.

"Okay, let's make a deal. You tell me what you are looking for, and I will try to find articles or books for you. I will not ask any question. I promise you. How does that sound?" Brittany said to him.

"Fair enough. Since you already know that I am reading about cloning. I can tell you this much. I want to know if human cloning has been done or not. I also want to know if there are rumors of successful human cloning. I want to know if there is a way to detect if a person is original versus a clone.

Are they completely identical or are there some differences genetically? Can you find answers to these questions for me?" Alfred asked.

"I have tons of questions now, but I promised you I wouldn't ask questions, so I am not going to. I will find answers and share with you soon. Also, I must tell you again, you need to find a geneticist. You may have to confide a few things about you to him, so he can help you," Brittany said to him.

Alfred was way over his head with science. He was trying to learn genetics. He had learned a lot about chromosomes and modes of reproduction. He read about parthenogenesis, asexual reproductions, etcetera. However, there was still so much more to understand. Brittany may be right.

The next day, Alfred went to the library. Brittany was waiting for him. She told him that she had a break in a few minutes and if Alfred wanted to go out for a walk, she was fine with that. Alfred agreed. She went back to work.

About fifteen minutes later, Brittany came back, and they went outside. She told him that she had found some material on cloning that he might find interesting. She had made a folder of some articles she had printed off the Internet. She also had a couple of books for him to read.

Alfred said to her, "Thanks, Brittany, when we go back to the library give the material to me. I will read those articles and books as soon as possible."

"Yes, you must. There is a wealth of information in them. I think you will get answers to the questions you have in mind. You know, I found cloning to be a very interesting subject matter. I read that with the help of cloning they may be able to bring back many extinct species."

"I didn't know that. Bringing back extinct species with the help of cloning is a brilliant idea," Alfred confessed.

"Besides Dolly the sheep, they have successfully cloned other mammals too from cells of adult animals. Scientists have cloned horses, cows, cats, and of course dogs. The first dog cloned from an adult dog's cells was named Snuppy, and he was cloned in South Korea in the year 2005. Do you know why they named the dog Snuppy? It took place in the Seoul

National University or SNU. They combined the initials SNU and the word puppy and named the dog Snuppy," Brittany was excited.

"That's very clever. I am curious. Are you excited about it because it happened in South Korea?" Alfred asked.

"I think it's a fair question. If I had not been to South Korea, it won't have made any difference to me. But since I have been there, I feel different. Yes, I can say it makes me feel good about it. To some extent, though, after my visit there, I feel closer to the Korean people rather than South Korea as a country."

Then, Brittany's expression changed and she told Alfred, "Unfortunately, Alfred, there is a whole other side to this achievement by the South Korean scientists."

"I don't follow," Alfred confessed.

"Hwang Woo-Suck, who cloned Snuppy, was embroiled in ethics violations. He committed fraud, breached bioethics laws of South Korea, and embezzled funds. He is a discredited man now," Brittany lamented.

"Then how do they know if Snuppy really is a clone? Maybe, that too is fraudulent."

"No, that's the thing. Snuppy was extensively studied and proved to be a clone by scientists of other countries. It has been proved beyond a shadow of a doubt that Hwang successfully cloned a dog from the cells of an adult dog. Incidentally, Snuppy also became father to some puppies proving that a cloned animal can reproduce. Hwang is a brilliant scientist and has many achievements to his name, but at the pinnacle of his career, he made bad choices and went from, 'pride of Korea' to a 'pariah' in the scientific world. Apparently, he could not uphold the status he created for himself."

"That's very sad. It must be devastating for the reputation of his university and the country," Alfred opined.

They were silent for few moments then Alfred asked, "How was your visit there? Can you tell me about it? But please, tell me only if you are comfortable talking about it," Alfred asked.

"I think I can talk about it. As I told you before, my parents took my brother, my sister, and me to visit South Korea. They wanted us all to know where I came from. We went to Seoul, which is the capital of South Korea. Its official name is Seoul Special City. South Korea was quite different than I had pictured."

"Going there from the United States, it must have been a cultural shock to be in a third-world country," Alfred said.

"Actually, it was completely opposite, Alfred. South Korea is an advanced, urbanized country. Seoul could compete with any metropolitan city of a westernized country. It is crowded, but it is very clean and very organized. The standard of living is pretty good too. We went to the orphanage where I was dropped off by my biological mother. I had expected to see a dilapidated building with no modern facilities, but I was stunned to see how beautiful the place was. We looked for Sister Miriam who was the contact person for my parents when they adopted me. Luckily, she was still there."

"Did she remember your parents, I mean, your adoptive parents?" Alfred asked.

"I don't think so. She didn't mention anything to that effect. She was also very old when we met her. My parents showed her the adoption papers they had received when I was adopted. Sister Miriam was nice enough to go through my records. She told us that I was almost three months old when I was dropped off. There was a paper that mentioned my date of birth and the name my biological mother gave me. She had not mentioned her first or last names. She had named me Sun, which my parents kept as my first name. Brittany is my middle name as you already know. With the permission of Sister Miriam, we took pictures of that paper.

"After spending a few minutes there, my parents told me I should spend some time there by myself. They told me to join them outside of the orphanage when I was ready. That was a very thoughtful suggestion. I talked with Sister Miriam about how the orphanage was when I would have been there as an infant and what changes were made in the building since then. She gave me a tour of the place. It was very nice of her to walk around with me despite her bad knees. She was using a walker. I saw the well-kept rooms, the bassinets, the mattresses, etcetera. It was kind of overwhelming. Then she told me to walk around on my own and ask the staff if I had any questions. I looked at some kids. They ranged from toddlers to teenagers. The strange thing was that all those kids, irrespective of their age groups, were quiet. They were very well-behaved."

"The kids were obviously well trained. That speaks of the dedication of the staff in the orphanage," Alfred opined.

"That was my first reaction too and that's what most people would think. When I mentioned that to my parents they told me they noticed it too, but their opinion was different. They found it depressing. They told me that the kids in the orphanage behaved like robots. There was no spunk, no spirit on their faces. A toddler remains quiet and appears to be well-behaved, when he is deprived of love and interaction with his parents or caretakers. So a quiet child is probably a child who is withdrawn. I tell you, Alfred, looking back I realized that the place was very gloomy."

She continued, "Anyway, I walked to the playground behind the building. There were swings and slides there. You know, Alfred, there I did something spontaneously. I've never told anyone about this," Brittany was emotional.

"What did you do? Is it something that you can share with another person?" Alfred asked hesitantly.

"Yes, I will tell you if you promise not to tell anyone else."

"I promise," Alfred hesitantly agreed. He was expecting something really weird.

"In the playground, I took my shoes and socks off and touched the ground with my bare feet. That's when I felt that I was from that soil. Until then I was confused about who I was, but that moment I *became* Korean. I started crying. It's hard to describe that feeling," Brittany said as she wiped tears from her eyes.

Brittany remembered the event as if it had happened only yesterday. She was standing barefoot in the middle of the playground. Her sneakers and socks were lying next to her feet. She was wiggling her toes to feel as much of the soil as possible. There were slides and swings around her. Some kids were running around in the playground. They were staring at her as if she were an alien. When they saw her crying, the kids got scared and ran inside the building. She was suddenly all alone in the middle of that vast open space. It was a very lonely feeling. On a planet with seven billion people, she was standing in a barren play-ground, alone, sobbing. She had relived those moments a million times since then.

"My God, that's something. You know, Brittany, a few months ago, I won't have understood it. I might have even laughed at the person who would say something like this. Now I can relate to it. Half a world away in a strange country, standing alone in the playground, you discovered your identity," Alfred's eyes were welling up with tears, too.

"Well, after I spent some time barefoot in the playground, I put my socks and shoes on and went back to Sister Miriam. I gave her a big hug and thanked her for taking care of me and so many other kids. Then I walked out of the orphanage. When I joined my family, nobody said a word. I am sure my mom figured I had cried a few minutes ago, but she didn't say any-thing. No one ever asked me about the alone time I had there. My parents are very understanding that way. The visit to South Korea also helped me understand what Korean people do."

Brittany again wiped the tears and continued, "Before we went to South Korea, I had only known Koreans who lived in the United States. They were doctors, scientists, engineers, or storeowners. In South Korea, I saw Korean people who were police officers, postal workers, street sweepers, and wait-ers in restaurants. In essence, I saw people who looked like me, running a whole country. That made me very comfortable with my ethnicity. Before my visit to South Korea, every time we would go out here in Columbus, people would look at my parents, my brother, my sister, and then they will stare at me. That made me uncomfortable. After I came back from Korea, things were different. I felt normal. I didn't care about people staring at me."

"That's incredible. How did your siblings treat you when you were growing up?" Alfred asked.

"Man, you are being nosy. My brother, Eric, my sister, Amy, and I fought off and on, as all kids do. We would hit one another, hide one another's books; you name it and we did it. First time, when during a fight,

Eric commented on my looks—he said something about my eyes—Mom spanked him hard. She told Eric and Amy that if they ever made fun of my looks, she would break their bones. She also told me never to joke about my siblings' looks or for that matter anyone else's. She told us that she did not care if she had to spend time in jail for beating us up, but she would not tolerate if her kids made fun of somebody's skin color or appearance. It never happened again. My mom is a helicopter-mom and a tiger-mom rolled into one."

Brittany continued. "If someone in school commented on my looks, Eric would pick a fight with them. In a way, I think my ethnicity defined the outlook of my family. On the dining table in our home, there is never a negative comment about people's skin color, religion, or nationality. I do not think it is out of respect for me only. But because my siblings and parents see me as a normal person, they are able to see people of different ethnicity as normal too. My mom told me that I was free to choose my religion. She is sensitive of the fact that many people in South Korea practice Buddhism. I decided to stick to Christianity, because that's what everyone in my family practices. Actually, I don't care much about a person's religion. I think a person of another religion is as normal as anybody just like a person of different skin color or ethnicity is. In our house, mom has put a plaque over the breakfast table which reads, COEXIST. Each letter is written using symbols of different religions. Mom tells us that we all should learn how to live peacefully with people who are different than us," Brittany explained.

"Wow, you have taught me a lot. Brittany, you are a special person. I am tempted to say, you are comfortable in your skin," Alfred said.

"Well put, Alfred. I will use that in future," Brittany answered. After a brief pause, she said, "Alfred, I want you to have dinner at my house this Saturday."

"Thanks for the invitation, but I think I will be out of place there."

"No, you will be fine. It will be nice to have you there and meet my family. They already know a lot about you. They will enjoy meeting you." Alfred could not find a reason to decline the invitation. He agreed to be there.

They went back to the library. Alfred collected the material Brittany had picked out for him. He checked out some books and left. Marilyn called Brittany and told her, "You know that young boy you just went out with? I think his name is Alfred. He is very nice. Initially, I thought he was obnoxious, but lately I find him very respectful and polite. Most people who come here, look at me like I were a specimen in a museum, but not him."

Brittany said to her, "It's very nice of you to say that, thank you." She figured that Alfred's behavior with Marilyn changed after he knew about her medical condition. She still felt good to hear something nice about Alfred.

* * *

Alfred went to Brittany's home for dinner that Saturday. Brittany proudly introduced him to her parents and siblings. Alfred had a good time. Brittany's dad, Anthony Wilson, was very funny. He asked Alfred about Canadian slangs. He asked why they say, "aboot" and "eh" with every sentence. He also mentioned hockey and, of course—Tim Hortons, Canada's restaurant chain. One could tell that he had surfed the Internet to learn some common things about Canada. Alfred enjoyed listening to the stereotypes about Canada. Brittany's mother appeared very calculative. Alfred noticed her studying him with a penetrating gaze and asking him questions pertaining to his future goals.

Every time she tried to probe him about the purpose of his stay in Columbus, Brittany changed the subject. Brittany's siblings seemed to be supportive of her. After the dinner was over, Alfred offered to help with the dishes.

While in the kitchen, he noticed the plaque over the breakfast table about which Brittany had mentioned to him. The word COEXIST was written on it. It looked beautiful. Alfred liked the idea of spelling the word COEXIST using symbols like the Star of David, Hindu word Om, a Cross, a crescent moon, and so on.

Coexist, thought Alfred, *Yeah, I guess that's all we can do.*

16

What's a Homunculus?

The greatest single achievement of nature to date was surely the invention of the molecule of DNA.

— LEWIS THOMAS, PHYSICIAN AND SCIENTIST

One afternoon Brittany and Alfred were walking out of a restaurant after enjoying a cup of coffee. Brittany was off that day and Alfred had come back from his shift in the housekeeping department in the Beth Israel Hospital. Brittany was talking about the clothes she had bought from her paycheck. Alfred was half listening.

Suddenly, Brittany pointed at a car and exclaimed, "Oh my God, look at the license plate on that car!" Alfred had no idea what she was talking about. He looked at the car; it was a black Toyota Camry.

He asked, "Brittany, the license plate number is 1CE 959. What is so unusual about it?"

"I was reading about genomes, and I read a chapter about a worm called *Caenorhabditis elegans*. This worm is less than one millimeter long. The number 959 is interesting, because the scientists have calculated that in an adult hermaphrodite form of this organism, there are exactly 959 cells. 1CE kind of represents one *Caenorhabditis elegans* organism."

"I can honestly say that I didn't know it," Alfred confessed. "Why is that worm so important?"

"Oh, I will tell you. Biologists have studied this organism in extraordinary details. They have not only determined the number of cells in the adult hermaphrodite form but also discovered how each cell is formed from the original single cell. Each cell divides into two daughter cells and never more than two. The organism develops because of asymmetric cell division. This asymmetric cell division results in the differentiation of tissues, which ultimately result in the adult organism. For each cell in the adult organism, scientists have determined after how many cell divisions it forms. In most organisms, the cell development is not so well-defined. In complex animals, the development of cells is different in different individuals of the same species. Actually, John Sulston received a Nobel Prize for his research on this organism." (*Sulston shared Nobel Prize in Physiology or Medicine with two other scientists*).

"That's fascinating. You come up with some interesting things, Brittany," Alfred said.

"Thank you. Speaking of interesting things, I have to apologize to you," Brittany said.

"Apologize to me? For what?" Alfred did not understand.

"Remember I made fun of you when you told me you were lactose intolerant? Well, it turns out that it is normal to be lactose intolerant. At birth, mammals drink mothers' milk so they need the enzyme lactase to digest the milk. Adult mammals of other species don't drink milk, so they don't need that enzyme anymore. Therefore, actually it is normal for an adult to be lactose intolerant. Since human beings continue to consume milk and milk products, many of us continue to produce lactase. It is especially so in the countries where consumption of dairy products is more common," Brittany explained.

"Wow, that's a relief," Alfred answered.

"I hate to confess it, but there is something normal about you," Brittany joked.

"Thanks," Alfred said and continued. "I came across something really bizarre while reading about genetics. A few centuries ago, scientists believed that inside the sperm of a man, there is a homunculus.

"What's a homunculus?" Brittany asked.

"Homunculus is a fully formed, miniature human being in a sperm. They believed that a sperm is placed inside a woman's womb for growth of a person. Can you imagine how weird it is?"

"That is one of the stupidest things I have ever heard," Brittany gave her opinion. "This theory may explain why a child resembles his or her father but does not explain why a child would resemble his or her mother too. Also, when the homunculus is grown and a son is born, how is he going to have his kids?"

"Well, they claimed that inside that homunculus there is another homunculus and another and so on. That's why I said this is bizarre. In today's world, a child in fifth grade would understand how ridiculous this theory is. But, apparently, it survived for quite some time," Alfred explained. They were quiet for a few moments.

"I think you need to meet doctor Betty Sue Lawson," Brittany suddenly told him.

"What are you talking about?" Alfred was clueless.

'Remember, I told you, you should speak to a geneticist?" Brittany asked.

"Yes. What about it?" Alfred was still puzzled.

"Dr. Lawson is a geneticist. She has done lot of work on the genetics of twins. I read a book written by her and I was very impressed," Brittany explained.

"Where does she work?" Alfred asked.

"She works in Cleveland. Her office is in the famous Cleveland Clinic. It is about 150 miles from here. She has published many weird cases. She has worked on life histories of twins separated at birth. She herself has lived a very interesting life. I was impressed when I read her biography."

"Wait a minute. You are jumping from her work to her own life. I don't see how her life story is going to help me," Alfred was confused with this distraction. He knew that Brittany couldn't make simple, straightforward talk.

"Give me a minute and I will explain. Betty Sue Lawson was a twin. She was the younger and smaller twin. While growing up, she felt neglected by her family. Her life was strongly affected by the way she grew up. Her biography, *The Invisible Twin, Incredible Life of Doctor Betty Sue Lawson*, is a fascinating book. The author, Katherine Gill, interviewed her, her family members, relatives, teachers, coworkers, and many other people while researching for the book. Check the book out from our library and read it. Anyway, I think you should contact her. She can advise you regarding the tests you need to undergo."

"I will definitely look into it. I think whatever secrets I am keeping, I will have to reveal them to a geneticist to get the answers," Alfred answered. That was something that Alfred was not looking forward to.

*   *   *

Michael Kincaid invited some guests for a weeklong retreat to his own private island. Among the guests were Hollywood actress Dodie Lockhart and her husband Richard Perkins. According to *People* magazine, Ms. Lockhart was one of the fifty most fascinating people of the decade. Mr. Kincaid flirted with Dodie in front of her husband and other guests. On her part, she enjoyed the overtures from a billionaire. Her behavior made her husband feel emasculated in front of all the guests. The poor guy pleaded with her not to create a scandal and offered to divorce her if that was what she wanted. She ignored his pleadings and continued her shenanigans in front of everyone. Ten days after returning from their island vacation, Richard Perkins filed for divorce. Three months later, Mike ended his romance with Dodie Lockhart, leaving her with scandalous reputation and no husband. Patricia remembered what John had told her about Mike. She felt bad for Dodie's husband and their kids.

17

The Invisible Twin

We've had cloning in the South for years. It's called cousins.

— Robin Williams, comedian

Betty Sue Lawson grew up in southeast Kentucky. She was born into a stereotypical Appalachian family. Her poor, illiterate parents lived in a shack. It was no surprise that her parents were related prior to their marriage. They were second cousins, once removed. Consanguinity was prevalent in the culture at the time and it still is. When her mamma was pregnant with her, she already had two boys and a girl.

Betty Sue was born at home just like her other siblings. Her mamma did not visit a doctor during any of her pregnancies. When she went into labor, a midwife came to her home and helped her deliver the baby. After one baby, a girl, was born, the midwife saw a tiny leg sticking out in the birth canal. That's when she realized that there was a second baby. The excited midwife gave the good news to the mother, but instead of being happy, she was upset. The second twin, also a girl, was born ten minutes later. Neither the parents nor the midwife had expected twins. The midwife explained that when she examined her belly, she could not tell there were twins. Maybe, the bigger first twin was hiding the smaller second twin, she argued.

Mamma was not ready to handle two newborn babies. She had no difficulty bonding with the first twin, mainly because she was expected and partly because she was the healthier of the two. She couldn't bond with the second twin. To make matters worse, the second twin was two pounds lighter than the first. She was small and emaciated. The mother named the first baby Samantha Lou. It took her ten long days before she accepted the name Betty Sue for the second baby. Her neighbor suggested the name since the mother would not even care to name her. She breastfed both babies but fed Samantha Lou first. Betty Sue was fed next if any milk was left. As if this were not enough, she asked her cousins and other relatives if they wanted to adopt Betty Sue. They didn't, because she was not attractive, and she was so scrawny. As an infant and a toddler, she was neglected by her family.

Her older siblings remembered that Betty Sue had to wear clothes discarded by her twin sister. Having to wear hand-me-downs was not necessarily unusual in rural America in those days, and it still is a common practice in many parts of the world. However, when the hand-me-downs came from your twin it was awkward. Betty Sue resented it. Samantha Lou and her friends didn't miss a chance to tease and torment Betty Sue. When Samantha Lou's friends visited her home, she shunned them. She would hide in the closet or under the bed when they were home. She learned how to be invisible to survive.

Physical fights were common among the siblings. Betty Sue would be at the receiving end due to her short stature and inferior status in the family. Samantha Lou grew up to be a spoiled brat because of the favorable treatment from her parents. The siblings attended school but received mediocre education in the public school system.

At the age of thirteen, Samantha Lou started going out with boys. Betty Sue didn't have time for that because she had to help mamma in house work. Two years later, their daddy died of a massive heart attack. He was obese, diabetic, and hypertensive. The family became poorer. To make ends meet, mamma forced the twins to find some work. Older siblings had already moved out. They were doing whatever work they could find.

Samantha Lou started working as a stripper in a nearby town. Every now and then she bragged about the money she was earning and made Betty Sue feel inferior. Betty Sue was finding it difficult to land a job because of her small physique and introvert nature. There were hardly any jobs available anyway.

One day she heard about a job opening in a coalmine a few miles away from her home. It was almost impossible to find a woman working in the mines, but as luck would have it, a woman from her village, Peggy Mae, worked there. Betty Sue met her. Peggy Mae encouraged her to apply for a job and advised her to lie about her age because as a minor she wouldn't be eligible for such a job. Betty Sue applied for a job there and to her surprise, she got it. The supervisor was too drunk at the time to realize that the applicant was too small to do manual work.

Working hundreds of feet underground felt "natural" to this invisible twin. She had survived all these years by hiding from everyone. Betty Sue tolerated insults and harassments from men working in the coal mine. They resented the presence of women, but legally couldn't do anything about it.

For some time, Betty Sue was satisfied with her job. She made a decent wage; she was able to help her mamma out. However, after a while, Betty Sue realized that it was a dead-end job. Peggy Mae, who helped her find the job in the coalmine, was in her fifties and was still doing hard work with no prospects of any improvement in her status. Samantha Lou was always flaunting her monetary success every chance she got, not to mention the bragging about her "successes" with men. Betty Sue knew that she had to get out of there or she would be Peggy Mae after forty years. She could no longer live in the shadow of her twin or in the underground world of coalmines. She had to rise above this. *Being "invisible" is worse than being dead*, she reckoned.

Among these hillbillies and coal miners, there were some success stories too. She had heard of people who went to college, received a professional education, and made something of themselves. True, most of them were men, but why couldn't a woman be successful too, she wondered. In the Appalachian regions of Kentucky, West Virginia, and Tennessee, there were doctors, lawyers, and politicians. Every now and then, a diamond was discovered in a coalmine. Why couldn't she be one of those diamonds?

Betty Sue was now seventeen years old. She went back to school and obtained a high school diploma. Then she went to college while working part-time. Her ten-minute older twin sister, Samantha Lou was always on her mind. She was her alter ego. *I can't be invisible forever, I had to show off to her*; Betty Sue repeated this mantra over and over again.

Betty Sue decided to go into medicine. During her undergraduate studies, she received scholarships. She supported herself with part-time jobs. When she was accepted into medical school, she received a full scholarship and statewide recognition that included monetary awards. The Governor of Kentucky personally congratulated Betty Sue. The "invisible twin" was on local news. Even her mamma started bragging about her *favorite* child. Betty Sue was becoming visible, slowly. Samantha Lou was furious. She was still working as a stripper, had a two-year-old child, two abortions, and a drug addiction. She had no chance of getting out of that rut. She resented her little twin for being successful, but she could do nothing about it.

Betty Sue's years in medical school were not easy. She was subjected to insults and jokes due to her hillbilly background and her Southern accent. She tried to change her appearance and lose the accent, but she was ridiculed more and more as she attempted to disown her heritage. In the end, she learned to ignore the comments people around her made and focus on her goal of being more successful than her twin was. She specialized in genetics. She wanted to learn about twins. She had heard the stories of how parents didn't treat the twins as two separate individuals. They will dress them alike, constantly compare them to each other, and favor one twin over the other. She had also similar experiences in her own life. She wanted to educate people on raising twins and triplets.

Betty Sue Lawson became a geneticist. She published papers in medical journals and also published life histories of many twins and triplets and discussed their grievances about the way their parents had raised them. Many of these twins insisted that when their life stories were published, their actual names were used. They wanted to show the world what they had gone through. In Dr. Lawson, they found a true friend. For them, she was one of the few people in the medical field who would understand their plight. Critics argued that vast majority of twins or multiples grow up fine. They were not stigmatized by the way they were raised. Dr. Lawson agreed with that sentiment, but her crusade was for the small number of twins who were not treated as individuals. She stated that some parents don't treat their kids as individual persons even when they are not twins and that can cause life-long trauma to those kids.

Doctor Betty Sue Lawson also wrote extensively against the Twin Days celebration. Twin Days is a festival to celebrate twins, triplets, and quadruplets. It takes place every year in August in the City of Twinsburg, Ohio. Dr. Lawson argued that people should notice the twins and multiples as separate individuals and not as curiosities. Her criticism backfired because more people learned about this event and embraced the idea. Celebrating multiple births for one weekend a year was not going to cause any harm, instead it would be fun, they believed. People told Dr. Lawson to lighten up and let them enjoy the festival. On her part, she enjoyed the publicity.

Her biographer, Katherine Gill, asked Dr. Lawson about her personal life, specifically her plans to raise a family. She told her that she had no plans of marrying somebody and she definitely didn't want to have kids. She wanted her gene pool should evaporate with her death.

In the midst of all these achievements, there was a dark chapter in Dr. Lawson's life. After she got a well-paying job, she offered financial help to her siblings. She told them she wanted to improve their lives. While the older siblings politely declined, Samantha Lou couldn't bear this insult. Her boyfriend found her dead just three days after Betty Sue made that generous offer. There was no suicide note. The Medical Examiner ruled that Samantha Lou died of accidental overdose. Dr. Lawson's biographer asked her if she felt avenged by her twin sister's death. She denied it and insisted that her objective was to help her family. Then in reply to a question, she admitted that she knew that any offer of financial help from her could cause distress to Samantha Lou, however, she emphatically denied that she wanted her twin sister to take her own life or even hurt herself. In her book, the biographer added that she could see a faint smile on Dr. Lawson's face when she talked about her twin's death. Dr. Lawson didn't make any public comment about the biographer's claim. In the interviews she did after the publication of this book, Dr. Lawson refused to discuss the death of her twin sister. This incident was a blot on her otherwise phenomenal career.

* * *

Alfred thought the way Dr. Lawson took revenge on the person who had wronged her was innovative, but absolutely revolting. He believed that Dr. Lawson had to know that her twin sister would do something horrible when she would offer money to her. He concluded that in her own subtle way she was getting back at her twin. After all, he himself had entertained the idea of causing harm to people who had wronged him. Of course, in his heart, he knew he could never kill or even harm anyone.

Alfred also read a book written by Dr. Lawson. When he read the cases published by Dr. Lawson, it dawned on him that there was no way anyone involved in his case would keep it a secret. A paper in a scientific journal about a proven case of cloning was a gold-mine, professionally speaking. A book written on a case of cloning was worth millions of dollars to the author and the publishers. Why should he just give it away? He decided that he had to hire a lawyer. He remembered Robert Newman who was hired by his mother, Angela Johnson, years ago. A lawyer will also help him protect his own interests from the book's author.

Alfred was not sure if Mr. Newman was still practicing law and if he did, whether he was still in Columbus. When he Googled his name, he found his office address and phone number. He also found links showing that Mr. Robert Newman, attorney at law, had married his longtime lover, John Peterson. They took their vows in the State of Massachusetts soon after same-sex marriage became legal in that state. Alfred remembered his mom telling him that Mr. Newman was gay.

Alfred called Mr. Newman's office and made an appointment to see him. In his office, there were pictures of Mr. Newman with his spouse. Alfred informed him that Angela Johnson was his mother and she was his client many years ago in a case of surrogate pregnancy. He remembered her thanks to all the troubles she had caused him. He told Alfred that Angela Johnson gave him lot of grief when she disappeared. Alfred explained to him that Angela wanted to keep the baby and thought that leaving the country was the only option she had, so she had run away to Canada. Then, Alfred informed Mr. Newman that the case of surrogate pregnancy was not what he thought it was. There was lot more to it than he could imagine. Mr. Newman didn't follow.

Alfred told him his story including his suspicion about cloning and the involvement of Michael Kincaid. Due to his facial hair, Mr. Newman couldn't see the resemblance between Alfred and Steven Kincaid, but when Alfred showed him his driver's license, he was speechless. So Michael Kincaid was behind this so-called surrogate pregnancy! Mr. Newman was very surprised!

He agreed to hire Alfred as a client. He explained to him that although his main practice was in divorces, his office would love to take this challenge. Alfred mentioned to him that Mr. Drake tried to scare and possibly kidnap his mom and him when he was few months old. It was news to Mr. Newman.

"Well Mr. Drake passed away, so we can't ask him why he did that," Mr. Newman informed him.

"I didn't know that he has passed away. Anyway, I am not interested in finding out why he tried to harass my mom. Can we get any information about my case from his office?" Alfred wondered.

"I don't think so. Even if they have the information you need, they will not release it due to attorney-client privilege. By the way, many people hated Mr. Drake. About fifteen years ago, a prisoner broke out of jail, stole a car, and ran over Mr. Drake while he was jogging. He then called police and surrendered. He claimed that Mr. Drake had ruined his life by wrongfully putting him in jail. Many attorneys and other people who knew Mr. Drake were not surprised that someone killed him."

Alfred told Mr. Newman that he would want doctor Betty Sue Lawson, a geneticist working at Cleveland Clinic, to advise him in this matter. Mr. Newman's office contacted Dr. Lawson. Three days later, he and Alfred went to meet with Dr. Lawson in her office in Cleveland Clinic. Mr. Newman had informed her that the meeting was pertaining to an interesting case in the field of genetics and a possible book deal.

Dr. Lawson was a small woman. She was barely five-feet tall and was very skinny. She welcomed Alfred and Mr. Newman in her office. Her attorney, Mr. Fujiwara, was also present.

"Dr. Lawson, I am trying to find my roots and I need your help. But before I lay down my cards, I need some understanding between us," Alfred tried to explain.

"Of course," Dr. Lawson agreed.

Mr. Newman proposed that his client, Alfred Johnson, will give details about his life and Dr. Lawson will have rights to publish them in a scientific journal and/or write a book about it. In lieu of that, he demanded one million dollars flat or 50 percent of her earnings from books and movie deals. Mr. Fujiwara was not willing to have his client part with one million dollars without having more information. Dr. Lawson also was uncomfortable with it. They asked for some clues or some more information from Alfred and from Mr. Newman. They wouldn't budge.

Finally, after a few emails and phone calls, and a threat by Mr. Newman to see another geneticist, they agreed to pay 50 percent of the future earnings to Alfred if his story would prove worthy of publishing. If Dr. Lawson felt that it didn't, Alfred would have to pay Dr. Lawson for her time. Alfred and his lawyer agreed. In return, Dr. Lawson will help him with all the genetic tests he would need. Robert Newman and Alfred were very happy with the deal.

After all the necessary papers were signed, Mr. Newman explained the case scenario to Dr. Lawson. He proposed the theory that Alfred is a twin of another person, but they were born more than one year apart. He added that his client would like to investigate if he is the product of cloning. Doctor Lawson assured Mr. Newman and Alfred that cloning is extremely unlikely and that to her it appeared a waste of time but promised to obtain necessary genetic tests. Thanks to Alfred's moustache and beard, neither Dr. Lawson nor Mr. Fujiwara suspected that a famous billionaire was involved in this mess. She agreed to explore the issue. She advised the tests needed to prove their theory. There was one problem. Alfred had to take a sample from Steven Kincaid. Without that, there was no way of proving anything.

The invisible twin was about to achieve worldwide recognition, but she didn't know it yet.

18

Brittany Learns about Steven Kincaid

I was born by myself but carry the spirit and blood of my father, mother and my ancestors. So I am really never alone. My identity is through that line.

— ZIGGY MARLEY, JAMAICAN MUSICIAN

Brittany was reading about cloning. She read about the methods used to clone animals. She figured that in humans there wouldn't be much difference in the methods used to clone them.

She read how they take the cells from an adult animal, they remove an egg from a female and enucleate it and then implant it in the uterus. She read that, and she suddenly had a bright idea. She had to talk to Alfred. Maybe, there was a way Alfred can solve the problem regarding cloning in his life. He can prove whether he is a twin or a clone. She called him. Alfred picked up the phone.

"Hello?" Alfred answered.

"Hi, Alfred, how are you? I have to tell you something urgently," Brittany was talking fast. Alfred wondered whether this was really urgent or if Brittany found something weird about Wendy's restaurant or that stupid worm with 959 cells. Anything was possible with her.

"Are you okay? You are talking so fast, it scares me," he told her.

"Listen, I found something that will interest you. Can we meet somewhere?"

"Sure, but it's three in the morning in my universe. I don't know about yours. Can we wait till, like four?"

"Everything's a joke for you, isn't it? But you are right. It's too late in the night, and I can certainly wait till morning. How about at seven?"

"Yes, that's better. I like to sleep in on Sunday mornings, but I can make an exception. I can meet you at McDonald's on Main Street at seven."

"Okay, that's fine," Brittany agreed and hung up the phone.

Seven o'clock in the morning, they met at McDonald's. Brittany seemed very excited. After picking up their food, they sat in a booth.

"Do you know what mitochondria are?" Brittany asked.

"Yes, I have studied about mitochondria in my biology class. They are small structures in the cells that produce energy," Alfred answered. Maybe, she will come up with some weird stuff she may have read last night. *Instead of wasting time with those things, I should tell Brittany about my life*, Alfred decided.

"Before you talk about mitochondria, I want to tell you that I met Dr. Lawson," Alfred mentioned.

"Good for you. Now let me tell you what I came here to inform you. It's very important."

"In a minute," Alfred stopped her. Hesitantly, he took out his wallet. With hands shaking, he removed his driver's license from his wallet. "Brittany, you can tell me about mitochondria, but first let me show you something. I want you to keep your composure. I will show you how I look without any facial hair. I am sure you will see similarities with someone that you might have seen before. I want you to tell me what you think. Whatever you do, for God's sake, do not scream. People are eating here." He showed his driver's license to Brittany.

A look of horror came over Brittany's face. Alfred urged her to keep silent by putting his finger over his own lips. Brittany was shaking. Finally, after a few seconds that seemed like a few hours in Brittany-time, she said, "Alfred, what on earth is going on? You look like Steven Kincaid. He was in the news a few weeks ago because he almost died in a skiing accident. Everybody has seen his pictures. Oh my God!"

"Yes, I told you, it's shocking."

"Steven Kincaid!" Brittany whispered.

"Yes, Steven Kincaid. I believe I am his clone," Alfred whispered back.

"You are in big trouble. This is heavy. Your mom ran away with a clone of Michael Kincaid's son? You have no idea who you're dealing with. Michael Kincaid is a very dangerous man. I can't believe what's happening here. Steven is most likely a nice person, but Michael Kincaid? He is not right. He has destroyed people right and left. Alfred, whatever you do, please for God's sake be careful. If he gets upset about this whole saga, he will ruin your life. Can you put your driver's license back in your wallet before anyone sees it?" Brittany cautioned him. Alfred put the license in his wallet.

"I know some of the things Mr. Kincaid has done. I want to know if I am a clone of Steven Kincaid or not. If I am, then I want to know why Mr. Kincaid cloned his son. Basically, I want to know why I was created," Alfred tried to explain.

"I heard in the news that Steven is admitted in Beth Israel Hospital for some surgical procedure related to his skiing injury. Isn't that one of the places where you work?" Brittany asked.

"Yes, I too heard that he is admitted there. I work in the housekeeping department there."

"I see. Let me ask you something. If you can't answer that, then just say so. What are you after? You know that Mr. Kincaid is worth billions. How much money are you expecting to get from him?" Brittany asked him point-blank.

"Again, I want to know the circumstances around my birth. I have lived my life not knowing who I am. I want to know my roots and embrace them," Alfred mentioned.

"You didn't answer my question. The general public is not familiar with the children of every billionaire in this country. People know what Steven Kincaid looks like because he was in an accident in which he almost died. Until Steven Kincaid had his skiing accident, you didn't know you had anything to do with him. Until that time, your life was as normal as anyone else's. Of course I understand you grew up without a father, but that's not too uncommon in today's world. So why are you now making a big deal out of it?" Brittany asked.

"It's not that simple. My mother was hired as a surrogate. When she was pregnant with me, she decided to keep the baby. At least that's what she told me, and I believe she is telling the truth. To keep the baby, she ran away to Canada, where I was born.

"I remember growing up with different names, both first and last names. She did that to keep us from being detected by the people who had hired her as a surrogate. We changed our apartments frequently, and I was forced to change my schools frequently too. I was even home-schooled from time to time. I did not have a steady life until I was ten years old. I have been confused about my identity all my life. When Steven Kincaid got into an accident and nearly died, his pictures were on the Internet, television news, and newspapers. When I saw the similarities between the two of us, I confronted my mother, and she told me that she carried me as a surrogate for some couple. She decided to keep me because when she felt me move in her belly, she fell in love with me like a mother would love her child. That's why she ran away to Canada, and she moved from place to place. I want to meet Mr. Kincaid and his son. I can't get over the resemblance between Steve and me. It's uncanny. Look at this." Alfred tried to show his driver's license to Brittany.

"Alfred, please put it away. Don't let that picture get out of your wallet. If you are caught speeding in this town, and police officer asks you for your driver's license, you have no idea what will happen to you. My advice is that if you are stopped by the cops, you should not show your license. Just tell them that you cannot find it. You haven't answered my question. Are you in this for money?" Brittany persisted.

"My mother asked me that question too. If Mr. Kincaid did anything wrong, I will love to teach him a lesson. To teach a lesson to rich people, you part them from their money. So I would like him to lose some of his money. On the other hand, all I want is to belong somewhere. I want recognition. Remember you stood barefoot in the playground of the orphanage in South Korea? I want to do the same thing in a place that I can call mine. I want to stand barefoot in my father's home. I don't want his money to ensure a comfortable life for me. Certainly, I don't want Steven to lose what rightly belongs to him."

"I think you need to really give this a lot of thought. Once the cat is out of the bag, you will not be able to control anything. Decide what you want for yourself. Don't care about teaching anyone any lesson. Don't care about Mr. Kincaid, Steven Kincaid, your mother, or anyone. Think about yourself. Ask yourself what you want. More importantly, ask yourself how far you are prepared to go to achieve what you want."

"So you want me to be selfish?" Alfred asked.

"Yes. No, no, no, that's not what I'm talking about. Don't try to focus on what Mr. Kincaid deserves or what his son deserves. I want you to think what the right course of action for you is. If you can deprive him of his money, it will teach Mr. Kincaid a lesson, but if it means selling your soul to the devil, then you must ask yourself if it was worth it. Whatever you do, please don't lose your integrity."

"You know what, Alfred? Take as much time as you need. Take a day, a week, a month, or two, before you take your next step. Why don't you think about it and then call me with your decision," Brittany gave an ultimatum and got off her seat.

"Wait, wait. What about mitochondria?" Alfred asked.

"They can go to hell," Brittany answered and left. Alfred slumped in his seat.

19

Who Am I?

How do you eat your roots?

— Kamila Shamsie, Pakistani novelist

Alfred returned to his apartment and went to bed. It was early morning, but he didn't have much sleep since Brittany had called him at three in the morning. In his half-awake, half-asleep state of mind, he started thinking about what had happened that morning.

Brittany was right. If he would prove that Steven and he were genetically related, then he may be able to deprive Michael Kincaid of half his money. It would certainly teach him a lesson. It will be a well-deserved punishment to him for all his evil deeds. After all, Mr. Kincaid had hired Angela to be a surrogate but didn't tell her what it was for; he cloned his son even though it was illegal, immoral, and essentially against the laws of nature. He played with God for his own selfishness. He should be taught a lesson.

Brittany had cautioned him. She wanted him to decide the right course of action from his point of view. *If he gets half of the Kincaid fortune, he would be a billionaire before he is even twenty years old. But Michael Kincaid's money is blood money. He should not take any part of it.* He remembered how he admired Howard Roark, the hero of *The Fountainhead*. Roark's uncompromising integrity of character was the kind of life he aspired to live. Taking someone's money meant losing that integrity. That's not who he was.

Nevertheless, someone needs to be punished. *What if Steven Kincaid is killed and he shows up as a substitute?* If Steven is dead and Mr. Kincaid knows that Alfred is available and is threatening to declare him as a clone of Steven, then he will have two choices—either to let Alfred go public and live with the chaos or to accept him as Steven and cover up his death, cloning, and everything else. Alfred tried not to think about all the impracticalities of that idea and enjoyed the thoughts of damage he could inflict on Mr. Kincaid.

The more he thought about it, the more it sounded like the right course of action. He must kill Steven and confront Mr. Kincaid with those choices. That's how Dr. Lawson taught a lesson to her twin sister. She had to know that the monetary offer from her would devastate her sister. Even if Mr. Kincaid does not accept him as his son, it would teach him the worst lesson of his life. He would have to live with the knowledge that his son died because of his own actions.

After a few hours of a disturbed state of mind, he finally got up. He started thinking about his plans. He remembered what his friend Jagdish had told him. He knew in his heart that he could not kill or hurt anybody. That's not who he was, and no person or event in the world could change him. At the same time, he was honest enough to admit to himself that he enjoyed thinking on those lines.

* * *

Brittany had left the restaurant in tears. She drove her car a few blocks from McDonald's and parked in a street. She was overcome with emotions. She started crying. Alfred's revelation was shocking. Not only could he be a product of cloning, possibly the only such person in the whole world, but also in a situation that involved Michael Kincaid. Alfred had told her that his mother ran away while pregnant with him. Obviously, Mr. Kincaid would still be mad about that betrayal. Now, after all these years if Alfred goes to Mr. Kincaid and introduces himself, he would not take it kindly. Mr. Kincaid could destroy him and the people around him. Not only Alfred's family but also her own family could be affected.

What a mess Alfred's life has become and how much worse it may get . . . she wondered. What can happen to people when they don't have normal lives? Immediately Brittany thought about her own life.

What would her life have been like if she were not plucked out of the orphanage by a rich American couple suffering from white man's guilt? She would have received some rudimentary education and, around the age of eighteen, would have left the orphanage to be on her own. She would have found some menial job, got married, and lived the life of a poor woman in South Korea. But at least she would be with her "own people," on her "own soil." She understood Alfred's quest for his identity. There were hundreds of thousands of orphans all over the world who were adopted, so her case was not unique. She had heard of many Korean, Chinese, and Indian babies adopted by Westerners and raised thousands of miles away from their homelands. So while she was struggling to find out who she was, she had company. There were precedents in her case. Alfred's case was one in a billion or rather one in seven billion. She felt sympathy for Alfred.

What about her? Would she have been better off if she had grown up in South Korea? Why are babies left in the streets or in the orphanages by their own mothers? Why are orphans not adopted by people within their own countries? How many people realize the agony these kids go through when they find themselves being raised, albeit lovingly, in other countries by people of other races? Brittany had come to terms with her life some time ago, but today's events hit her like a bolt of lightning. She was now questioning her own identity. After crying for an hour, she drove home.

Brittany didn't want to talk to anyone at home. It was Sunday morning and the rest of her family would be at the breakfast table drinking coffee and reading the newspaper. She parked her car in the driveway and walked to the main door. She didn't have the key, but if it was open, she would sneak in and directly go to her room. Unfortunately, it was locked. She walked back to the garage, opened the garage door via the keyless entry, and entered the house. As soon as she walked in, her mom, Lisa, saw her. She asked Brittany if she would like to join them. She didn't want to make eye contact, so she looked up above the breakfast table on the wall.

Her eyes fell on the wooden plaque that read, *COEXIST*. Lisa had put the plaque there so the kids will see it every day and it will remind them to respect members of all religions.

People who came up with the concept of this plaque had to be quite ignorant of religions. Religious scriptures teach that their God is the only true God. The First Commandment preaches intolerance to other gods and, thereby, to other religions and to people who follow them. Many scriptures strongly claim that people who practice other religions are condemned to suffer in eternal hell. As if this were not enough, many religions actively proselytize.

How can a Christian be expected to coexist with a Buddhist? Christians are taught that the only way to receive salvation is to accept Jesus Christ as their personal savior. Buddhists, on the other hand, do not believe in a god or a superpower. Coexistence can occur if people are willing to forgo their "identity" as a Christian or a Buddhist or a Hindu. Those who believe that people of different religious affiliations can coexist also believe that all religions are essentially the same. Nothing can be farther from the truth. The degree of tolerance (or lack of it) is different in different religions.

We can coexist because most of us, despite being religious, pick and choose parts of the scriptures we can follow while obeying the law of the land. We know that we cannot follow the scriptures blindly. The scriptures are designed to prevent coexistence. It will be easier to coexist if people limit their religious identity within the confines of their homes and churches. Coexistence should be stressed based on nationality or skin color and not on the basis of religion. The plaque should be designed with the letters of the word COEXIST written with pictures of people of different races or ethnicities or maps of different countries and not with religious symbols. Thankfully, Brittany or anyone in her family never thought about it, just like hundreds of thousands of other people who put that sign in their homes or as bumper stickers on their cars.

Brittany told her mom she already had breakfast and started climbing up the stairs to go to her room. Her mom had a quick glance at her face. She immediately figured something was wrong. Brittany's face was swollen; she looked upset. She figured something must have happened while she was out with Alfred, her *lactose-intolerant Canadian boyfriend. Damn Canadians!*

Lisa signaled her husband, Anthony, to keep quiet. Then she ran after Brittany. "Are you all right, honey?" she asked. Eric and Amy also figured something had happened to their sister, but they were not going to interfere while their mom was on the case.

"Yes, Mom, I am fine," she answered in a weak voice and kept walking.

"Please, tell me what's going on," Lisa persisted and followed her up the stairs.

"Mom, everything is fine. I just want to be alone for a while," Brittany answered.

"I'll leave you alone once I find out that you're okay. Did Alfred say something to hurt you?"

By that time, they were already on the second floor and in front of Brittany's room. Brittany hesitated. She didn't know whether to open the door of her room and risk her mom enter the room or to say something now to end the conversation. She chose later.

"Mom, I promise I will tell you what happened when the time comes. Right now, I want to be alone."

"Okay, that's fine."

Brittany thought she would get her privacy now, but she was wrong. Her mom gave her a hug before leaving her. Immediately, Brittany broke down and started sobbing. She hated herself for being so weak.

"Brit, I can't walk away while you are hurting. Please tell me what's going on, and I will try to help you."

They were in her room now. Brittany slumped on her bed. Lisa sat next to her. To make matters worse, her dad finally figured there was something going on, so he walked into the room too. *Why don't we call Eric and Amy, so I can discuss Human Genome Project and cloning with everybody in the family!*

Lisa asked her husband to go back downstairs and assured him that if it became necessary she would call him. Anthony left and continued his breakfast. Within seconds, he was back reading the newspaper and was oblivious of the world around him. Men are blessed with short attention spans.

Lisa asked Brittany what was going on. Brittany told her it was too complicated, and there were certain things she could not tell her because Alfred had told her those things in confidence.

"So this is something to do with Alfred and not with you?"

"Yes, something complicated is going on with Alfred, and he has come here from Canada to resolve those issues. I can foresee that it's not going to end well for him," Brittany tried to explain.

"Will that affect you too?" Mom asked.

"I have asked him to find answers to certain matters and when he gets back to me with the answers, I will decide if I will see him again."

"Can you give me some information, so I know what's going on? So far, from what you have told me I can't give any opinion."

"Mom, you don't understand. This is something I need to take care of myself."

"Well, as a mother, I can't see my daughter suffer. I want to help you," Mom persisted.

"I am not two years old anymore. It's about time I make my own decisions."

"Brit, Sun, for me you will always be a baby. Even when you are sixty and I am in my eighties, you will be my baby and I will try to make things right for you."

"Actually, I like to hear that, Mom. Can I ask you for a favor?" Brittany asked. "I like it when you call me Sun. Can everyone in the family call me Sun? I don't care if outside of the home people know me as Brittany."

"Sure, I will tell dad, Eric, and Amy to call you Sun," Mom agreed. In that instant, she realized that Brittany's problems were deeper than what could possibly be going on with her boyfriend, Alfred. She was missing her roots.

"Sun, you need to tell me what happened today. I respect your decision to honor the trust Alfred has placed in you, but I think what is bothering you is something else. Please, tell me."

"Mom, I will tell you, but for God's sake don't misunderstand me. I have the utmost respect for you and Dad. I fight with Eric and Amy, but I love them to death," Brittany started opening up.

Now we are getting somewhere. "I appreciate that. You can always tell me what's on your mind."

"I have some questions which were probably in the back of my mind for some time. Today, while having breakfast with Alfred, those questions started bothering me. Can you tell me, why Dad and you decided to adopt a child? And why did you go to South Korea?" Brittany asked, crying.

"Oh my God! What's going on? What did you and Alfred talk about?" Lisa asked. *Why she couldn't ask questions about sex like a normal teenager.*

Lisa continued, "Maybe, you don't want to tell me. Anyway, I will answer your questions. We decided to adopt a child, because we wanted to make a difference in somebody's life. Eric was already born when we adopted you, so it was not because we couldn't have children of our own. Whenever Dad and I heard about kids living in foster homes or orphanages it broke our hearts. When we saw babies abandoned in the streets of China or when we saw the dismal conditions millions of children lived under in the third-world countries, it pained us. We knew we could donate some money, but we thought it will be better to adopt a child and make his or her life better. We decided to adopt a child from South Korea or China."

"We were told that it would be easier to go through the bureaucratic process with the South Korean government than with the Chinese government. So we decided on South Korea. I think there may be some hidden guilt on our part for being better off than millions of people in the world. I don't deny that. As far as ethnicity or nationality or race was concerned, Dad and I didn't care," Lisa explained.

"Mom, actually there is no genetic basis for race. People of different races have very little genetic variation among them," Brittany tried to explain.

"I don't know about genetics. Whether it's right or not, but the first things we notice when we see someone is their skin color, their ethnicity, and their race. If genetically we are all so similar, then why our appearances are so different?" Lisa questioned.

"What they say by similarities in our genetic makeup is that there are very few variations in the genes between different people. Not only that, but our genes are almost 97% similar to the genes of chimpanzee."

"Irrespective of the scientific explanations, I think we should treat all human beings equally. I think the way the world is changing, even the borders between countries are becoming meaningless," Lisa opined.

"Mom, what made you decide to pick me and not any one of the other hundred kids in that orphanage?" Brittany asked.

"Brittany, Sun, we have been through this many times in the past. We liked you because you were friendly, you had a cute smile, and for some inexplicable reasons I felt I bonded with you. I am not talking about anything supernatural or mystical. I just felt good when I picked you up. Does that answer your questions?"

"Yes, it does. Dad and you have been the best parents a girl can have. What's bothering me is something different. I am thinking how my life would have turned out if I had grown up in Korea, whether in the orphanage or outside of it. I feel that there I would have been with people who looked like me. I would be with 'my people' so to speak." She said with air-quotes. "Please, don't feel that I have any complains about you or Dad. I just feel that by living a better life in the United States, I am betraying my own people," Brittany tried to explain.

"Sun, I am sorry if somehow by uprooting you from your birth place we have affected your life negatively. I have always told all three of you that when you grow up, you can decide where you want to live and what you want to do with your lives. Thanks to your presence in this family, we have learnt to see a person for who he or she is and not be obsessed with their color, religion, or nationality. So if you feel guilty living in the United States, you can move to South Korea in the future or you can help people in any corner of the world without leaving this country." Lisa paused to see if Brittany was all right.

Then she added, "You don't need to feel guilty for growing up here. First of all, you were a baby when we adopted you. So you didn't have a say in that. Second of all, millions of people from other countries live in the United States or hundred other countries in the world. Imagine what would happen if all their children felt guilty for being born in countries other than where their parents were born. You can decide where you want to live in a few years. Of course, in my eyes, you will always be that three-month-old baby. You will never grow up in my eyes. You don't have any options there. Do you get it?"

"Yes, Mom, I do get it. I am glad I talked to you. I am also glad that if I had to be adopted, then it was by you and Dad. Thanks for making things better for me. When I can, I will tell you what I decide about Alfred," Brittany told her.

"Sure, I am here whenever you need me," Lisa said as she was getting off the bed.

"Mom? Who am I?" Brittany asked.

"*Who am I?* Sun, if by that question you mean the philosophical aspect of our existence then I can tell you, even the sages have not been able to answer that question. I am just a college graduate, I can't even begin to answer that," Mom explained.

"But did you ever think about it?" Brittany asked.

"I sort of did when I started college. I was thinking about the purpose of my life. I was wondering whether I was destined to do something to make the world better or not. After thinking about it for a while, I asked my dad. He told me that I could think on those lines until the cows came home and I would still be the same person, a pseudo-intellectual. Then he laughed. Of course, he was trying to be funny," Lisa answered. "After his obligatory semi-funny remark, he gave me good advice. He told me that I should live my life in such a way that I live happily and I make people around me happy. If I do that then the world will be a better place for those people. Thinking on those lines helped me decide what I wanted to do with my life. I think it's healthy to think about such things and we need to understand that a human life is more than just eating, drinking, and sleeping."

"Mom, I agree. I miss grandpa. He was a very loving and kind person. I always remember him as a very big man with white moustache and gray hair. He passed away when I was six, but I remember how playful he was around us. Do you know, behind your back he let us eat things that you did not allow us to eat? Whenever we had a sleepover at his house, we had no rules. We stayed up till midnight. It was always exciting," Brittany commented.

"I knew that, and I didn't like that, but he wouldn't listen to me. I miss him too. Grandma was nice with you all too."

"She sure was. She tried to teach me English. It was hilarious. She believed that because I was a foreigner, I would not speak proper English. She would point at an object and tell me, '*In English, it is called table*'. She assumed that English was a second language for me."

"I know! I explained to her many times that you were only few months old when we adopted you. You had not learned to talk. Since English was the only language spoken in our home, you were going to learn English as your first language. But she could not grasp that," Lisa explained.

"Amy and I laugh when we watch old videos. Those videos show that I could speak more words than Amy could because I was older than her, but when grandma talks to me she speaks slowly, separating each syllable. With Amy, she doesn't do that. Even now, if I don't follow something, Amy and Eric mimic grandma and explain to me slowly. We all laugh when that happens."

"I didn't know that. One day I will have to hear them mimic Grandma."

"Mom, I have one more question. Would it be all right with you if I explore Buddhism?"

Brittany asked. She expected to see some disappointment on mom's face, but she was wrong.

"It's up to you. I had told you about that in the past also. Whatever makes you happy is fine with me," She said calmly and then added, "Are you interested in Buddhism because of your Korean roots?"

"Yes," Brittany answered. For a brief moment, Lisa had a smirk on her face. Brittany noticed that. "Why are you smiling, Mom? I saw it on your face."

"Oh, nothing, I was just wondering what it would be like if I had adopted babies from three or four different countries where different religions were practiced."

"Then you would be Angelina Jolie," Brittany answered laughing.

"Yes, that's true. I won't mind it if Dad looked like Brad Pitt," Lisa replied laughing as she was leaving the room.

"Mom . . .!" Brittany screamed and hurled a pillow at her.

That evening at dinnertime, Lisa informed the family that from now on everyone should call Brittany by her Korean name, Sun. She explained that that's her wish, and it should be respected. No one objected. The next day, Brittany started studying Buddhism. She also began attending cultural programs in Korean community. She desperately wanted to belong in her community.

* * *

Alfred decided not to approach Brittany until he had resolved issues regarding his identity. He sent her a short e-mail:

Brittany, I am sorry; things have taken a bad turn for us. I want to find some answers for myself before I call you. I believe you deserve to know where I stand in this mess. I hope you will understand. I won't visit the downtown library until then. I am looking at the license plates of cars now, and I find them interesting. I thank you for that. – Alfred.

Alfred received the kits to obtain samples for genetic tests. He had to get Steven's samples somehow. For reasons he did not understand, Dr. Lawson had requested two samples from each person. He took the kits for Steven's samples to the Beth Israel Hospital where he was admitted. That day, late in the evening, he went to the private room where Steve was recuperating after a surgical procedure. A nurse saw him enter the room and stopped him. She asked why he was cleaning the room so late. It might disturb the patient's sleep.

"My supervisor has asked me to do it. He is in a bad mood, and he just fired somebody for not doing the job to his satisfaction. If I don't do it now, my job is on the line," he answered. He promised to be very quiet.

The nurse informed him that she would have to check with her supervisor. Alfred guaranteed that no one would even know that he was there. The nurse relented. Alfred heaved a sigh of relief.

Alfred entered Steve's room with his cleaning supplies. Steve was sleeping. Light in the room was dim. He increased the brightness a little, so he could see his victim's face. Alfred noticed that they both really looked alike. He found it rather unsettling. But he had to do his work. He put his supplies on the floor and took out the plastic cups to collect samples. On the desk, he saw some "get well soon" cards. There was an envelope from his girlfriend, Stephanie Anderson. He found a card inside it. He put the envelope in his pocket. He wanted to know more about Steven's life. He collected the garbage and placed a new garbage bag.

"Mr. Kincaid, it's time for your samples," Alfred announced. Steve did not move. Alfred slowly shook Steve by his shoulder. Steve opened his eyes. He was groggy from painkillers.

"Mr. Kincaid, I want to collect samples. Please, sit up," Alfred said softly. Steve stretched his right arm out for collection of blood sample.

"I am not collecting blood samples, Mr. Kincaid. I want to collect your saliva. Alfred opened the kit and held it in front of Steve's mouth. He asked him to spit in it. When the sample was collected to the fill level, he brought out the second kit. Alfred told Steve that by mistake he spilled the sample, and he will need another sample. Steve was annoyed but Alfred told him that it was either saliva or blood. Steve again spit in the kit and gave the sample.

Why I should not kill him, Alfred asked himself. *What does he have that I don't? Why can he live a stable life and I can't? Maybe, if I kill him and lie down in his place, I might be able to live his life.* For a second, Alfred thought about all the money he will have if he were in Steve's shoes. He hated himself for thinking about Mr. Kincaid's money. He resolved that he will not be tempted again by his money. He was shocked to discover that he had that weakness. He came back to his senses quickly and left the room with Steve's samples.

20

You Are a Clone!

We wish to discuss a structure for the salt of deoxyribose nucleic acid (D.N.A.). This structure has novel features which are of considerable biologic interest.

— ROSALIND FRANKLIN, SCIENTIST AND CONTRIBUTOR
TO THE STRUCTURE OF DNA

D r. Betty Sue Lawson was confused. For a long time, she kept staring at the results. One belonged to Alfred Johnson and the other belonged to Christopher Smith, possibly a fictitious name Alfred had given to the second specimen. After she met with Alfred and his attorney, Robert Newman, she had suspected something interesting in the laboratory samples, but this was not what she had in mind at the time. If this was true, then it was the most unusual thing she had ever seen.

It began as an ordinary day. She woke up at her usual time, had breakfast, got ready, and drove to work. Her commute to work was taking a little longer due to construction on Interstate 77. She remembered that when she first moved to Cleveland, she had inquired about the winters in Cleveland. One of her colleagues had told her that Cleveland had only two seasons; winter and road construction. Every time she saw road construction, she thought about Cleveland's weather.

First thing she did after entering her office was to have coffee. Then she looked at the papers on her desk. She went through some mundane laboratory reports. There were reports of the paternity tests and correspondence from journals. After taking care of the snail mail, she turned the computer on and started checking her emails.

There were emails from the hospital regarding a software upgrade, honoring some employees for their outstanding work, and some spam emails. Then she saw an email from a genetics laboratory. She opened it. It mentioned that the results were attached in a file. Dr. Lawson opened the attachment thinking in few moments she would know what Alfred and his attorney were talking about. The pdf file of the attachment opened. She was looking at the STRs (Short Tandem Repeats). They matched exactly in both samples. There were only two possibilities to explain the results; the samples came either from the same person or from identical twins. The laboratory's interpretation was that the samples must have come from the same person and requested a repeat sample. In addition, there was a cautionary note that those results were not valid for legal purposes.

Of course, there was a third possibility, a very remote one—Cloning. Cloning can explain the results too. *Think Occam's razor*, Dr. Lawson told herself. Unless proven otherwise, it's a sample error.

Then she looked at other emails. There were two more e-mails from two different genetics laboratories. She opened them. The first email had the results of Alfred's sample and second Christopher Smith's. These samples were analyzed to detect maternal markers. Interestingly enough, they were not identical. These two samples, if obtained from same two people who gave the first set of samples to detect STRs, clinched the case for cloning. *So much for Occam's razor!*

Dr. Lawson printed all the results. She looked at them one more time. She knew that Alfred may not have given the correct name of the second person. Also, she suspected that the dates of birth could be wrong in one or both samples. From the outset, she and her attorney had suspected that something huge was at stake.

The first thing she had to do was to collect the samples again. Unless the results were repeated, she cannot claim that she had established a case of human cloning. To obtain proof of cloning, the samples had to be repeated in her presence. She wondered if she should look at the telomere sizes in both the samples. If there is no major difference between the ages of the two persons concerned, then it won't matter. But she will need to explain to Alfred why correct age of both persons is important. Maybe, this time she will also look at the Y-chromosome markers.

She closed her office door and called Alfred. She told him that the tests were inconclusive and must be repeated. Alfred asked her what the tests indicated. Dr. Lawson was not sure what she should tell him. She gave an evasive answer.

Several minutes later Mr. Newman called Dr. Lawson. From his talk with Alfred, he knew that the test results must have confirmed their suspicion of cloning and Dr. Lawson wanted some more tests before she could say it with conviction. He asked Dr. Lawson to explain the results to him. When Dr. Lawson started being evasive, he reminded her about the contract they had signed and told her that it will get ugly if she would not tell him what she knew so far and that they may have to consult another geneticist.

Dr. Lawson told him that she will call him back in few minutes. She called her attorney, Mr. Fujiwara. She discussed with him that possibly Alfred was someone's clone. They had a long discussion on the ramifications of this discovery and finally concluded that Mr. Newman and Alfred can be informed about what was known up to that point.

She called Mr. Newman back and told him that possibly Alfred made mistakes in collecting the samples. He could have used his own saliva for both samples. Mr. Newman assured her that he can guarantee that it didn't happen. He asked her to explain how she would interpret if they were from two different individuals.

Dr. Lawson hesitated briefly and then explained that the first set of samples looked at STRs or short tandem repeats. They matched exactly; therefore, if they were collected from two different people, then those individuals must be identical twins. But the second set of samples was definitely from two different persons; therefore, there were only two possibilities. Either there was an error in collecting the samples or the samples came from clones. Since there were no known cases of human cloning, the results should be confirmed by repeating the tests on both persons. She explained that maternal origin of these two samples was different. Mr. Newman thanked her for her help and told her that he agreed with her and will arrange for the repeat samples as soon as possible. He also requested her to fax the results to him, so he can go over the results with his client.

Within five minutes, Dr. Lawson personally faxed the results to Mr. Newman. After the fax went through, she put all the papers in her briefcase and locked it. Mr. Newman called Alfred and asked him to come to his office to discuss the results. He dropped everything and rushed to his lawyer's office. Mr. Newman showed him the papers faxed by Dr. Lawson. Alfred looked at them but didn't know how to interpret the results. Mr. Newman called Dr. Lawson again and requested her to explain the results for Alfred's benefit.

This time, Dr. Lawson was excited to explain the results. "Okay, Alfred, the first column shows the markers. These markers are called STRs or short tandem repeats. STRs are short sequences of two to thirteen nucleotides, which are repeated a number of times in a DNA molecule. An individual receives one copy of an STR from each parent. The parents may or may not have similar number of repeats of these markers. These markers are of smaller sizes as the name suggests, therefore, they are useful in cases where the DNA in a sample may be degraded. As a matter of fact, STRs are used by FBI to solve crimes where the DNA is frequently degraded. They have created a national database of thirteen STR loci, known as CODIS, which stands for Combined DNA Index System. These thirteen CODIS loci are used all over the world for identification of a person. In your samples, the laboratory has looked at those thirteen loci and a few more."

"Dr. Lawson, if you give a specific example, it may help," Mr. Newman suggested.

"Sure. Look at the report. Under the first column which is the list of the markers, find a marker called FGA. It is approximately in the middle of the list."

"Yes, I see it," Alfred answered.

"Good. Now in the STR marker FGA, the sequence *cttt* is repeated. Of course, it does not say that in the report. This marker is located on chromosome 4. As you can see on the report, it is repeated twenty-one times in both samples as indicated by second and third columns. Similarly, the marker D7S280 is on chromosome 7, and the sequence repeated is *gata*. The number of times these markers are repeated in an individual depends on their inheritance. In individuals who are related, the STRs match. Depending on how many STRs match, probability of how closely the two individuals are related can be calculated. These markers are not identical in any two people unless they are identical twins. Next column shows your results, and third column shows the results of Christopher Smith. Next two columns show FSI and HSI, respectively. By the way, who is Christopher Smith?" Dr. Lawson asked.

Mr. Newman and Alfred looked at each other. Then, Mr. Newman answered, "Dr. Lawson, actually it's a name Alfred has made up for the other individual. He suspects that this other person is his clone."

"I see. Can you tell me his real name?" Dr. Lawson asked. Alfred looked at Mr. Newman and shook his head.

"Dr. Lawson, in due time Alfred will reveal his name," Mr. Newman answered.

"After I discuss these findings with that person, I will reveal his name," Alfred added.

"Okay, I understand. For the repeat samples, I will like to know the real name of the person and meet him personally. I must collect the samples myself," Dr. Lawson insisted.

"Yes, we agree. We should get back to you shortly regarding this matter," Mr. Newman assured.

"Dr. Lawson, you mentioned FSI and HSI. What do they mean?" Alfred asked.

"FSI means full sibling index, and HSI means half sibling index. Both samples match for all the STR markers, so these two samples are either from the same person or they are from identical twins. Third and very remote possibility is that they are clones. Second and third set of the fax I sent to Mr. Newman show the results from two different laboratories. I looked at the maternal markers in both these individuals. They are different. Assuming that the samples were obtained correctly, the maternal markers in your sample and that of Christopher Smith are different, even though you both are genetically identical. For cloning, if an ovum was obtained from a woman who is not related to the person who is cloned then these markers will be different. I cannot stress enough that before I can confirm the results, I must have repeat samples taken by me personally in my office. To prove that we are dealing with cloning, I cannot leave anything to chance. I also want to make sure that I have correct age of both candidates. If there is a significant difference in the age between them, there are some other tests I will need to perform. It is to measure telomere length. I will fax some more information to show what the maternal markers indicate."

"The age difference between me and the other person is less than two years," Alfred replied.

"In that case, I may not need to worry about telomere lengths."

"Dr. Lawson, can you explain a little bit about telomeres?" Mr. Newman asked.

"Of course. Telomeres are small pieces of DNA located at either ends of a chromosome. They are made of repeat sequences of base pairs. Each time a cell divides it loses a small number of base pairs making the telomeres shorter and shorter until the cells become senescent and can no longer divide. Differences in the telomere lengths can indicate differences in the ages of two individuals. Since both of you are almost of same age, there is no need to investigate telomere lengths. If for cloning, the cells were taken from a much older individual then the telomere lengths will be significantly different," Dr. Lawson elaborated.

Alfred promised to meet her for the repeat tests. He thanked her profusely for her help. As far as he was concerned, there was no need to repeat the tests. They had to be done only for academic interests, as they say.

His quest to discover, *Who Am I*, was finally over. His suspicion that he was the product of a clone was confirmed. He stared at the genetic test results, the Holy Grail of a person's identity. Whether he liked it or not, Michael Kincaid's blood was flowing in his veins. He had inherited Kincaid genes.

Mr. Newman realized that Alfred was too emotional to say anything. He excused himself for a coffee break and left the office for few minutes. Sometime later, when he returned, Alfred had regained his composure. He told Mr. Newman that it was about time he confronted Mr. Kincaid. Mr. Newman reminded him that the geneticist wanted another sample to confirm cloning.

Alfred told him that after he speaks with Michael Kincaid and Steven Kincaid, he will take the next steps. Alfred informed him Steven Kincaid was out of the hospital for more than two weeks now. Steven had to agree for the repeat tests. Somehow, he had a feeling that Steve would not object once he asked him.

After going back to his apartment Alfred shaved his beard and moustache off. He was ready to accept himself for who he was.

21

Alfred Meets Mr. Kincaid

All discomfort comes from suppressing your true identity.

— Bryant McGill, author and activist

Alfred decided to meet Mr. Kincaid in person. He did not know how to approach him. He wondered whether he should make an appointment to see him. He remembered that Mr. Kincaid knows him by name thanks to his attorney's, Mr. Drake, efforts to find him when he was little. He decided that he should just walk to his office and play it by the ear.

Alfred drove to downtown Columbus. Mr. Kincaid's office was located on N. High Street. He parked his car across the street from the office building. Then he walked to his office. He had a fake mustache, beard, and a mole on his face. He was also wearing dark glasses. He entered Mr. Kincaid's office feeling very unsure of himself.

"Hi, I am Suzy Thomas. May I help you?" The receptionist asked.

"I want to see Mr. Kincaid," Alfred told her.

"Mr. Kincaid is busy. Do you have an appointment?"

"No, I don't. Can you tell him Alfred Johnson wants to see him?"

"What is this about?" Suzy asked.

Alfred didn't know how to answer this question. "I am Steve . . .," Alfred realized what he was about to say. He stopped mid-sentence and corrected himself, "I am Steven Kincaid's cousin."

"You are Mr. Kincaid's nephew? I have not heard of a nephew named Alfred." Suzy was used to people coming up with all sorts of reasons to try to meet her boss. Her job was to screen them properly.

"Whether you have heard of Steve's cousin or not does not make any difference. If you tell him Alfred Johnson from Toronto, Canada, is here to see him, he will agree to see me," Alfred persisted. He was mad at himself for almost blurting out to the receptionist that he was Steve's clone.

Suzy picked up the intercom and spoke with Mr. Kincaid. She told him that someone named Alfred Johnson from Toronto, Canada, was there to see him. She also mentioned that he claimed to be his nephew. Mr. Kincaid did not say anything for a few seconds. For a moment, Alfred wished Mr. Kincaid would refuse to see him and he would not have to go through the whole ordeal, but Mr. Kincaid told Suzy to send him in. The receptionist was surprised. Alfred smiled nervously as she escorted him to Mr. Kincaid's office. As she opened the office door, she heard Mr. Kincaid speaking on the phone, ". . . yes, after a long time. You need to be here right now." Then he hung up the phone.

While Suzy introduced Alfred to Mr. Kincaid, Patricia entered the office. She was now vice president of operations. Patricia appeared emotional, as if someone had shaken her mind violently. Suzy figured that Mr. Kincaid was talking to Patricia on the phone and he wanted her to be present when he talked to Alfred, *Steve's cousin from Canada*. Suzy stood there waiting for further instructions. Mr. Kincaid thanked her and asked her to leave. *This must be something big*, she thought and left the room.

As she was leaving, Patricia told her, "Suzy, please hold the calls for me and for Mr. Kincaid. Don't disturb us unless it's an emergency." Alfred noticed that Patricia had a British accent.

"Certainly," Suzy answered and closed the door behind her.

Alfred looked around Mr. Kincaid's office in awe. The office was huge. It was beautifully decorated. Standing in the middle of this enormous room, Alfred felt very insignificant. *If Mr. Kincaid's intention was to intimidate someone visiting him in this office, then it worked*, he thought.

"Can I help you, young man?" Mr. Kincaid asked.

"Yes, Mr. Kincaid. But I will like to talk to you in private. It's a personal matter," Alfred answered, pointing at the lady sitting in the room.

"Oh, it's quite okay," Mr. Kincaid reassured Alfred. "Let me introduce you. This is Patricia Sharp, vice president of operations. You can say anything you want to say to me in the presence of Ms. Sharp, even if it pertains to personal matters." Then he turned to Patricia and announced, "This is Alfred Johnson. He is from Toronto, Canada, and he claims to be Steve's cousin."

Alfred shook hands with Patricia. He could not quite figure out why, but she looked at him with some weird curiosity. It looked like she was thrilled to see him.

"I don't know quite how to begin, so let me just lay my cards on table," he announced.

"That's the best way," Mr. Kincaid agreed.

"Well, let me ask you, Mr. Kincaid. Do you know who I am?" Alfred asked.

"I know that you are not my nephew?" Mr. Kincaid answered.

"That's true. I am not your nephew. But I am related to you somehow. Why did you have your son, Steve, cloned?" Alfred dropped the bombshell. He was surprised by what he said. *I should have started the conversation differently*, he thought. *I should have done homework before my meeting with Mr. Kincaid.*

"What? What kind of person asks a question like this?"

"I see you are not answering my question."

"Can you tell us who you are and what you want?"

"Sorry. I am Alfred Johnson from Canada. Angela Johnson is my mother. Does her name ring a bell?" Alfred asked. Sure, it did. Patricia knew that this was Steve's clone and that her egg was responsible for his existence. It was this memory that made her feel an emotional connection with Alfred.

Alfred continued, "I want to know why you cloned your son and created me?"

"This is ridiculous," Mr. Kincaid wanted to know the motive for his arrival.

"Well, Mr. Kincaid, let me make it easier for you." As he said it, Alfred removed his glasses, fake mustache, fake beard, and the fake mole. Mr. Kincaid was trying to show no reaction, but Patricia was visibly stunned. She could not hide her emotions. The stranger standing there was an almost exact duplicate of Steve. *This could have been Chuck, if he were alive today*, she thought. Patricia had tears in her eyes, which Mr. Kincaid noticed. He was not happy to see her react that way.

Mr. Kincaid asked him to sit down. Alfred sat in front of him. Mr. Kincaid studied Alfred's face for a few seconds. The resemblance was uncanny. But then, that's what you would expect from a clone or an identical twin.

"Alfred, I admit there is some similarity between you and Steve. It must be a coincidence. What makes you think you are a clone?" Mr. Kincaid asked.

"Mr. Kincaid, please don't insult my intelligence. I don't know how powerful the Internet was when you cloned your son, but these days things are different. When Steve was injured in the skiing accident, I saw his pictures on TV and in the newspapers. Immediately my mother, Angela Johnson, and I knew something was wrong. I put all the pieces of the puzzle together and figured out what must have happened."

He continued, "How could you do this to me? How could you do this to your son, Steve? How could you cheat the woman you hired as a surrogate by telling her it was for in vitro fertilization? If she had known it was a clone, she would not have done what she did to keep the child," Alfred was angry.

"Listen, Alfred. First of all, I have never met a woman named Angela Johnson. Based on what you are telling me, she was hired to carry a baby. So it's her fault for what happened to you. A surrogate is supposed to give the child to the biological parents after his or her birth, irrespective of whose child she was carrying and how the child was created. I don't know whether she had signed a contract and what were the terms of the contract if there was one, but even morally she was supposed to give the child to the rightful parents after delivery. She is the one who cheated you from your life with your biological family, whoever that family is," Mr. Kincaid was not admitting that he was responsible for this mess.

"Do you have any idea what I have gone through my whole life? My mother was afraid that your minions will kidnap me any day. She lived in constant fear and kept running from place to place. I did not have a normal childhood. I was given different names while I was growing up. Half the time, I didn't know what my real name was and what name I was supposed to use that week. I grew up without a father, without a proper family, and without a steady place. I essentially grew up without any roots. When Steve had an accident and I saw his pictures, I realized that somehow he was related to me. Thanks to you and my mom, I was cheated out of a normal life," Alfred blurted out.

"Alfred, first of all, the fact that you and my son, Steve, look alike does not mean anything. There are more than seven billion people on earth. It's not impossible to find two people who look alike."

"You don't get it, do you? I had Steve's DNA compared with mine. I have a geneticist involved who went through the results of samples from Steve and me and has confirmed that we are clones."

"How did you get Steve's sample? Don't you have to get his hair or blood or something? How did you obtain it?" Patricia asked. She was going to ask more questions, but Mr. Kincaid signaled her to stop.

"How I got his sample is not important. Let me tell you something else. I didn't see it mentioned anywhere in the news or on the Internet that Mrs. Lucy Kincaid was part American Indian. Please explain, how do I know that?"

Mr. Kincaid laughed. He laughed as if he had heard the funniest joke in his life. Obviously, it was not true, or he would have known it. Patricia, on the other hand, had a puzzled expression on her face. She didn't know if Lucy had Native American blood either, but she believed that Alfred must have a reason for making that claim. Mike's laughter only showed that he wanted to convince Alfred that he was not a clone of Steven even though she and Mike both knew he was.

"Alfred, dear, I have never heard such baloney. I'm glad you mentioned that. Now I know what to make of your claims. I know why you didn't say

160

I was part Indian because then I would know for sure that you are making things up. You claim that my late wife was part Indian because I can't prove you are wrong. I admire your audacity. Here's Lucy's picture. Does she look Native American to you?" Mr. Kincaid showed the picture.

Alfred could see that Mrs. Kincaid didn't look Native American. He was certain that Dr. Lawson had explained to him and to Mr. Newman that Steve's maternal markers showed that his mother was part Native American. He couldn't comprehend the discrepancy. He tried to remember what else Dr. Lawson had told him, but he could not. He was so overwhelmed with the results of the genetic tests that he could not pay attention to what she was explaining. She had said something about some genes passing through maternal lineage only. She had also told him that his maternal marker came from a British woman. She had said something about Cambridge Reference Sequence. He didn't remember enough to explain to Mr. Kincaid how he knew Lucy's heritage. But he was sure of what he claimed.

"Whether you know it or not and whether she looks Indian or not, Mrs. Kincaid had Native American blood. But that's not important," Alfred answered. Mike looked at Patricia to see if she knew what Alfred was talking about. Patricia gestured she did not know.

"Alfred, I don't get it. Are you upset because you think you have some Native American blood? Take it from me, no one in a million years will tell you that you look Native American," Mr. Kincaid assured him.

"No, Mr. Kincaid. I didn't say that *I* look like Native American. What I told you is that Mrs. Kincaid was part American Indian. Besides, if I looked Native American or if I were Native American, why would that upset me?" Alfred clarified.

"You believe that you are Steve's clone or his twin. I understand that you are mad because you did not get the chance to grow up as a son of a tycoon. If what you claim is true, then it's your mother who robbed you of the life of luxury," Mr. Kincaid clarified.

"Hold on, Dad," Alfred was furious. "Are you implying that I am upset because I was raised in an ordinary middle-class environment and not in a billionaire's mansion? That's insulting. I don't care about your money. I wanted recognition, I wanted parents, and I wanted a normal family life."

161

"Well, Alfred, listen. I am sorry for what you have gone through. I cannot undo what happened to you. Let us say hypothetically that I cloned Steve. If I did that then it would be to have more children. I would also have hired a surrogate to carry the pregnancy. If Angela Johnson was that surrogate then after giving birth to the child, she would have given the child to me instead of running away. Then I would have raised him as Steve's brother. Even if you are Steve's clone, now how can I make you a part of my family? Don't you think it will be an injustice to Steve? How would you like it if suddenly you had to cut down your inheritance by half because you had a twin or a clone or a sibling that you knew nothing about until then?" Mr. Kincaid explained.

"Alfred dear, why are you here? What exactly do you want?" Patricia asked. Obviously, she understood that Alfred was not interested in money.

"I want acceptance. I want identity," He tried to explain.

"I have no idea what you are talking about. Again, let me explain to you. Angela Johnson is the person responsible for your situation. The fact that she was a surrogate woman means, whoever is responsible for conceiving you must have been rich. It implies that you were destined to be born with a silver spoon in your mouth, but she took that out of your mouth and made you . . ."

Alfred interrupted him. "Mr. Kincaid, are you listening? I am not after money. All I want is to 'belong' somewhere. No man is an island. A man needs to have someone that he can belong to. Trust me, I feel like I am a drop in the ocean. In this world of seven billion people, I feel like I am without roots. Do you understand that?"

"Yes, I do get that. I can't undo what she has done. But I can change your life now. I will give you a check for five million dollars. It's life-changing money for you and Angela. It's obvious to me that you are after half my money, but it's not going to happen," Mr. Kincaid made his offer. Patricia was visibly uncomfortable when she heard this.

"Mr. Kincaid, I resent the implications that I am here for your money. Again, I want recognition. I will like to be invited to birthday parties, Thanksgiving dinner, to go fishing and camping with you and Steve. I want acceptance. You know, I mentioned that I am not after your money. Let me take it back. I am not after your billions. I would like to have hundred dollars occasionally for pocket expenses like a dad would give his son. I would like to have my Christmas stocking filled with some gifts that would cost less than fifty bucks. Can you spare a few dollars like that?"

"Listen, I am offering you a chance to live in luxury. You can attend any college with this much money. You can buy a nice house and live comfortably. You can essentially be set for life with so much money. You don't want that, and you want to catch couple of fish with me and Steve? Okay, I get it. You want to split my money with Steve. I am sorry, I cannot do that. I would have done it with someone I had raised from birth. I can give you ten million dollars. How about that?"

"Mike, I think you don't understand what he's trying to say," Patricia tried to reason with him. She could not believe someone would be so insensitive. She had always known that Mike saw everything in relation to money and had learned to live with it. This time it annoyed her. "Alfred wants a family. He wants name and social acceptance. I believe that's all he is after."

"Thank you, Ms. Sharp. Mr. Kincaid, when you can comprehend that money cannot buy everything, call me. Here's my card. And no, I am not going to the tabloids to sell my story. Don't worry about that." Alfred left his card on the table and walked out. As he was walking out, he put his fake beard and moustache on.

After Alfred left, Mr. Kincaid asked Patricia about Alfred's visit. Patricia told him that she thought he was genuine, and he was not interested in his money.

"Pat, you are naïve. You know what your problem is? You have an unhealthy respect for people. That's your biggest flaw. Young men at Alfred's age are idealistic. They love to talk like this. But one visit with an attorney and he will change his mind. I anticipate a letter from a lawyer within a few days. Alfred will demand half of my money. You will see. I will enjoy watching my lawyers fighting it out," Mr. Kincaid explained.

"Mike, I looked in his eyes and saw a man hungry for affection. I don't believe that he will talk to an attorney. If he does it, then in my opinion, you could have prevented it by giving him a hug. That's what he wanted and that's what he deserves. As an immigrant, I can put myself in his shoes. He feels alienated. He has felt that way all his life. When he finally got a chance to have a family, you took it away from him," Patricia gave her opinion.

"We will see. I am sure this is not the last we have heard from him. You need to consider how this will affect Steve. All he knows is that he had a brother named Chuck and he died of an illness. He does not know that Chuck was a clone and that there is another man in the picture. If I were to accept Alfred in my family, it will open Pandora's Box. I could not do that to Steve." Mike looked at Patricia and noted some uneasiness on her face. It was because he mentioned Chuck, but Mike didn't know that Chuck's memory bothered her.

"I think you need to talk to Steve before it's too late. He needs to be told about Alfred," Patricia warned him.

"Pat, I don't want Steve to ever find out about Alfred. By the way, do you have any idea what he was talking about when he said something about Native American blood?" Mike wondered.

"No, I have no clue. Interestingly, he specifically mentioned Lucy. It means the genetic test showed that Steve has a Native American ancestor on his mother's side. I don't understand it. I will have to look it up," Pat confessed.

"Well, at least there is something you don't know. Let's see what Edna has to say about it." Edna Dent was Lucy's mother. Mike kept in touch with her even after so many years had passed since Lucy's death. Patricia also got along well with Edna.

"You want to talk to Edna, but you don't want to talk to Steve! That's peculiar," Patricia was surprised.

"Yes, I think she would know the answer to this puzzle. It is important to know that Alfred is wrong about this Native American blood. It will be helpful to us if he goes to the court to demand money from me," Mr. Kincaid said and dialed her number and put her on the speakerphone.

"Edna, how are you? It's me."

"Hi, Mike. I am fine. How are you doing?" Edna answered cheerfully.

"I am fine too," Mike answered.

"How's Patricia?"

"Fine, Edna. Thanks for asking," Patricia answered.

"Mike, you should not put me on speakerphone. Pat listens to everything," Edna said laughing.

"Edna, you always claim that I don't speak or understand American English. So you don't need to worry about me," Patricia joked.

"I know. It's your Cockney, British accent that makes it difficult for me to understand you and I like to pretend that you don't understand American English," Edna teased.

"Edna, I called you because something important came up out of the blue. You may know the answer to the question I am going to ask you, but if you know the answer and you don't want to tell me then it's fine with me."

"Mike, what are you talking about? I won't hide anything from you."

"Well, you need to know the question first. Today, I heard a cockamamie story that Lucy was part Native American. I had never heard it from her or from anyone in your family. Is there any truth to it?" Mike asked. There was a gasp on the other end. Patricia concluded that there was some truth to Alfred's claim.

"Mike, it's true. I don't know how somebody discovered it. I don't think even Lucy knew it. If she did, she would have told you. My grandmother was Native American. Her name was Malina. She was from northern Canada and was a member of Inuit community."

"Was that your dad's mother?" Mike asked.

"No, she was my maternal grandmother. She passed away when my mom was only three years old. My grandfather married again. Mike, there was no reason to hide it from you. It's a forgotten past of our family history. I don't understand how anybody could know it. Does this affect Steve's health in anyway?" Edna was confused.

"No, this has nothing to do with Steve's health. Don't feel bad that you didn't tell Lucy or me about it. Come to think of it, I even remember that your family celebrates Thanksgiving. People of American Indian heritage generally don't celebrate Thanksgiving."

"When my grandfather married again, he married a white woman. I guess, if my real grandmother had lived longer, we would have followed different traditions. My grandfather married her when he had gone to Canada for business. By the way, Malina means solar deity."

"Someone told me today that he analyzed Steve's genes and found that he had Native American blood from his mother's side. That's why I thought of asking you," Mike explained.

"Why would somebody want to look at his genes?"

"I will tell you. You will be shocked to know who that guy is. I am sure you remember Chuck. He died when he was only a few months old." Patricia felt her stomach churning.

"Do you remember another woman was pregnant at the same time, but she ran away to Canada?" Mike asked.

"Yes, I do remember that. But that was years ago," Edna sounded shocked.

"Someone came today to my office. He claimed that he is the son of that woman. He told . . ."

Edna interrupted him, "Oh, Alfred came to see you!"

"Yes, he did. You remember his name!" Mike was stunned.

"I think Edna remembers his name from way back when we were trying to find him," Patricia opined.

"Yes, Pat, that's true. I still remember how your attorney tried to bring him back. I am shocked myself that the name came to me in an instant. Well, no one can accuse me of losing my memory," Edna laughed.

"I am truly surprised that after all these years, you still remember his name. Anyway, Alfred Johnson came to my office. He claims that after Steve had the skiing accident, he saw his pictures in the news and suspected that he was related to Steve. He told me that he compared Steve's DNA with his and they matched, just as we would expect. He also told me that genetics is never wrong. If it was your grandmother who was Native American, then Steve would be only one sixteenth Native American. Not only could he discover that by examining Steve's DNA, but he also knew it was from Steve's mother's side of the family. How he could tell that is something I can't understand," Mike told her.

"I can't explain that. I don't know how genes work. Why don't you ask miss-know-it-all? The British encyclopedia is sitting right there," Edna needled.

"Edna, Mike already asked me. I have no clue," Pat quipped.

"Good, that makes me feel better. Mike, can I meet him?" Edna was excited.

"Edna, I can't publicly acknowledge that he has anything to do with Steve or me. My original plan was to have more kids and tell people they were born from frozen eggs of Lucy or from in vitro fertilization with a surrogate woman. When Chuck was born that's exactly what I did. Now, after all these years, that ship has sailed. Can you imagine the scandal it will cause if people find out how he was born?"

"Sorry, I forgot you hate scandals," Edna was being sarcastic.

"That hurts, Edna, but I deserve it. Let's wait and see how things turn out."

"All right, I would love to meet him, but I will wait until you are comfortable with it."

"Thanks, Edna, bye," Mike said.

"Bye, Mike," Edna replied and hung up. Mike looked at Patricia. She had a look of surprise on her face.

"What are you thinking about, Pat?" Mike asked.

"I just can't get over how much you respect Edna. I am also surprised to see that you didn't hide anything from her about Alfred."

"Pat, it's because of Lucy. Even after all these years, I have the same respect for Edna as I did the first time I met her. I can't thank her enough for giving me Lucy. I will never play games with Edna," Mike confessed.

"Had you ever imagined that Lucy's ancestor was an Inuk?" Pat asked.

"Pat, Edna said her grandmother was Inuit, not Inuk," Mike tried to clarify.

"Actually, Inuit is plural and Inuk is singular. Edna mentioned that her grandmother was from the Inuit community."

"So *that* you know, but you don't know about the genetics of maternal inheritance! Anyway, if you find the explanation, let me know. Also, from now on, I am not going to celebrate Thanksgiving," Michael announced.

"Mike, Edna celebrates Thanksgiving. Why won't you?" Pat was surprised.

"I cannot celebrate Thanksgiving after knowing that Lucy had Native American blood. It's one of those things that I can't explain," Mike answered.

"Mike, so many things happened today that you missed an interesting geographical irony," Pat mentioned.

"I don't know what you mean," Mike didn't follow.

"You are in Columbus, the city that was named in honor of the great explorer Christopher Columbus. It was his discovery of the New World that heralded the ethnic cleansing of many Native American tribes. Your late wife was part Native American," Pat explained.

"You are right. I didn't see that," Mike confessed. Until now, he had been indifferent to the criticisms of Columbus and the colonization of the Americas by the Europeans. As far as he was concerned, the voyages of Columbus paved the way for European conquest and colonization of the new continent. In his mind, expansion of Western civilization was the legacy of Columbus. Now, he suddenly thought about the genocide of the natives by Columbus and his people, and also the spread of diseases, the sex slavery, and the eradication of Native Americans that went on for centuries.

"Well, Pat, I never considered the impact of Columbus's voyages on the people who lived here before 1492. Now that I know that my late wife and my son have Native American blood, I must reconsider my views about the history of the western world. After all, blood is thicker than water," Mike confessed.

Pat was truly astonished. In spite of all the cold-heartedness and destructive attitude, Mike had displayed since Lucy's death, he was going to honor Lucy's heritage by not celebrating Thanksgiving. When it came to Lucy or Edna, Mike was always respectful and decent.

* * *

After Suzy Thomas took Alfred in Mr. Kincaid's office she left for lunch. When Alfred was leaving Mr. Kincaid's office, she was returning to the office. She was still on N. High Street and was about to turn right to enter the parking lot when she saw Alfred walk out of the building. She stopped her car to watch him. Suzy noticed that his beard and moustache were crooked. He crossed the street to go toward his car. He appeared angry. Suzy was puzzled. Something terrible was going on with her boss. Maybe, this man is blackmailing him. Why would he say he was a cousin of Steven Kincaid? Why would Mr. Kincaid agree to see him immediately even though he was busy today? Why had Patricia appeared so emotional? When Alfred approached his car, Suzy noticed that it had a Canadian license plate. She took out her smartphone and took pictures of his car and the license plate.

When Alfred was driving away, on an impulse, Suzy followed him. Alfred drove toward OSU. A couple of blocks from OSU, he entered an apartment complex and parked his car. She parked her car on the street and waited. Alfred got out of his car and walked inside the building. Within two minutes, she saw him behind the window of a second-floor apartment. She could see him taking his beard and moustache off. She took some more pictures. Then Alfred walked onto the balcony. Suzy was stunned. He looked like Mr. Kincaid's only son, Steven. Maybe, Mr. Kincaid has an illegitimate son who is blackmailing him. She took more pictures. After few minutes, she returned to her office.

As soon as Suzy returned, she went to Patricia's office. She asked Patricia who Alfred was. Patricia gave her a dirty look and told her that it was something personal and she did not want to talk about it. Suzy told her that she saw him walk out of the building, and she believed that his beard and moustache were not real. Patricia looked straight in Suzy's eyes and reiterated that it was Mr. Kincaid's personal business, and she did not want to entertain any discussion regarding him. Suzy apologized and left Patricia's office in disgust. She would have shown pictures of Alfred without facial hair and told her where he lived, but all she got was a cold shoulder from Patricia. She felt slighted.

* * *

Late that evening, Patricia called Edna. "Hi, Pat, I was expecting your call. What took you so long?" Edna asked.

"I came late from work because there were a few things Mike wanted me to take care of. Surprise, surprise, after all these years Alfred's here."

"Isn't that something? I can't wait to see him. I am sorry I blurted out his name, but you saved me immediately. How does he look?" Edna asked.

"He is a spitting image of Steve. I will let you know when the time is appropriate to meet him. Alfred wants to be a part of the family, but Mike wants to pay him off to get him out of the picture. I think he is a genuine person and deserves our love and affection. I will try to support him as best as I can," Pat assured Edna.

"I think you should do that. You have done a lot to save him from Mike and that crooked attorney of his. Regardless of what Angela had done to Mike, I always think of Alfred as our own blood, and, therefore, he deserves to be protected. I don't blame Angela either for running away and keeping the baby. She must have felt like she was the real mother of this child when she was pregnant with him. I wish she had not done it, but now it's all water under the bridge."

"I agree. Mike thinks Alfred is after his money, and that he would demand fifty percent share of his empire."

"Even if that's true, he should be treated as a family member. That's just my opinion. God, I can't imagine how things would have turned out if Lucy had survived. Mike would never have turned into a controlling monster. How her death has destroyed his mind? I can't imagine it," Edna lamented.

22

The Deadly Girlfriend

Fighting for identity is something that is very much in my life.

— ANG LEE, FILM DIRECTOR

Alfred was frustrated. He knew that he could not hurt anyone under any circumstances. His meeting with Mr. Kincaid didn't go well. If Mr. Kincaid had been nice to him and apologized for making a mess of his life, he would have felt better. He could have called Steven to meet him. A little recognition was all that he wanted. Unfortunately, Mr. Kincaid couldn't think outside of the context of money. Alfred knew that he didn't want to replace Steven and that he won't be accepted by Mr. Kincaid as a family member, so what he wanted to do now was to embarrass them. *Why I want so desperately want to be accepted by this man who is pure evil*, he asked himself. Then he remembered the sleepless nights he had spent imagining a normal family, a father who could have mentored him or a brother to play and fight with. As bad as Mr. Kincaid was, he would like to be part of that family. His half brother Jeff and his friend Jagdish were luckier than he was. Maybe, he could show Mr. Kincaid that even though he is decent enough not to black-mail him, he could embarrass him and his son. *It was time for plan B.*

Alfred decided to pay a visit to Steven's girlfriend, Stephanie. He suspected that Mr. Kincaid would not have told his son of his existence. Most likely Steven or Stephanie may not have known anything about him.

Stephanie Anderson was at Miami University in Oxford, Ohio. Alfred knew that because when Steve had the skiing accident, media had interviewed his girlfriend, Stephanie. He knew her address from the card she had sent to Steve while he was in the hospital.

Alfred drove to her apartment and rang the doorbell. Stephanie opened the door and looked startled.

"This is a big surprise. I didn't know you were coming here to see me," she said.

"I just wanted to surprise you," Alfred answered.

"I thought you were supposed to rest in bed for a few more days after your recent surgery." Stephanie was puzzled.

"I am feeling better, so I came to see you," Alfred replied.

"There is something different about you, Steve. I don't exactly know what, but something is definitely different. For one thing, you are wearing different clothes."

"No, I do have a terrible toothache that is making my face swell a bit, so I might look and talk a bit differently," Alfred explained. Alfred was trying to cover part of his face by placing the palm of his hand over his supposedly sore tooth.

"Maybe, but that shouldn't be a reason not to kiss me. How could you forget that?" Stephanie wondered.

"It's the toothache," Alfred answered.

"I don't care," Stephanie insisted. He kissed her on the lips very gently. Then he moved away and put the palm of his hand on his jaw, pretending it was hurting. Stephanie pulled him back and kissed him on the lips. She showed more passion in the kiss than he had expected. He had to kiss her back.

"Wow, your toothache makes your kiss sexier," she told him. Alfred blushed. Stephanie exclaimed, "My goodness, this is the first time I have seen you blush! Maybe I should pay you compliments more often."

Stephanie's approval of his kiss made Alfred think of taking the next step. *That would be his revenge.* It would embarrass Steve forever once he finds out. *Does that make him a rapist? Possibly, it does.* No, he could not do that. Even if Steven and Michael Kincaid deserve such humiliation, he should not lower himself to their level. *Why should he let others make him do something that he detested so much?* He also remembered Brittany had told him to decide how far he wanted to go.

He pushed himself away gently and told her that he was in pain and that he just wanted to spend a few minutes with her. He decided to leave as soon as possible. The fact that he came there, impersonated Steven, and fooled his girlfriend into kissing him was revenge enough. They can do the math and figure out how far he could have gone but didn't.

After a few minutes of chitchatting, Alfred told her that it was time for him to leave. He told her that he wanted to go back to Columbus and get some rest. Stephanie asked him to leave in the morning after a good night's sleep, but Alfred insisted on leaving right away.

"Okay, why don't we stop by this new ice-cream place? It's only three blocks from here. You can leave after we have some ice cream. They have a special selection of ice creams for handicapped people like you," Stephanie said, laughing.

"A toothache is not a handicap. Besides, ice cream may make my teeth hurt more," Alfred pleaded.

"I am not talking about your dental problem. You can eat it from the other side of your mouth or drink it after it melts. I don't care. I just want some company to get out of this apartment. Are you sure you are all right?"

"Yeah, why do you keep asking?" Alfred wondered.

"Because you didn't understand that when I said handicapped, I meant your stupid lactose intolerance and not your—"

"Oh," Alfred interrupted, "*he* is also lactose intole—" He stopped in midsentence. The sudden revelation that Steven too was lactose intolerant was too much for him to process without making a faux pas. Too many things happened at once. Alfred realized that his reaction to Stephanie's comment had blown his cover, and that scared him. Stephanie noticed that Alfred used the word "he" for Steven, then stopped talking, and looked petrified. It didn't take her more than half a second to figure out something was wrong with this person. She had suspected it from the moment he walked in her apartment. Before Alfred could utter a word or do anything for that matter, he felt a severe kick in his groin. He fell on the floor in agony. After kicking him, Stephanie ran to the kitchen, grabbed a knife, ran back to Alfred, and held the knife over his throat. He put his hand between the knife and his throat to protect himself.

Alfred looked at Stephanie. The determination on her face scared him more than the knife she was holding. He gestured that he wanted to say something. He was not able to speak for a few seconds. When finally he was able to speak, first he apologized to her. Then he asked the question that surprised him, "Why did you not run out of the apartment after I fell on the floor? Anybody in your shoes would have done that."

"Anybody would have done it, but I am not anybody. Now tell me, who you are, and what are you up to? Be careful, if you make me mad, I will not stop this time until you are dead," she warned him.

"You don't need to worry about it. I will tell you everything. You are going to find out soon, anyway. Yesterday, I met Steve's dad and talked to him. I had suspected that Mr. Kincaid would not have told Steve about me. So you wouldn't be aware of my existence either. Apparently, I was right."

Alfred told her his story. He described how he grew up in Canada, how he suspected something was wrong about his life when Steven Kincaid had an accident while skiing, how he discovered that he was a clone of Steve, and how his meeting with Mr. Kincaid went. He explained that the only thing he wanted from Mr. Kincaid was a little recognition, not necessarily a public one either. He told her that his birth certificate has a blank where his father's name should be. He also mentioned that for whatever it was worth, he was sorry, but she needed to understand how empty it was to grow up without knowing who you really are.

Alfred asked her, "What answer do you get when you ask yourself, 'Who am I?' I am sure you hear that you are Stephanie Anderson, daughter of so-and-so, etcetera. When I ask that question, I get nothing. I didn't know who my father was. I grew up thinking Angela was my real mother, but she is not. Of course she is a mother to me because she raised me and loved me. She still loves me. Lucy Kincaid, who can be considered my biological mother, died before I was even conceived. As a matter of fact, can a clone claim that the biological parents of the original person are his biological parents too? When you think about all this, you will understand why I am doing what I have been doing."

"I can understand what is going on with you, but that does not give you any right to behave this way with me," Stephanie said to him. She was still furious.

"First of all, I didn't do anything except kissing you back. I am in search of my identity, but I know what I am not. I am not someone who would take advantage of a lady just because I look like her boyfriend. Besides, you don't have to worry about this anymore. This will never happen again," Alfred reassured Stephanie.

"Oh, I am not worried at all. You lasted hardly fifteen minutes before you were caught impersonating someone else. For God's sake, you claim to be Steve's clone, and you still couldn't pull it off." Stephanie was angry.

"I learned my lesson today. From now on I am going to stay away from double X chromosomes. I would prefer people with forty-six XY chromosomes. I think it will be safer. I mean, I would rather be gay," Alfred assured her while trying to laugh.

"Well, Alfred, I know what you mean by that, but you don't know that a person's chromosomes do not tell you everything. If you knew more about me, you will know what I am talking about," Stephanie told him.

"What do you mean by that?" Alfred was confused. "You look like a normal woman."

"Yes, I am a normal woman. Remember what I just told you. Never mind. Why am I acting so stupid? Now get out of here before I kill you." Stephanie was mad at herself.

Stephanie opened the door. After Alfred left, she slumped on the sofa. She was angry at herself. *Why did I reveal anything about my chromosomes to Alfred? That's not like me. I am supposed to be in control. How could I not know that it was not Steven Kincaid who had entered her apartment? Women are usually smarter than that.*

She remembered her siblings teasing her about being masculine. She had always laughed it off, but now she seriously questioned if she was too much in touch with her masculine side! She remembered that her therapist, Isabella, had assured her that she was a normal woman despite having a Y chromosome.

After a few minutes, Stephanie called Steve on his landline phone.

Steve answered, "Hello."

"Steve, where are you exactly at this moment?" she asked.

"Steph, you know where I am. I am home. You are calling me on my home number for crying out loud," he answered.

She asked, "Steve, can you tell me what my dad thought of you when you first met him?"

"Steph, what are you talking about? What kind of question is that?"

"I saw someone who looks like you. If you answer my question, I can tell whether you are the real Steven Kincaid or not."

"Steph, what's going on? If it helps, I can tell you. Your dad thought that I don't have a personality. He believed that I don't have depth. I believe his exact words to you were, 'Steve is a no-good, one-dimensioned parasite living off his dad's money.' He also told you that thanks to my dad, his money, and his people, I don't have to think or work in my life. Does that help?" Steve was getting edgy.

"Yes, that's good enough," Stephanie answered. "By the way, my dad changed his mind after he got to know you better. He thinks 'you are normal.' My dad says that in spite of being born with a silver spoon, Steve is level-headed."

"Thanks, Steph. That was nice of him. I am sure that when he said I was normal, he didn't mean it as a compliment. Now tell me, where did you see someone who looked like me?"

"Oh, someone came in my apartment pretending he was you. I knew something was not right the moment he walked in. I should have trusted my instincts," Stephanie said. Then she repeated the story Alfred told her.

"Steve, you have a doppelganger." Steve was surprised to know that he had a clone. He told her that he remembered a brother called Chuck, who was born when he was a little more than one year of age, but he had died just a few months after his birth.

* * *

Suzy Thomas was obsessed with Alfred's identity. She went back to his apartment complex and, from her car, took some more pictures. When Alfred came back from his traumatic meeting with Stephanie, Suzy was waiting in her car. He was again wearing his disguise. The following morning in the office, she asked a couple of her coworkers if they had heard of Alfred Johnson. They had not. She told them about Alfred coming there to see Mr. Kincaid and that he looked like Steven Kincaid. They told her that she should mind her business and not poke her nose where it did not belong. She was getting more and more frustrated. So she went to Mr. Kincaid's office and asked him. "Sir, the other day a young man named Alfred Johnson was . . ." Before she could finish her sentence, she was interrupted by an angry Mr. Kincaid.

"Suzy, it does not concern you in any way. You should drop it. I know you have made some noise about this for the last couple of days. Don't ever mention it to me or to anyone again. Is that clear?"

"Yes, sir," she replied and left his office.

She felt jilted. Here she was trying to help her boss with the information that could be very useful to him, but all she was getting were insults. She decided to take the matter in her own hands. She thought that if Patricia, who was Mr. Kincaid's right hand, snubs her, and Mr. Kincaid himself insults her, then there was nothing wrong in making money out of this situation. She will teach Mr. Kincaid a lesson for ignoring her. She called *National Gossip Weekly*. She told them that she had a story about some rich person whose illegitimate son was blackmailing him.

When the tabloid heard from Suzy who that person was, they were interested. While she was on the phone with them, Suzy could almost picture the editor of the tabloid drooling. The following day, they sent their representatives to meet her privately. After looking at the pictures of Alfred, they were convinced that they were sitting on a goldmine.

23

Stephanie Discovers Herself

Certain defects are necessary for the existence of individuality.

— Johann Wolfgang von Goethe,
German author and statesman

Victor Anderson sat nervously by his wife, Bridget. She had been in labor for hours. Her desire for a "natural" childbirth was not going well. She was in pain, and she was totally exhausted. Her doctor assured her that in the first pregnancy, it was normal for the labor to be prolonged. Finally, after fifteen agonizing hours, Stephanie was born. The doctor placed her on her mother's belly. Victor looked at the newborn baby. A million emotions were running through his mind. The doctor asked him if he wanted to cut the umbilical cord. It's a special privilege granted to the dads by the obstetricians. Victor nodded in affirmative, but he was not sure if in his emotional state he would be able to perform that simple task. With his hand shaking, he picked up the scissors and managed to position the blades between the two clamps and cut the cord.

Baby Stephanie was covered in blood and some thick whitish cheesy stuff. Her head was misshapen because it was lying in the birth canal for hours. She looked like a cone-head. Her eyes were swollen. She was crying loudly. Yet when Victor looked at her, he could not imagine how a little thing like that could look so beautiful. That instant Victor realized why dads have special relationships with their daughters. He resolved that he will do anything for the "*happiness of my daughter.*"

Stephanie grew up in a loving family. She had one brother and one sister. Her parents were very proud of her, and she knew that. Her life was so perfect that it could have been from a storybook. Sadly, it all ended when she was fourteen years old.

Stephanie failed to have menstrual periods. From the time she was twelve, her mother was waiting for this important landmark in a woman's life. She had been asking Stephanie almost every week if she had any bleeding "down below." Stephanie kept on telling her that she would know if she had her period and that she and other girls in her class had received the education from their teacher. When she was fourteen and had yet to get her first period, her mom took her to a gynecologist.

Dr. Susan Tackett examined Stephanie. The physical examination was normal. Then she ordered ultrasound to look at her internal organs. An ultrasound evaluation did not show a uterus or ovaries. After explaining the results of the ultrasound, she ordered more tests. She sent blood sample to check her chromosomes. When the report was received, Dr. Tackett called Stephanie and her mom to her office. She explained that genetically Stephanie was male. She had the chromosomal makeup of a boy. A girl should have two X chromosomes, but Stephanie had one X and one Y chromosome just like a boy would have. The doctor explained that some people have what is called "testicular feminization syndrome" or "androgen insensitivity syndrome." Their organs fail to respond to androgens or male hormones. They do not have ovaries or uterus. These patients look and develop like normal women, but they cannot menstruate or bear children. Young Stephanie was devastated. She was facing a major crisis.

Dr. Tackett very patiently explained to Stephanie that she was biologically female. She was a woman with the exception that she won't have menstrual periods and she couldn't have children of her own. Stephanie never felt like anything other than a woman. Never in a million years had she imagined that she was not a *normal* woman. She had read in the books and heard from her friends that monthly periods are a big bother to a woman.

Now, after she found out that she was not going to have periods, she felt she was missing out on a wonderful experience of being a woman. She did not know what to do. On the top of that, her parents advised her not to reveal this secret to her friends or teachers for fear of being stigmatized.

Stephanie and her parents were going through a nightmare. Victor and Bridget decided that Stephanie needed some professional help. They found a counselor for her. For months, she could not think of anything other than her medical condition. Her life revolved around this thought. Her counselor, Isabella, advised her that she should not let her medical problem consume her life. Per her advice, she devoted ten minutes every evening to think about her medical problem. Any time during the day, the thoughts of her inability to have periods or to conceive bothered her; she would make a mental note of it and decide to think about it at nine o'clock in the evening that day. Then she would continue to do whatever she was doing at the time. After a while, she was able to function without her medical problem bothering her every minute of her time. In the evening, she would calmly think about the problems and figure out how to handle them.

With the help of the counselor, she was still working on many issues related to her medical problem. One day Stephanie asked the counselor, "Isabella, what makes a woman a 'woman'?"

Isabella replied, "That's a loaded question. Can you tell me exactly what you are asking?"

"Until I knew my genetic makeup, I felt like a normal person. Now that I know that genetically I am a man, I want to know what I should do to be a normal woman."

"You are a normal woman. The only difference is that you cannot have monthly periods and you cannot have babies. Your medical diagnosis does not change anything else. You look like a normal woman, and you act like one too. You are a cisgender female. It means that you have the body of a woman and you identify yourself as a woman also. A transgender person is one whose gender identity and assigned sex are different. You are attracted to boys, so you are heterosexual. This makes you a cisgender, heterosexual woman like majority of women. So I don't understand why you need to ask such questions," Isabella replied.

"I know all that. But now that I know I am different, I want to define my role as a woman. I want to find out how a real woman should act," Stephanie elaborated.

"Steph, now I understand what you are saying. You are having an identity crisis. There are many role models around you. A woman is a daughter, sister, wife, and mother to different people. The way your own mother and your relatives live their lives can show you how a woman should or should not act. Your friends, your neighbors, and your teachers are also great examples. If that's not enough, then the scriptures and mythology also can guide you," Isabella tried to explain.

That evening, at nine o'clock, Stephanie thought about her mother's life. Her mother, Bridget, had a degree in computer engineering. Before she married, she was a project manager in a multinational company. She continued to work after her marriage. She managed her home and her career with great efficiency. Stephanie remembered that when she was about twelve years old, her mother quit her job. Stephanie's brother, Conner, was having troubles in school. He was dyslexic. The teacher warned that he would need a lot of supervision in his homework and that his parents would need to help him in his studies. Young Stephanie remembered that her parents were distraught when they heard about it. After discussing for a few days, they came to a decision.

Bridget quit her job so she could spend more time with Conner. At that time, Stephanie did not think much of her mother quitting her job, but now she realized that as a wife and mother, her mom had to sacrifice her career for her young son. She also realized that her father was not expected to make the same sacrifice. After all, he could have done the same thing and let his wife continue her job. How come this thought had never occurred to her until now, she wondered.

Overnight, her mother's status changed from project manager to a housewife. In the two years since she quit her job, she had lost interest in current events, politics, and, practically, the world around her, save the duties of a housewife. All she did was housework, drive kids around, and help her dyslexic son in his studies. To lessen her burden, Stephanie's dad started handling bills, bank transactions, and everything outside of the house except grocery shopping. She realized that her mother metamorphosed from a vibrant, well-informed lady to a woman dependent on her husband for every penny and every decision. Is that the price a woman must pay for having two X chromosomes? Stephanie didn't think this was right. Her mother deserved a lot more respect than she got.

Stephanie looked around. She found many families where the man was supposed to be the main bread-earner, while the woman brought a minor share of the family income if she worked outside of her house. She saw in many families that the wife went to work part-time after having kids. The husband was not expected to sacrifice his job so that his wife could have a better career. Barring a few exceptions, it was always the woman who sacrificed. On the other hand, Stephanie also knew many women like her aunt, her neighbor, and mothers of some of her classmates in school who identified themselves proudly as homemakers and were happy raising kids and keeping their families together. She acknowledged that there was nothing wrong with it if it did not happen due to the so-called traditional gender roles determined by the society.

Stephanie looked into the scriptures. She soon realized that the scriptures had to be written by men. If God had a hand in writing or inspiring the scriptures, then God had to be a man. She also found that the Holy Scripture allowed fathers to sell their daughters. She found that according to the Koran, a rape victim had to produce four male witnesses before she could allege that she was raped. *This is ridiculous*, she thought. Stephanie discovered that every religion had given secondary roles to women. God is misogynist. The Holy Scripture, religions, and laws in some countries were all skewed to favor men. Human civilization has systematically exploited half the population.

Luckily for Stephanie, she did not know that her own medical condition revealed how evolution has dealt a devastating blow to the female gender. She did not know and her gynecologist had not explained to her how sex determination takes place. Normally, females have two X chromosomes and males have one X and one Y chromosomes. It is not the number of X chromosomes, but the presence (or absence) of Y chromosome that determines the gender. An embryo develops as female by default, meaning absence of Y chromosome results in a female child and its presence results in a male child. A fetus with one X chromosome only (as in cases of Turner syndrome) or two X chromosomes develops as female. It is only due to the actions of the genes on Y chromosome, it becomes male. Not many feminists will like to know that! Of course, in her case, it was the insensitivity to the testosterone, which resulted in her biological gender to be female.

Stephanie read that in some communities in India, a woman not only takes her husband's last name but also the husband gives her a new first name after marriage. Your name is your identity. After marriage you lose that too. Almost every culture in the world has patriarchal societies. There are very few exceptions to that rule. It is always the woman who has to give up something; her family, her last name, her career, and her independence—basically, her identity. A woman is "miss" or "missus" depending on her marital status. What about a man? If it is all right for a man to not change his salutation after marriage, why not for a woman?

Why does a society have to be patriarchal or, for that matter, matriarchal? Why can't a couple marry and live on their own, keeping equal relations with extended families of both sides? Both genders can keep their identities by keeping their own last names and give their last names to their children based on their genders. A mother's last name can continue as her daughter's last name and a father's as his son's. No one has to lose their identity. This is the best way of breaking the marital glass ceiling. She vowed to keep her last name after marriage. She will not take her husband's last name.

In the wedding ceremony, why is the bride "given away" by her dad? A bride is not a transferrable property. She can walk by herself to the altar. She decided that she will not let her dad "give her away" in the wedding. Interestingly, that was one promise she was to renege on in the future. After all the things her dad had done for her, she could not deprive him of that privilege he had as a father of the bride.

When Stephanie looked at the condition of women in the modern times, she found that in the underdeveloped countries, women were illiterate and poorer than their counterparts in the developed countries. Being barefoot and pregnant was not just a cliché in those countries. There was genital mutilation practiced on millions of Muslim and Christian girls in many African countries. How can such a barbaric practice exist in the twenty-first century? "The hand that rocks the cradle rules the world" seemed like empty words.

Paradoxically, she discovered that in the third-world countries, women had become heads of states long before the developed countries could boast of that kind of gender equality. Corazon Aquino, Sirimavo Bandarnaike, Indira Gandhi, Benazir Bhutto, Sheikh Hasina, and a host of other women were presidents and prime ministers in the developing countries. There were very few such examples in Europe and other developed countries. The United States, in its 230-year-long history, had not elected a woman president even though they had elected an African American man as president, twice. The United States did not allow women to vote for decades after African American men were given that privilege.

True, there were laws in the books to prevent discrimination against women and minorities. Women and minorities! Does anybody realize how ridiculous it sounds? Yes, there is discrimination against minorities based on their color, nationality, ethnicity, and sexual orientation in many countries, and the laws to prevent that are important. But women could belong to any of the above categories, and they do. How can 50 percent of the population be lumped together with minorities? The only explanation for women to be considered minorities is the patriarchal nature of the society.

What has been happening to women is nothing short of "gender apartheid." She concluded that contrary to the prevailing views, Western cultures were not immune to this, either. Stephanie read that there were hundreds of thousands of cases of domestic violence in an advanced country like the United States. Domestic violence was something she had associated with third-world countries, but the United States? Why didn't they teach women to have self-esteem? Why can women not learn the basics of self-defense?

She read about some Asian countries where millions of female embryos are being aborted as a form of population control. This practice is so prevalent that in some places the gender ratio is almost 900 girls to 1000 boys. Millions of women are missing.

Then there was human trafficking. She was stunned when she looked at the numbers. It was a multi-billion-dollar industry. Millions of people, mostly girls, were the victims of this disgusting practice. Girls were sold by parents for debt relief in many parts of the world. She decided what type of woman—no, a lady—she would be. She resolved that she was not going to take any nonsense from men, society, or the church. The marital glass ceiling was perhaps the most damaging problem across the globe. It must be broken.

Late one night while she was reading about women's role in mythologies, her dad knocked on her door.

"Are you still up, Steph?" he asked.

"Yes, Dad, I am reading."

"May I come in?" he asked.

"Yes, sure," she replied.

"Why you are up so late at night? Are you preparing for exams?"

"No, Dad, I am just doing some casual reading." Victor looked at the books lying on her desk. There were books on anthropology and mythology. She was holding a book titled *World Mythology* in her hands.

"Why are you reading about mythology?" Dad asked.

"I want to learn from anthropology, mythology, and religions as to what type of a woman I should be."

Within seconds, Dad had tears in her eyes. "Dad, why are you so emotional? Did I say something bad?" She was puzzled.

"No, Steph, I am sorry about everything that you have had to endure and go through. If I could change it, I would do it in a jiffy," he answered. "I feel like I failed you somehow."

"Dad, it's nothing like that. My androgen insensitivity syndrome has taught me a lot. I am learning how to be a woman. If I didn't have that condition, I would have been just like billions of other women not knowing who we really are, what we are capable of, and how important we are in this world. I am actually using my medical condition to my advantage." Dad gave her a big hug and started to leave the room.

Stephanie stopped him. "Dad, you said you would do whatever it takes, right?"

"Yes, I said that, and I mean it." Dad turned around.

"Well, there is something I would like you to do. It has nothing to do with my condition directly, but I kind of thought about it because of my medical condition," Stephanie said.

"Tell me. If it's within my powers, I will do it."

"Dad, I want Mom to go back to work. We can all pitch in a little bit in the housework so she would have enough time to help Conner. I think she needs to spend some time outside of the house," Stephanie threw a curveball.

Victor had not imagined this in a million years. He stared at his daughter for a few seconds. "I don't know where this is coming from, but I will talk to Mom to find out what she wants. Ultimately, it's her decision," he said and left the room.

Within a few weeks, Bridget went back to work part time. Pretty soon, Stephanie saw the change in her mom. She was not a "housewife" anymore. Stephanie reasoned that if both genders are treated equally, most of the world's problems would go away. In this day and age of interracial and interfaith marriages, if women would keep practicing their own faiths after marriage, then prejudices for other faiths will disappear too.

From the time she was ten, her parents had been talking about celebrating her sixteenth birthday. The sweet sixteenth birthday party is a coming-of-age party for a girl. Many cultures celebrate coming of age for boys and girls. Bar mitzvah and bat mitzvah in Jewish communities and quinceañera in Hispanic cultures are examples of such events. Further, bark mitzvah is one that is celebrated by some people for their dogs when they are thirteen months old. In certain castes of Hinduism, especially Brahmins, the boys start wearing a sacred thread that goes from their left shoulders to the right side of their waists. Christians have Confirmation.

Stephanie had an amazing sweet sixteenth party. Her parents could not believe how their daughter had matured in the last two years. They celebrated the party with tears in their eyes. Their relatives and friends who came to the party thought that the parents were emotional because their daughter was becoming a woman.

Stephanie's parents were relieved that if their daughter could deal with this crisis with such dignity and grace, then nothing in life would be impossible for her. Instead of overpowering her, her genetic problem had made her stronger. Nietzsche was right: That which does not kill you, strengthens you.

Stephanie Anderson had grown up to be a very strong, very determined, and a very beautiful lady. She had come a long way.

24

Tweedledum and Tweedledee

The best thing you've got going for you is individuality.

— RICHARD THOMPSON, MUSICIAN

Patricia was right. Michael Kincaid should have talked to his son before it was too late. When Alfred met with Stephanie and was exposed as Steve's doppelgänger, Steve knew it was serious. It sounded absurd that Alfred was his clone, but if Stephanie could be fooled by him, then Alfred must be at least his twin.

Steve asked his dad about Alfred. Mr. Kincaid told him that maybe he had an affair with Alfred's mother, and the mother and son were trying to extort money from him. He didn't mention cloning. Steve asked him if Alfred was his clone. Mr. Kincaid told him to mind his own business. He told Steve that if he were to meet Alfred, the consequences will be disastrous for everyone involved.

"Dad, I think Alfred wants to be a part of our family. I believe he has every right to expect that. I want to meet him," Steve insisted.

"Why? So you and Alfred, Tweedledum and Tweedledee, can socialize? Is that what you want? It's not going to happen. Again, this is something that does not concern you," his father was firm.

Steve told his dad that by cloning him, he had violated his rights. Mr. Kincaid was surprised. "Let's suppose that I had cloned you. How are your rights violated? You are going to inherit my entire estate whether Alfred is your clone or not. So how does this affect you?"

"Dad, you violated my right to be left alone. I had a right to my own identity. You deprived me of that right by cloning me. Cloning has robbed me of my genetic identity. Some parents do not want to know their kids' genomes because they believe it's a violation of their privacy. They want the kids to decide when they are adults whether they want to know their genomes or not. This is not about money, so I don't expect you to understand it," Steve said.

"What is with you kids and your identities? Spend one day in the unemployment line and you will know your identity," he replied and stormed out of the room. Steve was shocked that his dad would blackmail him with his money. But he knew his dad well. There was no way he was going to get anything out of him unless it was to his benefit. He decided to approach Patricia.

Next day he met with Patricia privately. He asked her, "Pat, I have a question. I think you are the only one who can answer it."

"Steve, what is bothering you?" she asked.

"I think you probably know what I am going to ask you." Steve waited for her reaction. He desperately wanted to know about the circumstances around Alfred's birth, but he also did not want to hurt Pat, the only person he trusted, other than his girlfriend, Stephanie.

"I kind of have an idea. I will try to answer if I can," Patricia answered.

"Thanks, Pat. I want to know about Alfred Johnson. I have heard that he is my clone. Is it true?"

"How did you hear about him?"

"He met Stephanie pretending to be me."

"Oh, dear. Alfred should not have done that. You know if Alfred has any connections with you then your dad is the person you should talk to, not me." Patricia was looking for a way out. On the one hand, Michael Kincaid was her boss, but on the other hand, it was Steve, who was like her son. She also knew in her heart that Steve had a right to know everything. If Mr. Kincaid didn't want to tell something to Steve, then she was the only person who could do it and still get away with it. Plus, it is the right thing to do.

"You know my dad more than I do. He can't understand the relationship between that of a father and son except in the context of money. I would rather learn about Alfred from someone closer to me than from the media. I am sure it's a matter of time before it will be out in the open. That's why I am asking you," Steve persisted.

"I guess you are right. The way things have turned out after your skiing accident and Alfred's visit to your dad, I don't know what the right course of action is. I honestly believe that you should be told everything about this matter. But it's your dad who should talk to you and not me or anyone else, but that's not going to happen. I guess that leaves me."

"When your mom passed away, your dad was devastated. He could not function for months due to overwhelming grief. It was his love for you that gave him reason to live. Your parents wanted to have three kids. Your dad loved your mom so much that he did not want to marry again. He . . ." Patricia was interrupted.

"Yes, I know all that. You can fast forward."

"I am coming to the point. He wanted things to go back the way they were before your mom passed away, but that was not going to happen. Then he heard about cloning. He was excited when he learned that an exact genetic duplicate of a person could be created by cloning. He talked to a genetics professor from OSU about cloning. His name was Dr. Jihoo Lee. The professor explained about in vitro fertilization, parthenogenesis, test tube babies, etcetera."

Professor Lee explained to your dad that even if he were to clone Lucy, the clone will have to start her life as an embryo. That's when he realized that cloning Lucy was not going to bring everything back to normal, so he decided to clone you. At that time, you were a few months old. Long story short, he found someone who could do it, but he wanted utmost secrecy. You see, there are laws against human cloning and there are many ethical issues in this matter."

"The people involved in this process hired Angela Johnson. She became pregnant with your clone. A few months into her pregnancy she disappeared. Apparently, she wanted to keep the baby. She didn't know that it was Mr. Kincaid who had hired her as a surrogate and neither she nor her obstetrician knew it was a clone. She ran away to Canada where Alfred was born."

"Then you had the skiing accident and your pictures were in the news. That's when Alfred and Angela found out that Alfred looked like you. It was going to happen sooner or later because you are the son of a billionaire. Your pictures were going to be everywhere and Alfred or his friends would have seen them and become curious," Patricia spilled the beans.

"What was the name of the scientist who did the cloning?" Steve asked. Immediately, Steve thought about Chuck. He figured that Chuck must be a clone too. He resisted the impulse to ask Patricia about him. His first concern was to know about Alfred.

"Steve, that's not important. I believe you deserve to know that Alfred is your clone and I can confirm that."

"I think that's fair. Pat, I appreciate your help and your honesty. You have always been there for me. When Alfred came to meet my dad, you were there. Can you tell me what he wanted?"

"Alfred feels like a man without roots. He grew up not knowing who his dad was. He wants recognition. He wants identity." Patricia explained.

"Wow. My dad thinks that Alfred is after his money."

"I know. I don't think Alfred cares about your dad's money."

"You mentioned that Alfred wants recognition. He told Stephanie the same thing," Steve said.

"Why did he meet Stephanie?" Patricia was curious.

"After he met with my dad and you, he went to Stephanie's place. As I mentioned, he pretended to be me. He wanted to embarrass me and my dad. Stephanie was fooled for a few minutes, but Alfred made one mistake, so she figured out that he was not me. She kicked him in the groin. Alfred apologized to her and then told her who he was and how he is connected in all of this."

"My goodness. I know Stephanie. She is tough. She could be dangerous."

"You don't have to tell me that. She is strong-headed. After all, how many teenaged girls can change a flat tire?" Steven asked.

"That's right. Not many people would bother to learn how to change a tire," Patricia replied.

Two years ago, on a wintery evening, Steven was stranded on I-71 with a flat tire. While any road assistance was not forthcoming due to snow storm, he was shocked to see a well-dressed young girl stop there to offer help. She not only knew how to change the tire, but she insisted on teaching him how to do it. Steve was truly impressed. After the tire was changed, she introduced herself, "By the way, I am Stephanie Anderson."

"Nice to meet you, Stephanie, I am Steven Kincaid." Steven was used to notice a reaction on the face of strangers when they would hear the word "Kincaid." But he didn't see any such reaction on the girl's face.

"Michael Kincaid is my dad," he added.

"So? I am shocked to think that if I had not stopped to help you, you would have called your dad to rescue you."

That was the first time in his life that Steve was told on his face how dependent he was on his dad and his money. He was impressed by this girl's self-confidence and the way she carried herself. He called her after couple of days to thank her. After that encounter, they started dating. Steven loved that she didn't care how rich he was and how famous his dad was.

"Steve, what are you thinking about?" Pat asked. She found him lost in thoughts. Steve suddenly realized that he was silent for a few seconds. He asked, "Pat, are there other clones besides Alfred?" Steve asked.

"I can tell you that Alfred is the only clone, so you and Stephanie don't have to worry about anyone else impersonating you," Patricia assured.

"That's good to know."

"Alfred told your dad that he would like to be considered as part of this family. He said he would rather have a birthday gift or a Christmas present worth a few dollars than a few million dollars to keep his mouth shut. Your dad offered him millions of dollars so that he would go away." Patricia was becoming emotional.

"I cannot even begin to imagine what he is going through. Maybe, I should meet him," Steve mentioned.

"What will you tell him if you meet him? Do you have any idea what the media will do if they see you two together? Some avenues are better left unexplored, Steve," Patricia cautioned.

"I know. Somehow or other I must meet him. Maybe if I talk to him I can resolve the stalemate. If I accept him, then my dad may change his mind. I don't know. Whatever happens, it's time Alfred and I meet."

"Perhaps you should start with a phone call. In my opinion, it is less risky. After you speak to him on the phone, you both can decide if and when you two should meet in person," Patricia reasoned.

"Pat, it's not the same thing. We need to see each other eye to eye for our first meeting."

"I understand that. I have an idea. Why don't you use FaceTime? You can see him and talk to him without leaving your home," Patricia gave an idea.

"Yes. That is a great idea. I'll do that," Steve agreed.

"Good. Here's his phone number. Go for it, Steve." Patricia gave a piece of paper with Alfred's phone number on it.

"Pat, thanks for your help," Steve was delighted.

"Anytime, Steve," Patricia replied.

25

Boy Meets Clone

I have done everything I can to make sure my daughter knows her father because you form your own identity by rebelling against your parents—but first you have to know them.

— GRETA SCACCHI, ACTRESS

Steve called Alfred not knowing what they would talk about. Alfred answered, "Hello?"

"Hi, Alfred, I am Steven Kincaid. I hope you don't mind my calling you."

"Hi, Steve," Alfred stumbled, surprised at who was on the other end. "No, that's fine. How are you? I was wondering when you and I will talk," Alfred began to recover from his initial shock.

"I want to talk to you in person, but if someone sees both of us together then it would cause some problems. Can we do FaceTime?"

"Yes, absolutely," Alfred replied.

"Very well. I will hang up and call you on FaceTime," Steve responded. In few seconds, they were connected.

"Wow, I didn't know I was so handsome!" exclaimed Alfred.

"Very funny, Alfred. Very funny."

"I wanted to break the ice," Alfred confessed. "Actually, I have seen you before."

"I have never seen you. I didn't even know of your existence," Steve confessed. "This is so unusual for both of us. Perhaps there is no precedent for this situation," Steve admitted.

"True. You know I met your dad?" Alfred started the ball rolling.

"Yes, I know. Patricia told me a little bit about it. Can you tell me how the meeting with my dad went?"

"Sure. I told Mr. Kincaid that cloning has been responsible for disturbing many lives. Regardless of the ethics of cloning, if he had been upfront with Angela Johnson, things would have been different. I have believed all my life that Angela was my biological mother, but now it turns out that she was a surrogate. It's very complicated. She fell in love with the unborn baby and she wanted to keep him, so she ran away to Canada where I was born. Then, she ran from place to place to escape from being kidnapped or worse. To make a long story short, I have lived without knowing who I really am or where I really came from. I grew up thinking that she was my mother and that my father was someone she had a brief affair with. Growing up without a father, I felt incomplete. Then you had a skiing accident and I found out that we looked alike. So I confronted my mom. That's when I learned about the surrogate pregnancy. It really confused me. I want to discover my identity. I tried to explain to your dad all that. I don't know, in this situation, whether you are my brother or not and whether your dad is also my dad, or he is my grandfather. Since I didn't have a dad while I was growing up, I have created weird image of a dad in my mind."

"What do you mean by creating a weird image of a dad? I don't understand that," Steve was confused.

"When I was little, I used to think that my dad would be highly accomplished and famous. Sometimes I would think of my dad to be a politician or an athlete. Frequently I would dream that my dad would be a fire fighter or a police officer. I have spent literally hundreds of nights half-asleep, trying to figure out how my life would have turned out if I had a dad. I have also imagined my dad to be someone like actor Martin Sheen or game-show host, Alex Trebek," Alfred answered. "I have been fantasizing about where I came from and who I belonged to. I told your dad that what I want is to belong somewhere," Alfred lamented.

"That explains why you would want to be a part of the family."

"Yes, Steve, I am not after your money. I made it very clear to your dad that I would like to be invited to a birthday party, to a Christmas dinner, and so on. I don't think he understood because he kept on offering me more and more money."

"Yes, that's my dad. Most people speak English, my dad speaks money. I apologize for his actions. I can't force him to invite you, but we can meet from time to time. Personally, I don't know how an invitation to a birthday party should make any difference to you," Steve answered him.

"No, you can't understand that. Unless someone is in my shoes, they wouldn't comprehend this. You were born with a silver spoon. Your dad and his people have taken care of your every need. You have not experienced unhappiness or loneliness or an identity crisis," Alfred said.

"Alfred, that's what everyone thinks. But you are forgetting something. When I was growing up, I realized that I didn't have a mother. I don't remember when I noticed that, but maybe it was around the time I was three years old. Eventually, I was told by my pediatrician, my counselor, Patricia Sharp, and little bit by my dad that my mother died due to something that happened to her during the later part of her pregnancy and childbirth. Do you know who she was pregnant with? *Me*."

"So Alfred, I grew up with the knowledge that I was responsible for the untimely death of my mother. Clearly, if she was not pregnant with me, she would not have died from the complications of pregnancy. I've lived with the knowledge that before I was born I made my mother so sick that she lost her life. I must carry that guilt with me for the rest of my life. Now, tell me, how many people in the world can relate to this kind of tragedy?" Steve told his story.

"Sorry, I didn't think of that," Alfred said.

"My point is that we have to make the best of what we have. We all have problems, and we have to live with them. We all have to bear our cross, so to speak." Steve replied. Alfred remembered that Jagdish and Brittany also told him something to that effect. We all have issues, they had told him.

"I agree, Steve. I didn't see it from your point of view. You've given me lot to think about," Alfred did not know how to handle the issue of Lucy's death. He wished they were talking on the phone instead of by FaceTime. He did not know what emotions were appropriate for such a situation. Luckily, Steve broke the silence.

"You want to hear something else? You may be the first human clone, but that makes me the first person to have a clone. I am different than most of the people in this world. I have been cloned. I am the only one whose identity has been stolen this way. Can you imagine how creepy it is?" Alfred was speechless.

Steve continued. "Alfred, we will figure out how to meet in person sometime. We both have a lot to think about and process right now." Steve paused lost in a thought. "I have never met a person who would not be interested in millions of dollars. I am beginning to lose interest in my dad's money, thanks to you."

"Steve, I am not trying to deprive you of your inheritance. I had no right to his money in the past and I don't want to claim any such right now or in future. I am curious. How do you deal with not having your mom around? You don't have to answer it if you are not comfortable talking about it. No, you know, never mind, forget I asked," Alfred hesitated.

"Wow. No one has ever asked me something like that, and I have never talked to anyone about it. I guess, I should tell you. If I can't confide in you then who can I confide to? After all, we share the same genes. You met Patricia Sharp, right?" Steve asked.

"Yes? I think she's a very remarkable lady," Alfred was beginning to understand where Steve was going with this.

"She's a mother figure to me. The way she took care of me when I was a baby, I have always thought of her as my mother. I have imagined that if my mother had survived, she would be like Pat. But, Alfred, this is strictly between you and me. I am sure, Pat knows that she is like a mother to me, but we have never talked about it. Under no circum-stances will I jeopardize my relationship with her," Steve said. As he was talking about Patricia, he understood why Alfred looked for his dad in different people.

"Your secret is safe with me. I appreciate you being so candid with me. Where is Ms. Sharp from? I think she has a slight British accent. Is she from England?" Alfred asked.

"Yes, she is from a small village located southeast of London. Her accent is mixed Cockney and English," Steve answered.

"I didn't ask the most important question yet. Do you know why your dad cloned you?" Alfred asked.

"That's the million-dollar question. Actually, it may be a multi-million-dollar question. Pat told me that initially Dad wanted to clone my mom. When he was told that the clone starts as a newborn baby, he decided to clone me. He wanted more kids with my mom. He loved her so much that he could not bear the idea of having children with another woman. By having more kids, he wanted to make sure that her legacy would stay alive," Steve explained.

"So he was creating Horcruxes, right?" Alfred asked.

"I wouldn't go that far. First of all, in those days, the word Horcrux didn't exist. There was no *Harry Potter* then. Second of all, that word is connected with dark magic. Therefore, any association of that word with me makes me uncomfortable. Having said that, I must confess that my dad is capable of doing things that will remind you of the Dark Lord, the-one-who-should-not-be-named," Steve clarified with a laugh.

"Sorry, I didn't want to invoke Lord Voldemort when talking about your dad. That's not why I used the word Horcrux. I was just joking."

"I know that. I had a brother named Chuck. I think he might have been a clone too. He passed away at about six months of age."

"I came across his name on the Internet. By the way, I am sorry about Stephanie. I should not have met her like that," Alfred said.

"That's okay. Steph can take care of herself. She told me everything. Sorry, she kicked you so hard. She is something. After you met her, we have devised a plan to make sure she is with me and not with you or any other clone that my dad and his crazy assistants may have created. Although, Pat informed me that except you there is no other clone," Steve replied.

"Well, you don't have to worry about me. I can guarantee that I don't want to deceive her again. I learned my lesson."

"I am curious about something, Alfred," Steve mentioned.

"What is it?" Alfred asked.

"How did you prove that we are clones?"

"Oh, that's a long story. But, essentially, I had to take a sample to analyze your DNA. While you were in Beth Israel Hospital few weeks ago, I worked there in house-keeping. One evening, I entered your room and pretended that I was from the lab and I needed some samples. You were heavily sedated. I asked you to spit in a cup. I had a beard and moustache on so no one thought we looked alike," Alfred explained.

"That's sneaky and illegal," Steve answered. "Oh, so that's where you have seen me before."

"Yes, that day in Beth Israel Hospital when I entered your room was the only time I have seen you. Sorry for obtaining your samples under a false pretext."

"How did you know what tests were required?" Steve asked.

"I got help from a geneticist. After obtaining the samples, I mailed them to her," Alfred answered.

"So she knows that you and I are clones."

"No, not really. I didn't tell her your real name. I used the name Christopher Smith for your samples."

"How did you come with that name? It has no relation with my name," Steve wondered.

"I used Christopher because it is the first name of Columbus, in whose honor this city was named. I used the last name Smith because it's the most common last name. By the way, it reminds me of what my geneticist told me. She wants more samples from both of us to compare the DNA for confirmation," Alfred said to him.

"Very interesting. You apologize for taking a sample of my DNA surreptitiously and then you tell me that you want another sample!" Steve said.

"Yes, again sorry to put it that way, but I had to send the first sample under an assumed name. My geneticist, Dr. Lawson, wants another sample with correct names. She is planning to publish the results in a scientific journal," Alfred explained.

"You can send the prescription or the kit to me, and I will take care of the samples," Steve assured Alfred.

"I think it will be best if you make an appointment with Dr. Lawson. She is in Cleveland Clinic. She can obtain some history from you and personally take the sample. I will also do the same soon."

"Good. That's fine with me. Bye, Alfred," Steve said.

"Bye, Steve," Alfred answered.

*   *   *

After his meeting with Alfred, Steve called Stephanie. He told her that he FaceTimed with Alfred. He enjoyed talking to him, but he did not see the resemblance between him and Alfred to the extent other people saw. He even sounded different than him, but that was expected.

Stephanie told him, "The reason you do not see the resemblance between you and Alfred is simple. You are talking about two different persons here. When you saw Alfred on FaceTime, you were looking at yourself. But when you see your reflection in the mirror, you see Narcissus."

"Very funny," Steve said to her. "That's not even how the mythology mentions Narcissus."

"Like I care," Stephanie answered laughing. "If I can identify myself as a normal woman, I can twist anything to suit my needs."

"You *are* a normal woman. No one thinks otherwise. You know, you are making a bigger deal of your genetic condition than you should," Steve responded.

"Steve, again, like I care," Stephanie answered.

Next day, Steve talked to Pat about his FaceTime with Alfred. He told her about Alfred's desire to be part of the family and his lack of interest in his dad's money and his frustration with identity because he did not know his father.

"Steve, how did it feel when you looked at Alfred? I don't know how many people get a chance to stare at their clone?" Pat asked.

"You know, Pat, it's funny. We are supposed to look alike, but I don't think we do. Other than some similarities, I can't see him as my clone."

"Steve, I think the reason is simple. When you look in the mirror, you see a mirror-image of yourself, so right and left sides of your face are switched. We believe that our face is symmetrical, but in reality it's not. There are always subtle differences between the two sides of our face. So when you see yourself in the mirror, you are actually seeing your right side as your left side and vice versa. When you see yourself in a photograph you are seeing your face the way it actually is. That's why people think that they look different in their photographs. In pictures, they appear correctly, but they don't see themselves in the pictures as often as they see themselves in the mirror. So when you saw Alfred, it was somewhat like looking at your photograph," Pat explained to him.

"Pat, your explanation is better than the one Stephanie gave me. She told me that the reason I think we don't look alike is because when I look in the mirror, I see Narcissus," Steve replied.

"That's funny. But Stephanie is wrong. You don't look like Narcissus. Narcissus was very handsome," Pat said laughing.

"Sure, join Steph in mocking me."

"Steve, do you think Alfred sounds like you?" Pat asked.

"No, he doesn't. I think he has a slight Canadian accent. But difference in speech, I can understand. I don't see how cloning would make us sound similar."

"That's true. I think with little training, he could sound like you," Patricia said. Then immediately she screamed, "Oh my God. Don't tell anyone what I just said. I am still thinking of him as your copy instead of as an individual. No wonder he has problems with identity. Please don't say a word about this to him. I should treat him as his own man and not as someone's clone. I am sorry. It was a horrible thing to say."

Then she continued, "Anyway, just as we see ourselves differently, we also hear ourselves differently. When we speak, our sound is conducted through air as well as through our skull bones. So we hear our own sound as a combination of the sounds conducted via air and bones. The quality of sound conducted by bone is different. Therefore, when we hear our speech through a recording, it sounds different to us because then the sound is conducted through air only. Of course, the recording device itself produces some variations. But to other people, it sounds similar. So our perception of our looks and our speech are different than those of others." Pat clarified.

"Wow, I didn't know that. How come you know all these things?" Steve asked.

"It's not difficult. You would know a lot too if you would pick up a book occasionally," Pat laughed.

"Yes," Steve said and then under his breath, he added, "Mom."

"What! What did you say?" Pat asked.

"Oh, I said, yes . . . ma'am," Steve corrected himself.

"That's funny. I thought you said, 'Yes, Mom.' Must be my mistake," Pat answered.

"Must be," Steve answered. Pat looked at him with an odd expression.

"Bye, Steve."

"Bye, Pat."

*   *   *

Steve thought about what Alfred had told him. He respected Alfred for not being influenced by his dad's money. When his dad tried to buy him off, Alfred had enough integrity to not let that happen. He remembered what his dad had told him when he asked him about Alfred. Dad had told him that he would discover his identity when he spends some time in an unemployment line.

Essentially, his dad had told him that he was dependent on his money. In other words, his dad saw him as if he were one of his possessions; something that could be bought. Steve was shocked when he reached that conclusion. Obviously, his clone had more integrity than he had. How can he continue living under his dad's roof when he didn't agree with his ethics? He was an adult. It's about time he made his own decisions. All his life, he lived in the shadow of his powerful dad. Every aspect of his life was managed by people working for his dad. He had not lifted a finger to do anything in his life. Stephanie's dad was right about him. He had no personality. He had not thought about his future. He had accepted that, at some point in his life, he would join his dad's business. He must get out of this predetermined life. Whether he makes it in the real world or not, it should be on his own terms.

Steve called Stephanie. He told her, "Steph, I want to tell you something. I don't know whether you will like it or not."

"Steve, what is it?"

"I have made a decision. I am leaving my dad. You know Alfred told my dad that he was not interested in his money. I'm not interested in it either. I am leaving his house, his car, and everything that is his. What do you think?" Steve asked her.

"Steve, whatever you want to do, I will support you. What did your dad say when you told him?"

"I have not told him yet. I wanted you to know it first. I am going to tell him soon. I'll have to find an apartment and a job."

"That's good. I think your dad's money is tainted. If you want to stay away from him and his money, then there's nothing wrong with it," Stephanie agreed with his decision.

Steve packed up some important papers in a bag. He took a picture of his mother and some pictures of his childhood. Then he went to the living room. Mr. Kincaid was watching news on television. Steve sat down next to him. From his facial expression, Mr. Kincaid could tell something was up.

"Steve, what's going on? Are you all right?"

"I'm fine, Dad. No, I am not fine. Dad, I have made a decision. I want to leave this house. I want to live on my own," Steve blurted out.

"Why? What's going on? Listen, I'm sorry for what I said. I didn't mean it. If you want me to do anything, I will do it.'

"No, Dad, that's not it. I want to live on my own. I am an adult and it's about time I act like one."

"It's about Alfred, isn't it? If you want me to accept him as part of this family, I will do it," Dad was softening up.

"Dad, it's too late now. I am leaving my phone here so if you need to get in touch with me, you can email me," Steve told him. Then he hugged his dad awkwardly and left. As he left the room, Steve glanced one last time at his dad. He saw a man who had cared for him all his life, who had spent sleepless nights when he was sick, and a man who had always worried for his son's welfare. For a moment, Steve felt guilty leaving his dad. But then he also saw a man who was arrogant, a man who had no morals, a man who took pleasure in ruining lives of people just because he could do it, a man who measured everything by money, and a man for whom everyone around him was a mere pawn. Steve was not feeling guilty anymore. He knew he had made a right decision.

Mr. Kincaid was too stunned to say anything. By the time he realized what had happened, Steve was gone. Alfred had declined his offer of millions of dollars a few days ago and now the rightful heir of his billions was rejecting his fair share. *What is this world coming to?* he wondered.

Steve didn't know what he would do and where he would stay. He spent a night at YMCA. He called Stephanie the following morning from a payphone and told her how things went the night before with his dad. Stephanie told him that he did the right thing. She suggested coming to her place and staying with her.

"No, if I live with you, then it will be your dad supporting me instead of mine. So I can't do that," Steve explained.

"That's true. You are absolutely right. Steve, I have an idea. It's about time I live on my own too. Together, we can build a life of our own. How about that!" Stephanie was excited.

"No, I can't let you do that. Why do you want to interrupt your career?"

"Steve, we can both build our careers with our own labor. Of course, it will take longer, but it will be worth the wait. Also, you better agree with me. Do you remember what happened to Alfred when he got on my nerves?"

"Yes, I do remember. Since that day, I am also afraid of you," Steve joked. "I think it's a great idea."

Stephanie told her parents that she was leaving them. They tried to talk her out of it, but she was not going to change her mind. Her dad knew that if she was going to do it, then no one could stop her.

He confessed that Steve had more guts than he ever gave him credit for. Stephanie was happy to hear that. Before she left the house, her dad told her, "Steph, be careful. You and Steve are going to live together. If you are not careful, you will get pregnant before you know it."

Stephanie looked at him in bewilderment, "Dad, you know I can't get pregna—"

He was laughing. For a second, she thought that her dad forgot she can't get pregnant. When she saw him laughing, she realized that her dad was just joking, and he was proud of her decision. She also realized that finally her dad had come to terms with her genetic condition.

Stephanie and Steve rented a one-bedroom apartment. They dropped out of college and started looking for jobs. They didn't care if people would find out that Mr. Kincaid's son was living in a small apartment and was looking for a job paying minimum wage. They were lucky to remain incognito when they started a new phase of their lives. Unfortunately, it lasted only two days, literally.

26

From South Korea . . . With Love

We've discovered the secret of life.

— FRANCIS CRICK, CO-DISCOVERER OF STRUCTURE OF DNA

After his FaceTime with Steve, Alfred decided it was time to talk to Brittany. A few days later, he went to her home and knocked on the door. Her dad, Anthony Wilson, opened the door. Alfred was clean-shaved. Mr. Wilson did not know that Alfred was Steven Kincaid's clone, so he thought Steven Kincaid was at the door. He was surprised to see him.

"Hi, can I help you? Are you Steven Kincaid?" Mr. Wilson asked.

"Mr. Wilson, I am not Steven Kincaid. I am Brittany's friend Alfred, Alfred Johnson. I have met you before, but that time I had a moustache and a beard. Is Brittany home?" Alfred clarified.

"Oh, Alfred! I recognize you from your voice. You look like that Kinkaid Kid. That's odd. She is home, but I don't know if she would want to see you," he replied.

"Sir, I know she is upset with me, but I must speak to her. There are certain things I need to discuss with her," Alfred clarified.

"Alfred, Sun has been devastated since the last time she saw you."

"Who is Sun?" Alfred asked.

"Oh, I meant Brittany. At home we call her Sun. Why don't you come in?" Mr. Wilson let him in. Alfred remembered that Brittany's first name was Sun.

Brittany's mom, Lisa, was sitting in the living room. "Lisa, Alfred has come to see Sun. Since we are mad at him, he even disguised himself by shaving his face. Now he looks like Steven Kincaid." He seemed pleased with the joke he made. Lisa was also surprised to see that Alfred looked like Steven Kincaid.

"I didn't know at home she goes by her Korean name," Alfred said to him.

"Actually, we just started doing it," Mr. Wilson said.

"Honey, Alfred doesn't need to know all that," Lisa told her husband. Then she told Alfred, "You really do look a lot like Steven Kincaid? You know who Steven Kincaid is, right?"

"Yes, I know who he is and I also know we look alike," Alfred answered a bit put off.

"Does Sun know you look like Steven? Oh my God! She mentioned to me that there were some issues you were dealing with. Is Steven Kincaid one of them?" This realization shocked her.

"Mrs. Wilson, I don't know what Brittany, I mean Sun, has told you about me. I prefer that it comes from her rather than me. Can I please talk to her?" Alfred was uncomfortable. He wished he had not shaved his beard and moustache or at least had fake moustache and beard on.

Mrs. Wilson called Brittany. She came down. As soon as she saw Alfred, she screamed. "Why are you here? What do you want?"

"Sun definitely knows that he looks like Steven Kincaid," Mr. Wilson exclaimed!

"Brittany, I want to talk to you. Can we talk privately?" He pleaded.

"No, you can talk to me in front of my parents. It's about time they know what's going on," Brittany was firm.

"Okay, I will try."

Alfred took out a package from his pocket. It was giftwrapped. He gave it to Brittany and told her, "This is something I have brought for you as a peace-offering. Whether you like what I am going to tell you or not, I hope you will accept this small gift."

Brittany took the package and opened it. There was a small vial inside the box. On the vial, it was written, "From South Korea." It looked like it contained dirt. Brittany's face was beaming.

"Is it what I think it is?" she asked excitedly.

"Yes. It sure is. I hope you like it."

"I love it. Thank you for a lovely and thoughtful gift," she answered. Her demeanor changed instantly.

"Sun, what is it? It looks like dirt to me," Mrs. Wilson asked.

"Mom, *it is dirt*. It's from South Korea. I had told Alfred about our visit to my birthplace. None of you know this, but while I was in the orphanage, I went to the playground behind the main building. I took my shoes and socks off and stood barefoot on the ground. I wanted my feet to touch the Korean soil. I told Alfred about it. That's why he brought some dirt from South Korea for me," Brittany explained. "How did you manage to get it?"

"Long story. My roommate knows a Korean student in OSU. Upon my request, he talked to him who managed it through someone who was returning from his vacation in South Korea. I had to explain why I wanted it. Now, can we talk privately?" Alfred asked again.

"No, Alfred, say whatever you want to say right here. You can talk about anything. It's all right if you want to explain why you and Steven Kincaid look alike. I have no secrets from my parents."

"All right, if that's what you want. Mr. and Mrs. Wilson, I will tell you something that may be shocking. Please try to understand me before making any judgment. Steven Kincaid and I are clones. Actually, I am his clone. After his birth, his mom passed away. His dad wanted more children, so he cloned him. He . . ."

"Hold on, I have not heard of any such thing as cloning in human beings. Are you sure you know what you are talking about? Maybe, you guys are twins," Mr. Wilson interrupted.

"No sir. I have checked everything. My mother was hired as a surrogate woman by Mr. Kincaid's attorney, but she didn't know that she was to give birth to a clone. While she was pregnant, she decided to keep the baby. To avoid legal problems, she ran away to Canada. Long story short, I grew up there without knowing that I was a clone. When Steven Kincaid had the skiing accident, his pictures were on news. That's when I found out that he and I looked similar. I have done genetic tests to confirm that we are clones," Alfred explained.

"How did you get genetic sample from Steven? Did you tell him what was going on?" Brittany was curious.

"When last time we met at the McDonald's, Steven was admitted into Beth Israel Hospital. As you know, I used to work there. I obtained his sample from the hospital without his knowledge."

"That's a crime. You definitely have Kincaid blood," Mr. Kincaid joked.

"Dad, please," Brittany was annoyed at her dad for trivializing everything. Then she looked at Alfred and asked, "Do you remember that time I was telling you about mitochondrial DNA?"

"Yes, I remember," Alfred answered.

"Well, before I could tell you more about it, you showed me your picture and told me that you may be Steven Kincaid's clone. The mitochondrial DNA is..."

"Wait a minute. What DNA you are talking about? I don't follow," Mr. Wilson interrupted her.

"Honey, she can tell us later. Right now, why don't you let them talk?" Mrs. Wilson admonished her husband.

"No, that's okay. Actually, it's very interesting," Brittany was excited to talk about it anyway. "You know, Dad, besides the DNA on our chromosomes, we have some DNA material on our mitochondria. Scientists used to believe that we have about hundred thousand genes on our chromosomes. Now they have estimated that we have about 20,000 genes. On mitochondria there are only thirty-seven genes. Mitochondria are small organelles in our cells. There are thousands of mitochondria in each cell. They produce energy for the cells."

"Sun, what have mitochondria to do with cloning?" Mr. Wilson was confused.

"I am coming to that in a minute," Brittany answered. "Mitochondria are believed to be organelles, which were engulfed by cells. They are the 'powerhouses of the cells'. It is believed that chloroplasts in plants and mitochondria in plants and animals were independent cells or organelles and were engulfed by plant and animal cells millions of years ago. They are examples of endosymbiosis. Chloroplasts and mitochondria have independent genome, which is similar to the bacterial genome," Brittany explained.

Then she turned to Alfred and asked, "Do you know who proposed the theory that mitochondria were independent cells and were engulfed by plant and animal cells?"

"No, I have no clue," Alfred confessed. Of course, Brittany had to say everything.

"It was a biologist named Lynn Margulis. She was once married to the famous astronomer Carl Sagan." *Brittany always comes with interesting anecdotes*, Alfred thought.

"So long story short, DNA in chromosomes is separate from the DNA in mitochondria. When a clone is created, scientists take the cells from the animal or the person who is to be cloned. Then they take the ovum or egg from a female of the species. Ovum contains literally hundreds of thousands of mitochondria. A sperm contains only up to one thousand mitochondria. So when the fertilization occurs, the offspring receives half of the chromosomes from each parent. But, amazingly enough, in most cases, the offspring receives mitochondrial DNA only from the mother.

"Now, I will tell you what it has to do with your quest. You know there is a major difference between an identical twin and a clone? Identical twins share same DNA, including mitochondrial DNA, whereas, clones could have different mitochondrial DNA."

"That's interesting. I always thought that cloning is exact genetic replica of the original." Lisa was very excited now.

"That's what most people think too," Brittany explained.

"I remember something like what you said about mitochondria from my biology class," Alfred said. "Dr. Lawson, my geneticist, explained a little bit about it too."

"A boy or a girl receives one of each of the twenty-two pairs of chromosomes from each parent. A boy receives an X and a Y chromosome from the mother and father, respectively. A girl receives an X chromosome from each parent. But, regardless of the gender, the offspring receives mitochondrial DNA from the mother only. In fact, you can detect a person's maternal lineage by studying his or her mtDNA. Mitochondrial DNA is called mtDNA in short," Brittany's face was red as she was talking about this.

"That's something I didn't know," Mr. Wilson confessed.

"Dad, let me tell you about an interesting research project done based on mtDNA. It has to do with golden hamsters. Thousands of these animals are used in the laboratories across the United States. Many people keep golden hamsters as pets. Scientists investigated the ancestry of these creatures. With the use of mtDNA, they have concluded that maternal lineage of these animals can be traced back to one female golden hamster captured in Syria in the year 1930."

"Dr. Lawson explained to me about mtDNA, but I was dazed because I had just learned I was a clone," Alfred replied.

"He is already talking about birds and bees with our daughter," Mr. Wilson joked.

"If the egg used in the cloning process came from someone other than the biological mother of the original animal or person then the mtDNA would be different. If it came from the mother then it would be same," Brittany continued. "Did Dr. Lawson tell you whether you and Steve have different mtDNA?"

"Yes, she did. She discovered that our mtDNAs are from different persons," Alfred answered. Then he continued, "You know, I went to see Mr. Kincaid. I met him and his associate Patricia Sharp. I told them that I was Steve's clone. He didn't want to even acknowledge that his son was cloned. I told him that I have genetic tests to prove that. So he asked what I wanted. I told him that I just wanted to know who I was. I wanted recognition. He told me that he could understand that I was deprived of a life of living in a mansion and all that. He offered me millions of dollars," Alfred was explaining. Hearing this, Brittany's expressions changed. She was anxious to know what happened.

Alfred continued, "I got mad at him. I told him I would rather have him give me a fifty-dollar gift on Christmas than a bribe of millions of dollars to keep my mouth shut. He didn't get it. I told him when he understands what I was talking about, he can call me. Then, I talked to Steven. I assured him that I was not interested in his inheritance. I just wanted to be a part of his family."

"You know what kind of a person Mr. Kincaid is. Why in a million years you would want to be a part of his family?" Mrs. Wilson wondered.

"I understand your question. I want to know and embrace my roots irrespective of what they are. I certainly don't want Mr. Kincaid's money. Where I came from was not in my control, but I want to accept it because my roots tell me who I am. Whether to accept his money or not is within my control and I choose not to. I hope that answers your question, Mrs. Wilson?" Alfred replied.

"Yes, kind of," Lisa answered. "Obviously you have thought about it for a long time before coming to this conclusion. As long as you are comfortable with it there is nothing wrong in it."

"How was your meeting with Steven Kincaid?" Brittany asked.

"It went well. I told him about my meeting with his dad. I mentioned that his dad offered me lot of money and that I rejected his offer. Steve told me that his dad couldn't understand anything except money. He told me he would love to have me as a member of his family. Two days ago, he called me and told me that he has left his dad's home and is living with his girlfriend in an apartment."

"Have you met his girlfriend?" Mrs. Wilson asked.

Alfred hesitated for a moment. This was a touchy subject. He decided to come clean. He explained that he wanted to teach a lesson to Mr. Kincaid and to his son. To embarrass them, he met Stephanie pretending he was Steven. He told them what happened. He even mentioned how she hit him.

"Good for her; you deserved it," Mrs. Wilson told him.

"Mom, please don't be harsh on him; that's my job," Brittany scolded her. Then she looked at Alfred and told him, "Alfred, I understand what you did. I am glad that you are not a sellout. It's not easy to ignore millions of dollars, but I wouldn't touch Mr. Kincaid's money even if I were starving to death," Brittany declared.

"Alfred, clone or not, you are a good egg," Mr. Wilson said and chuckled.

"He sure is," Mrs. Wilson agreed. Then she told Alfred, "Alfred, it was nice of you to come and make peace with Sun. I am proud of you because you turned down Mr. Kincaid's money. That shows your character."

"Thank, Mrs. Wilson," Alfred answered.

Brittany got up and hugged Alfred. "Alfred, I am glad you stood up to Mr. Kincaid. You are my hero."

"Did he really offer you millions of dollars?" Mr. Wilson asked.

"Yes, Sir, he did. I explained to him that I grew up not knowing who I really was. I am searching for my roots, and I am not interested in his money. He didn't get it," Alfred explained.

"Alfred, Mr. Kincaid makes Donald Trump look like an angel," Mrs. Wilson told him.

Brittany's phone beeped. There was a text message. She glanced at it and gasped. "Oh my God!"

Mrs. Wilson asked, "What happened? Why are you so shocked?"

Brittany did not answer but picked up the remote control and turned on the TV. She switched the channel. The local news program was being broadcast. Then she announced, "I got a text from Marilyn, from the library. It says that in the news headlines, they just mentioned something about Alfred Johnson being Mr. Kincaid's illegitimate son. She asked me to watch the news."

Everyone had their eyes fixed on TV. In few moments, the news anchor broadcast the story. There were pictures of Alfred with his fake moustache and beard and his pictures without any facial hair with Steven's pictures juxtaposed to his, and a video footage showing him walking out of his apartment building. The story mentioned that *National Gossip Weekly* had investigated the story of Mr. Kincaid's illegitimate son named Alfred Johnson. The story claimed that possibly he was blackmailing Mr. Kincaid for money. It also mentioned that Steven Kincaid has left his dad's mansion because his dad has an illegitimate son. While the news was going on, everyone except Alfred was on their Smartphones surfing the Internet to find more information. There were exclamations from

Brittany and her parents. Alfred sat there quietly. A man at peace with himself.

The cat was out of the bag, finally. Whatever Alfred was planning for his future will be affected by this new reality. He knew instantly that paparazzi would begin stalking him. His days of living an anonymous life were over for good. But in the face of all these changes, he felt a sense of relief. It did not matter if people thought he and Steve were twins or siblings or whatever. It did not matter if people thought he was blackmailing Mr. Kincaid. Everything will fall in its place in due time. When the news broadcast about him and Steven was over, Brittany and her parents advised him on how he should handle this situation. Alfred thanked them and left.

After he reached home, Alfred thought about his maternal heritage. He remembered Dr. Lawson saying something about his mitochondrial DNA not showing any differences from the reference DNA or something. While she was explaining that he could not focus because he was digesting the fact that he was indeed a clone of Steven Kincaid.

The next morning, he called Dr. Lawson. By now, she had heard about the news of Alfred Johnson possibly being related to Steven Kincaid. She asked Alfred if the other samples came from Steven Kincaid. Alfred answered in affirmative.

"So it looks like you are his clone. Man, that's heavy. Can you explain to me how all this happened?" Dr. Lawson asked.

Alfred briefly explained why Mr. Kincaid had cloned his son, how the surrogate mother ran away to Canada and how he suspected that he was related to Steven Kincaid. He also told her how he took samples from Steve.

"Has Steve contacted you?"

"Yes. I have talked to him before the news came out yesterday. He was glad to talk to me. He also agreed to see you and give samples for repeat tests."

"That will be great. I would love to meet him."

"Dr. Lawson, I don't know about my maternal inheritance. You mentioned something about the other person having Native American blood from his mother's side. You also explained something about my sample not showing any differences. Can you explain it again?" Alfred asked.

"Sure, it's very interesting. Mitochondrial DNA in the sample with your name shows the so-called revised Cambridge Reference Sequence or rCRS. The name indicates that this genome sequence is used to compare other mitochondrial DNA samples to detect differences. It does not imply that it is supposed to be a normal DNA sequence. These differences are not necessarily mutations. People of European ancestry are more likely to have this type of mtDNA," Dr. Lawson explained. Immediately Alfred thought about Patricia Sharp. I must find who the egg donor was, he resolved. He thanked Dr. Lawson for her help and hung up.

27

Mitochondrial DNA

It's true that I run a multi-national group, but I have no interests in India. So please tell me, what should my identity be.

— LAKSHMI MITTAL, BUSINESSMAN OF INDIAN ORIGIN

Alfred called Patricia. He asked if she would talk to him privately. Patricia agreed to meet him because she wanted to know him better. After all, as an egg donor, she had contributed to his birth. She had also secretly helped Alfred and Angela with Edna's support. Question was— where could they meet? There were paparazzi outside of Alfred's apartment, Patricia's home, and where Steven and Stephanie lived. There was one location, which provided some privacy. With Mr. Newman's permission, they decided to meet at his office.

Alfred drove to his lawyer's office. The paparazzi followed him. Several minutes later, Patricia also arrived with nosy reporters following her. After preliminary chitchat, Mr. Newman left the room.

"Ms. Sharp, thank you for coming. I was getting nervous," Alfred confessed.

"Why should you be nervous? And, please call me Pat," Patricia tried to make him feel at ease.

"Okay, Pat. I don't know why I am nervous. You know my meeting with Mr. Kincaid did not go well. Since you work for Mr. Kincaid, I thought you may not want to talk to me."

As soon as she heard Alfred's comment, Patricia felt sad. She had developed a special respect for this young man because he was a man of integrity. How many times you will meet someone who was not interested in a ten-million-dollar bribe? She was also shocked at the callousness of Mr. Kincaid for not being able to understand where Alfred was coming from. Now, when Alfred tried to associate her with Mr. Kincaid, she resented it. She had practically adored Michael Kincaid since she had started working for him. She was blinded by his vision and his personality. She was not in love with him; it was more like she worshiped him. Even when her then-husband John tried to warn her about Mr. Kincaid, her respect for him had not wavered. Then one day, this teenager came from nowhere, declined an offer of millions of dollars and put the person she had idolized in his place. Now by associating her with Mr. Kincaid, he was treating her as if she was also like him.

She regained her composure. "Alfred, my meeting with you has nothing to do with my job. You can tell me what's on your mind."

"Pat, I am trying to figure out who I really am. Steve and I are clones, but part of our DNA does not match. I don't know how much you know about genetics, but clones are not necessarily exact genetic copies of each other. To put some pieces of the puzzle together, I want to know who was involved in this process." Alfred explained.

"Why do you think I would know the answers to these questions?" Patricia asked.

"Well, I have done my homework. I have learned a lot about the last two decades of Mr. Kincaid's life. You have been with him even before Steve was born. When Mr. Kincaid decided to clone Steve, you were working as his personal assistant. You would certainly know what was going on at the time. By the way, let us accept that we are dealing with cloning. Let's not beat around the bush regarding that. Can you tell me the name of the scientist who cloned Steve?"

"As part of my job, I can't reveal any such thing even if I knew about it."

"That's fair. I appreciate your loyalty to Mr. Kincaid." She did not like the word loyalty when it referred to her work relations with Michael Kincaid. She almost decided to tell him everything, but she stopped herself from running with that impulse.

"Alfred, I think I should leave now. Call me if you need anything else," Pat said as she was getting up.

"Pat, please sit down. May I ask something that's bothering me?" Alfred stopped her.

"Go ahead, ask me," Pat said as she was sitting down.

"How could you do this? How could someone like you work with Michael Kincaid for all these years? Didn't you ever think of leaving him? Didn't anyone advise you to leave him?" Alfred asked.

"Is that what you want to ask me? I think it's between me and Mr. Kincaid to figure out. If there is nothing else you want to say, then I am leaving," Pat was mad because Alfred was crossing the line. Patricia had been thinking of leaving Mr. Kincaid, but when Alfred mentioned that she got mad.

Despite her anger and frustration, Patricia remembered that Edna should get a chance to see Alfred. "Before I leave, I should tell you that Lucy's mother, Edna Dent, wants to see you. From the time Angela absconded to Canada, she has been worried about you. Edna considers you her family," Pat said to Alfred.

"Thanks. I have come across her name while searching for information about Mr. Kincaid. I would love to meet her too. Speaking of Steve's grandmother, I want to ask another question. You can answer if you think it's appropriate. If you don't answer it, it won't hurt my feelings. I told Mr. Kincaid that Lucy had Native American heritage. Is that true?" Alfred asked.

Patricia deliberated the answer for a few moments. Then she told him, "Yes, Alfred. You were right about it. Edna's maternal grandmother was Native American. Possibly Lucy never knew about it."

"How do I contact Mrs. Edna Dent?" Alfred asked. Patricia wrote down Edna's phone number on a piece of paper and gave it to Alfred. Shift of conversation from Mr. Kincaid to Edna, made Patricia more comfortable.

"I understand that the geneticist discovered Lucy's maternal inheritance by investigating Steven's mitochondrial DNA. I want to ask you something. What did your mitochondrial DNA show? If you don't mind, please tell me," Patricia asked.

"Sure, I don't have any problem sharing that information with you. My mitochondrial DNA has what is called, rCRS or Revised Cambridge Reference Sequence."

"Oh, I am surprised! So for the purposes of determining genealogy, the differences or mutations are measured against this so-called reference sequence, right?" Patricia asked.

"Yes, that's how I understand it. How do you know this?" Alfred was curious.

"After you came to see Mr. Kincaid, I looked it up. I wanted to learn how you discovered Lucy's genetic inheritance. It's a very interesting science," Patricia answered.

Patricia started thinking. John had told her that she didn't have a personality; that she had knowledge, but no opinion; that she was like a girl in awe of some Greek demigod whose worship was her only goal in life. She was devoid of personal ambitions. She was like a blank slate. She was a reference person who knew everything and helped others with her knowledge but did not know what to do with her own life. Now her mtDNA was a reference by which others could be compared. There was nothing exotic, nothing unique about her. It was about time she stood up for something.

Alfred had suspicions regarding Patricia's role in the cloning process. Ever since Dr. Lawson explained to him about revised Cambridge Reference Sequence and that it was sequenced from a woman of European descent, he was suspecting that his mitochondrial genes might have come from Patricia. He had to ask her directly.

"Pat, after I FaceTimed with Steve, I discussed with my geneticist about mtDNA. A question has been bothering me since then. You may be able to answer that. If you don't want to answer, I will understand."

"What do you want to know, Alfred?" Patricia tentatively asked.

"Did I inherit mitochondrial DNA from you? In other words, did you donate your eggs to clone Steven Kincaid?"

Alfred could see the signs of struggle on her face. Alfred hated that he was putting her through this ordeal.

If I want to be loyal to Mr. Kincaid at all costs, I should not answer the question. If I want to be my own woman, I should decide on the merits of the question itself. After all, I had helped Steve all his life and supported Alfred with Edna's help as and when I could. This is the moment. It is about time I thought of myself. She decided to come clean.

"Yes, Alfred, your suspicion is right. When Mr. Kincaid decided on cloning, I volunteered to donate eggs. I also was one of the women participating in the process and two of us, Angela and I, delivered babies. The baby I delivered was named Chuck. He died when he was a few months old. You deserve to know it," Patricia revealed the big secret. She felt a sense of relief after being frank with Alfred. A thousand pounds had been lifted off her shoulders.

"Wow, I don't know what to say. I feel like I am honored to have your genes. You are a very nice person. Steve also was full of praise when he talked about you."

"Thank you, Alfred."

"Pat, can you tell me who the scientist behind the cloning was? I didn't come across any names in my research on human cloning," Alfred asked.

"The geneticist who cloned Steve has disappeared. So his name is not important. I believe he worked under an assumed name when we contacted him. He may still be working with a different name and at a different location. Now, call your grandma. She wants to see you," Patricia said as she was getting up. Alfred got off his chair also. Then, he hugged Patricia.

"Alfred, dear, I can tell you one thing before I leave. I am going to leave Mr. Kincaid. I wish I had done it sooner, but your words have helped me make that decision. I have seen you only twice so far, but you have made me see what no one else was able to show me," Patricia promised him and left. *If I had, John would not have left me.*

So it was Patricia Sharp whose genes he was carrying. It was a very small part of his whole genome; nevertheless, it was a significant part. The quest for his identity was finally complete. Alfred sat in his chair for a few minutes. He had to let the information sink in. Then he called Edna. Fifteen minutes later he knocked on her door. The paparazzi were following him, but he didn't care. Edna opened the door and gave him a hug. Alfred felt that she was never going to let him go. They both had tears in their eyes. After a long minute, she released her grip.

"Oh my, you are so handsome!" Edna exclaimed. "I wish I had spent as much time with you as I have with Steve."

"I would have liked it too," Alfred agreed.

"My daughter's death has destroyed this man. He was so different while Lucy was alive," Edna lamented.

"I know. Thank you for accepting me as family," Alfred told her.

"Of course, you are family. For me you are as much a grandson as Steve is. Pat and I have talked about you a lot. Ever since that crooked lawyer, Mr. Drake, tried to kidnap you, I have been worried about you. I tried to talk Mike out of it, but Mr. Drake had some weird control over him."

"Well, you still did whatever you could," Alfred mentioned.

"Oh yes, I tried my best to thwart their plans. I made calls to Angela to warn her about Mr. Drake. I even sent her money every now and then. I could not reveal my name to her because I didn't want them to find out that Patricia and I were trying to save you."

"I understand. I can't thank you enough for your help. Can you tell me about your daughter? I would like to know more about her," Alfred requested.

"Sure, you have every right to know about her. She was a beautiful woman and a very successful model," Edna replied.

"How was she as a child?" Alfred asked her.

"She was cute and funny. Let me show you her pictures," Edna told him while getting off the couch. She left the room and came back with some photo albums. She showed him Lucy's pictures from her childhood. Edna also told Alfred about Lucy's life, her likes, her dislikes, that she wet her bed until she was four years old, that she would hide broccoli in her napkin while having dinner, and so on. Alfred loved to hear about Lucy's childhood.

"You know, Lucy would check under her bed for monsters before going to bed every night. It was so weird," Edna said to Alfred.

"I am sure many kids do that," Alfred found it normal.

"Lucy was afraid of monsters even as an adult. Mike always laughed at her when she would look under her bed before going to sleep," Edna explained in between her laughs. Alfred found it funny too.

"What is she doing with a pen and a notepad in her hand?" Alfred asked, pointing at a picture.

"Oh, when she was three, she would walk around with a pen and a notepad pretending to write down everything she heard. It was funny. All she could do was draw some lines on a paper. We all joked that Lucy would be a reporter when she grew up."

Then Edna told him about Malina, her maternal grandmother who was Native American. She told him that when her mother was an infant, Malina had passed away so no one had any direct knowledge about her. After spending some time with Edna and one more hug, Alfred finally went home.

28

The Bimbos and the Bastards

I don't cover my face because I want to show my identity.

— MALALA YOUSAFZAI, ACTIVIST AND HUMANITARIAN

Within days after the scandal of an illegitimate child broke, there were rumors flying everywhere. Mr. Kincaid wanted damage control done before it was too late. True to his self, he came up with a master plan.

The day after meeting Alfred, Patricia came to work late. She could not sleep much the night before. She came to quit her job. She had made up her mind. As soon as she got there, her assistant handed her coffee and told her that Mr. Kincaid wanted to see her for some urgent business.

She walked to his office with her coffee. She wanted to tell him she was leaving. She didn't care what urgent business he wanted to talk about. As soon as she entered his office, she was surprised. Mike had invited the Board of Directors. He was discussing how to control the damage his company was suffering due to recent developments.

When Patricia got there, Mike welcomed her and asked her to take a sit. There, in front of everyone, Mike explained the plan he had concocted. He told her that he was planning to take some steps to stabilize his business and her help was essential to accomplish that. Mr. Kincaid wanted Patricia to leave the company pretending that she was disgruntled with him. Then he wanted her to give interviews and publish a book about him. He wanted her to reveal some bad things about him and at the same time defend him of the most serious allegations, like bribing politicians in the United States and abroad, hiding wealth in overseas banks, inappropriately groping and molesting women, etcetera. The list was long. He had prepared a severance package for her too. She was to receive lot of money for helping her boss. She couldn't believe her ears. Her ex-husband was right about Mike all along.

Patricia looked at the faces of the Board members. They all seemed to agree with Mike's plans. She couldn't decide whether they were puppets who were being manipulated by a ruthless dictator or they were greedy millionaires willing to do anything to prevent the company from losing any more money and their own wealth with it. If all board members would accept such nonsense, then what was the point of having them in the first place? Then she realized that either way, it didn't matter anymore. Her time was up.

Her decades-long dedication was coming to an end. It was not the way she had pictured it. How much she had sacrificed for Michael Kincaid? She had donated her eggs, bore a child for him, ended up with a divorce, and took care of his son and the clone that he had created for his own selfishness; now he wanted her to lie for him to save his neck? *So in the end, I am also just a pawn in his game!*

John was right. After Lucy's death, Mike's personality had changed. He was more like Mr. Hyde than Dr. Jekyll just as he had warned her. Every warning and every prediction her ex-husband had made about Mike came out to be true. How could she not see it for all these years? Mike's own son, Steven, had left him and had chosen to live in poverty. Alfred had spat on his money. What has she done so far? She remembered what John had told her once. He had told her to punch someone on the face if she did not like what they said rather than compromise her life to keep everyone happy. John was right.

If she was to do it, this was the time. Patricia got off her seat. She took a few steps to go near him. Then she managed to bring all the hatred she could muster to the surface. Patricia Sharp slapped Michael Kincaid across his face. There was a stunned silence in the room. No one could believe what was happening.

"Mike, I came today to quit. I can't work with you anymore. You can put the severance package where the sun does not shine for all I care. I don't want to see you again. I am not your pawn. Good-bye."

When Mike and everyone in the room came to their senses, Patricia was gone. She walked outside of the building with her coffee. She had never been prouder of herself in her whole life.

"Miss Sharp, can you tell us if Alfred Johnson and Steven Kincaid are twins?" a reporter asked her.

"No comment," she said and continued walking.

"You must know it. You have been with Mr. Kincaid for a long time," another reporter yelled at her.

She turned her head toward him. His statement associating her with Mr. Kincaid irritated her. She looked at him with contempt. She was about to spit on him but changed her mind. Instead, she threw her hot coffee on him and screamed, "I have left Mr. Kincaid. Never, ever, mention that bastard's name in my presence." She continued to walk leaving the shocked paparazzi behind her. Video of her screaming at the reporter was posted on YouTube within minutes.

*   *   *

Within days, there were reports of illegitimate kids of Mr. Kincaid. Many people came forward claiming to be his sons or daughters. As if this were not enough, Mr. Kincaid was accused of more frauds and scandals. Many stories in the media were ridiculous but they were taking a toll on his image. The stock of his company plummeted more than 40% of its value. Many of his employees left him to sell their stories involving Mr. Kincaid. Most of those stories were made up.

Beverly Myers, an interior decorator, from Miami, Florida, came forward. She alleged that she had an affair with Michael Kincaid many years ago. She claimed that those days whenever Mr. Kincaid would visit Florida, he would invite her to his hotel suite. She further stated that her son, Robert, is the product of her liaison with Mr. Kincaid. Reporters asked her why she did not come forward until now. She replied that she had a boyfriend at the time and she did not want to jeopardize her relationship with him. According to her, the boyfriend broke up with her few years later due to his suspicions that she was unfaithful. She also made it clear that the reason she was doing it now was to make sure that "my Bobby" gets his fair share of his biological father's fortune. She showed some letters written to her by Mr. Kincaid, gifts he gave her, and checks he mailed her to support her and her son. She did not want to bring Bobby on television or show his pictures. Bobby was a minor, so no newspapers or magazines published his pictures. Media found out that Ms. Myers had fallen on hard times because her business had gone down, and she was in debt. They also found out that in last fourteen years, she had two failed marriages and many short-lived relationships.

Beverly Myers demanded half of Mr. Kincaid's assets. After Michael told his lawyers about his association with Ms. Myers, they didn't want to risk a paternity test. Mr. Kincaid's lawyers negotiated with Myers and her attorney. She insisted on paternity tests to prove Bobby was Mr. Kincaid's son, but Mr. Kincaid's attorneys convinced her to drop it with an offer of fifty million dollars. There were also threats on Bobby's life from unknown sources. Due to the threats, she couldn't refuse the offer they made to settle the matter out of court. She told the media that she wanted to do what was best for Bobby.

Mr. Kincaid's office dismissed all other claims of "Bimbo eruptions" and denied Mr. Kincaid having any illegitimate children. His office mentioned that whenever Mr. Kincaid was in the news, a few bimbos and bastards came forward and tried to make some money.

Within weeks after the story of Alfred being a twin of Steven Kincaid was in the news, people learned about the truth. Betty Sue Lawson, geneticist from Cleveland Clinic, called a press conference and published the news. She had personally collected samples from Steven and Alfred and had genetics laboratories analyze them. She had confirmed beyond a shadow of a doubt that they were clones. Her article in medical journals and a book about Alfred were just weeks away from being published.

Alfred went back to Canada for few weeks. He discussed with Angela his plan to settle in Columbus. He wanted Angela to come back to Columbus too, but she refused. She was not comfortable going back to the place where she had lived the life of a God-fearing, law-abiding citizen. She was happy for Alfred and understood his desire to settle there, but for her that ship had sailed. Alfred promised to visit her often. Before leaving Toronto, he went to meet his friend Jagdish. Jagdish, his parents, and his brother, Satyu, were happy to see him. For Satyu, Alfred was a celebrity. Alfred was pleasantly surprised to see Jagdish taking interest in his brother Satyu's life. Upon returning to Columbus, he joined OSU. Brittany too joined OSU to pursue her plans to become a pediatrician.

*   *   *

News of successful cloning captivated public attention for months. Religious organizations influenced governments in most countries to make experiments on human cloning illegal. North Korea and China declined to join rest of the world. They intended to make large sums of money from people who were desperate to clone themselves or their loved ones.

Time magazine declared "a clone" as a person of the year. Incredibly, they didn't declare "a person and his clone" as persons of the year. On the cover, they put a picture of a man looking at his clone in the mirror. The man was shown in silhouette, and his clone in the mirror was Alfred Johnson. In the article, the magazine admired Alfred for his courage, integrity, and perseverance.

29

Alfred Embraces His Identity

A tree without roots is just a piece of wood.

— Marco Pierre White, British chef and
television personality

Michael Kincaid poured another glass of whiskey. He was all alone again this evening in his huge mansion just as he was every evening. His reputation had tanked, his son had deserted him, stock of his company had crashed, many of his scandals had come to surface, and he had taken to drinking. His double identity was exposed to the world.

Angela Johnson was alone in her apartment watching sitcoms. Her son Jeff was mad at her for deserting him while she was trying to keep Alfred. His resentment for his mom had increased since the story came out that Alfred was not her biologic son. On the other hand, Alfred who was initially angry with her for lying to him about his birth eventually understood that whatever she did was because of her love for him and forgave her.

Steven and Stephanie were busy with their studies and their part-time jobs to support themselves. Steven stopped communicating with his father. Steven and Stephanie were bothered by the media for a while, but eventually they lost interest in their lives and left them alone.

* * *

228

Alfred knocked on the door. *I am coming home*, he thought. Patricia opened the door. They gave each other a hug. She helped him bring his bags inside the house.

"Did you have trouble finding the place?" Patricia asked.

"No, none at all," He answered.

"How is Angela? How did she take the news when you told her you were settling in Columbus?"

"Mom is fine. She thanked you and Edna for helping us. She was not very thrilled to see me leave, but she expected it once everything came out in the open," Alfred replied.

"Good. Alfred, I want you to consider this as your own home. I want you to stay here with me as long as you want," Patricia said to him.

"Thanks, I intend to stay for just a few weeks to get to know you better. Brittany and I are planning to buy a house." Alfred was financially secure thanks to the bestseller published by his geneticist, doctor Lawson.

"Alfred, I can't thank you enough for helping me see the truth. For more than twenty years, I was blinded by Mr. Kincaid's personality. I worshipped him. My ex-husband tried to make me see the truth, but I couldn't. It was you who made me see him for who he really is. I can never thank you enough for that."

"Well, what's a son for?" Alfred answered.

"Son! I like that. But, Alfred, please understand that even though I am old enough to be your mother, in reality, I am not your mother."

"I understand it. Angela is my mother for raising me for such a long time and going through many hardships in the process. I don't make light of that matter. Angela didn't know many things that happened around my birth, so I don't blame her for them, but she hid lots of things from me, therefore, I resented her for some time. I am over that now. You, on the other hand, have been different. After I met you in Mr. Kincaid's office, every time I have talked to you, I have felt very comfortable just like a son would be with his mother."

"Yes, me too. I have also felt very comfortable with you. You have also helped me know who I was and who I should be. Actually, I think of Steven as my son. You are his clone, so I guess it is all right."

"And you know what else? We are genetically related too." Alfred joked.

"True. But don't forget, it's only by mitochondrial DNA. It's not much to go by."

"No, it's not just mitochondrial DNA. It's *maternal* mitochondrial DNA. It's not for nothing that they use the word *maternal*."

"You are good. If I could think straight when you were little, I would have adopted you. Of course, Angela would not have let you go. It's ironic that most kids move out of their parents' house when they are eighteen. In my case, my son is coming home at that age." She started crying.

"Please. Don't get so emotional. I know you have been through a lot. There is no need to go back to the mistakes you may have made. Anyone in your place would have been impressed with Michael Kincaid."

"No, I am thinking about how different my life would have been if I had you many years ago."

"Well, I can help you with that. Would you sing a lullaby to me? If I had met you when I was a baby you would have done it," Alfred asked. She figured that Alfred was making the situation light by changing the subject, but she did not mind it.

"Sure," she said.

"When I found out that Angela was not my biological mother, I imagined that my mother would be from some exotic part of the world and would sing to me in a beautiful melodious voice in her native language."

"I know you are just making all these things up. Anyway, I am from England. So how about Queen's English in place of a native language from an exotic place?" Patricia asked.

"Sure, that's close enough," Alfred joked.

"I don't know any exotic song from my native country, so how about *twinkle twinkle little star*?"

"Never heard of it," Alfred joked again. Patricia sang the song and they both laughed.

30

Fifteen Years Later

Knowing yourself is the beginning of all wisdom.

— ARISTOTLE, GREEK PHILOSOPHER

Edna Dent, Lucy Kincaid's mother, passed away two years after the cloning scandal became public. Not only Michael Kincaid but Steven, Alfred, and Patricia had also kept in touch with her. At Edna's funeral, Michael Kincaid met Steven and Alfred for the last time. Patricia didn't bother to look at him. In Edna's honor, Michael donated a large sum of money to Native American charities.

Michael Kincaid passed away a year ago. He died an emotionally broken man. He suffered from obesity, diabetes, hypertension, and arthritis. Till his death, he could not understand why things turned out the way they did and why he couldn't buy Steve and Alfred with his money. In his declining years, the people who remained with him, continued to rob him. Steven, Alfred, and Patricia attended his funeral. Media ignored the last years of his life. Many people had forgotten about him until they heard the news of his death. Steven and Alfred both refused to accept money their "Dad" had left in his will for them. Money could not buy their integrity.

Angela continues to live in Toronto, Canada. She never returned to the United States. She has no friends, no family, and no church. Alfred visits her often. Jeff calls her and visits her rarely. He has not forgiven her for deserting him when he was a toddler.

Dr. Betty Sue Lawson, *The Invisible Twin*, has become legendary. She wrote papers in scientific journals about the cloning of Steven Kincaid. She also wrote a bestseller describing Alfred Johnson's life and his struggle to establish his identity. She is a Professor Emeritus in Cleveland Clinic. Due to her own amazing life, from the hillbilly background to a world-famous geneticist, she has become a motivational speaker and commands huge fees for her speeches. She travels all over the world. Dr. Lawson has received numerous awards and honorary doctorates. Of course, she bla-tantly exploits her Appalachian heritage and her Southern accent to her advantage. People, who know her, claim that she appears more Appalachian now than she did before.

Mark Baron lives a stable life. He has been dry since the time he first joined AA. He still considers himself a recovering alcoholic. Occasionally, he wakes up from the nightmares of Jeff being snatched away by CPS. Debra has told him that he probably enjoys punishing himself by think-ing about that dreadful event. She believes that we all must live with our demons; going through these nightmares is Mark's way of living with his. Debra also understands that if these thoughts didn't occupy Mark's mind then it would be occupied by thoughts of alcohol. In that case, it would be more difficult for him to stay sober. Mark holds a steady job. He and Debra are married. They have a girl. Mark's son Jeff also lives in Buffalo, New York, with his wife and two kids, a son and a daughter.

Steven Kincaid and Stephanie Anderson are proud parents of a six years old baby girl. Due to testicular feminization syndrome, Stephanie could not conceive. Her sister, Alexandra, is the biological mother of that child. She was conceived by intra-uterine insemination. Steven is the bio-logical father. They named her Athena, after the Greek goddess of wis-dom. The Goddess Athena did not have a lover; therefore, she was called Athena Parthenos or Virgin Athena. Their daughter was not conceived by parthenogenesis, but she was certainly conceived by asexual reproduc-tion, so Stephanie decided to name her Athena. Incidentally, Alexandra was unmarried at the time and was believed to be a virgin. Stephanie knew she was not, but she didn't care. She questioned why a woman's virginity is important, but not a man's. Stephanie's "virtual" mother-in-law, Patricia explained to Steve and Stephanie that although they named their daughter based on Greek mythology, it is not exactly the way Athena's story unfolds. Stephanie explained that she is aware of that, but she still wants to honor Athena and her own inability to bear children. Steve grew up as an heir to billions of dollars but refused to touch his dad's money. He and Stephanie live comfortable lives with pride.

Both Stephanie and her sister Alexandra have same mitochondrial DNA, so Athena also carries the same mitochondrial DNA that her mother, Stephanie, would have passed on to her if she could have children. Athena's last name is Anderson, same as Stephanie's. Steven and Stephanie both had decided that if they had a son, he would carry his father's last name and if they had a daughter then she will carry her mother's last name. Just as Nature passes Y chromosome (along with its mutations and markers) on the paternal line and mitochondrial DNA (along with its mutations and markers) on the maternal line, they concurred that that was the way children should be given their last names.

Stephanie has already planned Athena's sweet sixteenth. She wants it to be celebrated in the Parthenon, the temple created for the goddess Athena Parthenos—not the Parthenon in Athens, Greece, but its only exact replica in the whole world, in Nashville, Tennessee. There, in front of the forty-two feet tall statue of the goddess Athena, she will celebrate her daughter Athena's sweet sixteenth.

After she left Michael Kincaid, Patricia stopped working for the corporate world. She did some soul-searching and concluded that her knowledge would be most useful in the teaching profession. She teaches history to the high school students in Columbus, Ohio. She also spends time with her grandkids. After all, she has a "virtual" son Steven and a "mitochondrial" son Alfred.

Bobby Myers shared fifty million dollars with his mother when he was just a teenager. His mother wanted "my Bobby" to live as a wealthy individual. He did. Unfortunately, he became a drug-addict and died of a drug overdose at the age of twenty-three.

Jagdish Chandra Mathur married a Canadian girl of Indian ethnicity. They both went to India for their honeymoon. They saw the famous Taj Mahal. Jagdish also visited the village of his ancestors. If touching the soil was important to feel closer to his heritage, like it was for Sun Brittany Wilson, then Jagdish had plenty of it. Everywhere he traveled in India, he was covered in dust. Upon returning from India, he told Alfred that now he felt like an Indian. Like a card-carrying ex-patriate Indian (also known as NRI for nonresident Indian), Jagdish brags about achievements of Indian people every time he reads about them on the Internet.

Jagdish's brother Satyendra teaches world religions in the University of Toronto. He sees the good, the bad, and the awful in all religions. He has learned a lot about prejudices taught by different religions and has concluded that none of the religions could be right. He thinks of himself as an atheist Hindu.

Alfred and Sun are married. They follow Buddhism. Sun meditates regularly. She is a pediatrician. Besides practicing part-time, she devotes some time to treat impoverished children in third-world countries. Alfred is a genetic counselor. Sun treats Patricia as her real mother-in-law. She frequently resents her presence, ignores her advices, and does not talk to her for days! Patricia understands that she couldn't have a more authentic daughter-in-law than her.

Alfred and Sun have a son, Noah, and a daughter, Hela. Hela was named in honor of Henrietta Lacks whose cell lines, taken from her without her knowledge, have helped thousands of laboratories all over the world. Noah will pass the Y chromosome markers of Alfred, which Alfred got from Steven and thereby from the Kincaid family. Hela will pass the mtDNA that she inherited from her mother, Brittany. Alfred wanted to embrace his roots, no matter what they were. He did. His children's middle name is Kincaid.

Jayesh Shah was born in Gujarat, India. He immigrated to the United States in the 1980s. He is a practicing pediatrician.

He has been fascinated by scriptures of Hinduism and other religions. He is also interested in astronomy, mythology, and ancient cultures.

His hobbies include traveling and reading.

www.ingramcontent.com/pod-product-compliance
Lightning Source LLC
Chambersburg PA
CBHW071516110726
47908CB00003B/862